"You're [...]
assured her. [...] **B53** [...]
me."

[...]ause you let me."

[...]odded. "I don't want to hurt you."

[...]u did," Kate said.

"Not anymore," he said, lifting his head to close [...] distance between his mouth and hers. His lips [...]mmed across hers. "Now I just want you. . ."

[...]d she wanted him, her skin heating and tingling [...]rywhere they touched. The sheet had slipped [...]wn, so that her breasts were bare against his chest. His hair, that covered his impressive pecs, tickled and teased her nipples, bringing them to [...]t, sensitive points.

[...]d I want—" Kate struggled free of his loose [...]sp and grabbed up the sheet again, holding it [...]een them like a shield "—to arrest you."

TAMING THE SHIFTER

LISA CHILDS

MILLS & BOON

Published in Great Britain 2015
by Mills & Boon, an imprint of Harlequin (UK) Limited,
Eton House, 18-24 Paradise Road, Richmond, Surrey, TW9 1SR

© 2015 Lisa Childs-Theeuwes

ISBN: 978-0-263-91821-2

89-1115

Harlequin (UK) Limited's policy is to use papers that are natural, renewable and recyclable products and made from wood grown in sustainable forests. The logging and manufacturing processes conform to the legal environmental regulations of the country of origin.

Printed and bound in Spain
by CPI, Barcelona

Lisa Childs writes paranormal and contemporary romance for Mills & Boon. She lives on thirty acres in Michigan with her two daughters, a talkative Siamese and a long-haired Chihuahua who thinks she's a Rottweiler. Lisa loves hearing from readers, who can contact her through her website, www.lisachilds.com, or snail-mail address, PO Box 139, Marne, MI 49435, USA.

Prologue

The sweet, metallic scent of blood hung heavy in the air, and chimes rang out from the clock tower in the town square. Warrick James didn't need to know what time it was. He was already too late. He was always too late.

He pushed open the door and stepped into his father's den. He had known what he would find; he'd been warned. But still the scene struck him like a body blow.

His father lay back in his chair, blood gushed from a hole blown in his chest. Even with the bullet—that special bullet—in it, his heart continued to pump.

And his father's eyes stared—not up at the man who had taken his life. But at the man who had failed to save him. Warrick was used to the disappointment in his father's pale brown gaze. For thirty years, he had seen it every time the man had looked at him.

The chimes continued to ring out. Was that the eighth or the ninth? Just a few more chimes before midnight arrived...

Warrick reeled; his heart feeling as if a shot had been fired into it, as well. Maybe a bullet would pierce it next. Reagan—the man he'd known he would find standing over the body—held the gun yet, his finger against the trigger. And the barrel of that gun was pointed at Warrick.

"What kind of monster are you?" Warrick asked even as he felt his own body beginning to turn from man to beast. "How could you do this?"

"You don't understand," Reagan replied. "Let me explain..."

Warrick shook his head. He was beyond listening. He didn't even care that that gun—loaded with those special bullets—was pointed directly at *his* heart. Just as the clock chimed for the twelfth time, he launched himself at his father's killer.

Detective Kate Wever intimately knew the city she protected. Before being promoted to the major case squad, she had patrolled these streets. She knew the metropolis of Zantrax, Michigan, as well as she knew herself. As she knew her friends...

Or so she'd once believed. Now she wasn't certain what, or who, to believe. Except for Bernie...

She knew not to believe the vagrant. Yet she followed him into the dead-end alley between some of the tallest buildings in the city. The sun hadn't set, but it was dark in the alley. The air hung still and putrid above the asphalt.

Kate, following too close to Bernie, held her breath—

unwilling to breathe for fear of gagging. The man should have gone to the shelter instead of the police station. He could have used a shower. And probably a meal. Or at least some coffee. She held out a cup to him and pulled a sandwich from her pocket. "Here," she said. "You need to eat."

He needed to sober up. The stench wasn't just because he hadn't showered for weeks—maybe months. He also smelled strongly of alcohol. Or of strong alcohol...

She hadn't brought enough coffee. He reached for it, his hand shaking. The cover came off and the hot liquid spilled over the rim and splashed onto the front of his long trench coat. "Bernie, are you all right?"

His gray-haired head jerked up and down in quick, nervous nods. His dark eyes were wild. With fear or drunkenness?

"It's this place," he said with a shudder of revulsion.

"We didn't have to come here." She wasn't sure why he had insisted on her following him from the station to the alley. With no sun between the buildings, the air wasn't just still—it was cold.

She shivered. But not just from the cold.

One of those buildings had a bar in its basement—Club Underground. A bar where strange things happened...like Bernie had claimed happened here. Too bad her friend owned the place...

"This was my home first," he said, gesturing toward a Dumpster shoved against one of the buildings. "Then all of them started coming around—making trouble."

"All of them?" she asked. "Who are you talking about?"

"What," he corrected her, the word sharp. "They're not human. They can fly."

"What are you talking about?" she asked. And exactly how much had he had to drink?

"Those things," he said. "I've seen 'em fly out of the alley—straight up in the night sky like big, human-looking bats."

He had definitely gotten into some strong alcohol, but his words weren't slurred. So maybe he'd just been drinking so long that the alcohol had damaged his brain. Over her years on the streets, she had seen a lot of vagrants develop alcohol dementia. She wouldn't be able to reason with him; he was probably beyond that.

So she simply asked, "What do you want me to do about them, Bernie? Flying isn't a crime."

"They're killers," he said. "They kill humans and each other. If you're not careful, Detective Wever, they might kill you."

Kate smiled and opened her mouth to assure him that she would be fine. But the alley suddenly grew darker and colder. Along with a chill, a sense of foreboding rushed through her, and for a moment she believed Bernie. There was something out there—something not quite human—and it was coming.

For her.

Chapter 1

The murderous intent gleaming in the man's topaz eyes chilled Kate's blood. He was going to kill someone.

His hands, with wide palms and long, strong fingers, grasped her shoulders. Then he moved her aside and continued his pursuit of the man he had been chasing down the street before Kate had stepped into his path. But instead of knocking her down, he had caught and steadied her. Her skin tingled from his touch despite the layers of jacket and sweater that had separated his palms from her bare flesh.

She shook off the eerie feeling and forced herself to move, running after him. And as she ran, she reached for her phone and her gun. She wasn't on duty, but it was her job to stop him from killing.

In a metropolis like Zantrax, Michigan, a detective

was never truly off duty—no matter that her real shift had ended hours ago. Or that she wanted nothing more than a stiff drink and a soft bed and sweet oblivion.

"Where the hell did he go?" she murmured, unable to catch a glimpse of him ahead of her. This close to midnight the sidewalk wasn't as crowded as during the day—especially since this area consisted mostly of office buildings and warehouses.

Except for the underground nightclub in the basement of one of those buildings.

Club Underground was always busy, always full of people who were too beautiful to be real. She shook off the doubts Bernie had put in her head a few weeks ago.

He was crazy, she reminded herself.

And maybe so was she for not calling for backup before chasing after a man as big as the one who had nearly run her down. But she couldn't call in a crime in progress until she knew he was actually committing one. It was possible he'd just been running, albeit in jeans and a white sweater, and she'd just imagined that murderous gleam in his eyes.

Damn Bernie and his wild stories. But if she was being honest, she had to admit she'd had doubts about her city even before Bernie had warned her about flying nonhumans.

The man who'd nearly run her over had been human, though. And he had definitely been angry as hell. She couldn't see him now, but she couldn't get that brief image she'd had of him out of her mind. He was so tall and broad-shouldered, with a long mane of thick black hair that he would have been impossible to miss had he still been on the street ahead of her. But he couldn't have just disappeared.

She stopped and glanced around, peering into the shadows gathering outside the circles of light from the streetlamps on the sidewalk. A rage like his wouldn't have been easily suppressed or controlled so that he could hide silently in the shadows, though.

She cocked her head and listened. Grunts and groans and an almost inhuman cry shattered the quiet of the nearly deserted street and confirmed that her instinct to pursue the man had been right. Her pulse leaping, she tracked the sounds of the fight to the narrow opening of that alley between the building with Club Underground in the basement and the deserted furniture warehouses.

Lifting her cell phone, she reported the assault in progress. A unit would be dispatched for backup. But, remembering the gleam in those unusual topaz eyes, she doubted backup would arrive in time to prevent a murder. So she pulled her gun from her holster and, adrenaline and nerves coursing through her, stepped into the alley.

The two men grappled on the ground, rolling across the asphalt as they locked in mortal combat. The man with whom she'd collided swung his fists over and over into the face of another man. They were closely matched in size—tall and muscular. But one was clearly the attacker, the other the victim. The victim kicked and pushed, trying to get away. "Stop!" she yelled. "Zantrax PD. Break it up!"

The man on the ground murmured something, blood trickling from the corner of his mouth.

"Shut up. Just shut up! Or I'll tear your damn throat

out," the attacker growled, his hand reaching for the other man's neck.

"Stop!" Kate shouted now, panic rising. "I'm Lieutenant Wever, a detective with Zantrax Police Department, and I'm placing you under arrest for assault."

But he ignored her as if she had not spoken at all. She couldn't just stand there and do nothing while one man killed another—as she watched. So she fired. The bullet struck the man's shoulder and propelled him back. He shook his head and shrugged, as if shaking off a muscle twinge and glanced at the blood spreading down his sleeve and across his white sweater.

The victim struggled beneath the man she'd shot, but before he could get out of reach, his attacker caught him again. His hands, his long fingers stiff like claws, closed around the man's throat. Despite the bullet in his shoulder, he had lost none of his strength.

Was he on something? Drugged suspects were sometimes harder to subdue and apprehend because they tended to be more violent. And superhumanly strong.

So Kate fired again.

This bullet propelled him back farther, his hands slipping from his victim's throat. Finally, he turned toward her, as if just noticing that she'd joined them in the alley. With that murderous intent directed at her, he lurched to his feet, and she noticed the gun tucked into the waistband of his jeans.

He was armed and he was heading straight toward her.

Heart hammering with fear, Kate fired again. This bullet struck him directly in the chest—in his heart. He pressed his hand to it as if pledging allegiance.

Then he pulled it away and looked down at his bloody palm—seeming surprised to see the blood.

Had he thought she was firing blanks? Couldn't he feel the wounds in his shoulder? Blood saturated the sleeve of his white sweater and spread like a red wave across his chest. Finally, his legs buckled beneath him, and he dropped to his knees on the asphalt.

While he fell to the ground, another man rose from it—albeit with a lurch and a groan. The man he'd been pummeling stumbled forward.

Instinct had Kate swinging her gun toward him. But he had no weapon at his waistband and was in no physical shape to assault her or his attacker.

"Stay back," she said. She wasn't sure who she was protecting—herself or the man she'd shot. She stepped between them.

"He needs medical help," the beat-up man murmured, his voice weak—probably from nearly having his throat ripped out.

She'd had no choice. She'd had to shoot.

But even with three bullets in him, he was reaching out as if trying to grab for his victim again. "No…"

She put her hand on his shoulder. "I'll get you help," she said. She'd had to shoot him, but she felt guilt hanging heavily over her like the night sky. "Save your strength…"

However, he must have used his last because he slumped forward, his chest and head hitting the asphalt.

"Oh, God!" she exclaimed in horror. What had she done? She hadn't wanted to kill him. She'd just wanted him to stop. During her career, she'd had to shoot other suspects—had even killed a couple of them.

But she hadn't felt like this then. She hadn't felt any doubt and certainly not any guilt.

Her hand shaking, she reached for her cell. Where the hell was the backup she'd called? If she hadn't shot him, she might have been the one lying in the alley bleeding out if he'd grabbed for his gun. He still had his weapon on him, but he hadn't pulled it. He wouldn't have needed the gun to kill her, though; he could have used his bare hands like he had on his victim.

She gripped her gun tighter in one hand while she used her other to press the call button on her cell. Before anyone answered, she heard the sirens. Help had arrived.

But was it too late? Was he already dead? There was so much blood, pooling like tar beneath his body. She dropped down next to him. His face was to the side, his strange topaz eyes staring up at her. She couldn't help him. Her only medical training was CPR, and he was breathing. His heart was beating. She couldn't help him.

"You let a killer get away," he said.

She glanced around the alley. Even in daylight it was dark between these buildings. Now, close to midnight, the blackness was thick and impenetrable. The other man could have been standing beside her and she might not have seen him. But she knew he was gone. While she'd been distracted, he'd slipped away.

"A killer?" Had she shot the wrong man and let the real perp escape?

"Yes," he murmured, and blood gurgled from his mouth now. It was amazing he was still alive—given where she'd hit him. But he wouldn't last much longer.

"Hang in there," she implored him. "Help's coming…" Would they be able to find the narrow entrance to the alley? "I'll get them…"

She moved to stand up, but he caught her wrist in his hand. His incredibly large, strong hand. He could have easily snapped her wrist—if he'd wanted, if he wasn't near death.

"I'll get you medical help," she promised.

"You made a mistake," he said, his voice a low growl. "A fatal mistake…" He seemed less concerned about his wounds than the fact that the other man had slipped away.

His words—his last words—chilled her. His eyes had closed, and he was no longer breathing. She could administer CPR now, but it wouldn't be enough to save him. He needed the paramedics and a fast trip to an operating room. She pulled her wrist from his weak grasp and ran from the alley.

It wasn't until she returned with the EMTs and patrol officers that she realized her mistake.

He was gone.

"No!" As frustration and anger and shock rioted within her, she screamed the word. "No!"

The scream burned her throat and jerked her awake. Her heart pounded furiously, hammering at her ribs. She gasped for breath and clawed at the sheets that had tangled around her thrashing body.

No matter how many times in the past couple of months that she dreamed about that night, the intensity of that encounter never lessened. She relived every emotion as well as every action. But still, she could not figure out exactly what had happened to his dead body.

She had seen the blood gurgling from his mouth to join the dark pool of it lying beneath him on the asphalt. He had stopped breathing and closed his eyes.

He had died.

He hadn't walked out of that alley. But somehow in the short time that she'd gone to the sidewalk and led the uniforms back to the alley, his body had disappeared. Maybe the other man, the one he'd been beating, hadn't left the alley when she'd thought. Maybe he'd waited until she'd left.

And done what? Killed a man who was already dead? Dragged off his body? He hadn't been in any shape to do that.

But how had the body disappeared? The alley deadended into a third building; none of the doors opening onto it had been unlocked. There was nowhere he could have gone even had he been alive. But dead...

She had even tracked down the homeless man who'd admitted to living in the alley. Bernie had claimed to not have been there that night. In fact, he'd said that he didn't often stay in the alley anymore because he was scared that the humans—that weren't really human—would kill him. Like he'd warned her that they might kill her, too.

Hell, maybe Bernie's warning hadn't been so outlandish. Maybe there were humans—that weren't really human—that could fly. And that man had been one of them. That was about the only explanation for how he'd disappeared.

She shook her head, disgusted with herself for wanting to believe Bernie's wild, alcoholic dementia-influenced story. But what was the alternative? Angels? If she was spiritual enough to believe in them, they flew. But she doubted the man she'd shot—who had been so intent on killing his victim—was an angel.

"So where did you go?" she mused, pushing her sweat-dampened hair from her forehead. She had gone back to that alley nearly every night since it had happened, but she had yet to figure out how he could have just disappeared. "I looked for you everywhere…"

"Not everywhere," a deep voice murmured.

Kate jerked upright in bed, one hand clutching the tangled sheets to her chest—the other sliding under the pillow next to hers for her gun. She pulled out the Glock and directed the barrel toward the shadows in the corner of her bedroom.

He stepped away from the wall and moved into the glow of the moonlight streaking through the partially open blinds. His mouth curved into a mocking grin. "What are you going to do, Kate? Shoot me again?"

She shivered and tightened her grasp on her gun. She was too shocked over his appearance to ask any of the questions she should have. *Who the hell are you? How the hell did you get in?* All she could do was murmur, "I did shoot you."

Sometimes she had wondered if she'd missed. But that wouldn't have explained the blood. The crime techs hadn't been able to explain it, either—except to say that some animal must have been killed in the alley.

The man lifted a hand to his chest and patted it. "Did you?"

"I know I did. I saw you bleeding." Blood had gushed from the bullet wound in his heart. She swallowed the lump that had risen up the back of her throat.

She hadn't just shot him; she'd killed him.

"I saw you die."

So how was he in her room, stepping closer to her bed?

"Then I must be a ghost," he said. As totally unconcerned about the gun as he had been the night she'd shot him, he settled onto the mattress next to her, his muscular thigh rubbing against her hip.

"I don't believe in ghosts." But she couldn't deny that he was haunting her. With the glimpses of him she had been catching in crowds. With these strangely erotic dreams...

But she was awake. Wasn't she? So she couldn't be dreaming.

"Maybe I'm your conscience," he suggested.

"My conscience isn't bothering me," she said. But he was. He had been ever since she'd bumped into him on the street and looked up into those eerie topaz eyes. She had lost herself in that intense gaze of his, and she had yet to find her way back.

She should have already placed him under arrest for his older crimes—assault and leaving the scene of that crime—and his latest crime: breaking and entering. He must have come through her window; she felt the breeze blowing through it and she hadn't left it open—not this late in autumn.

But if she tried arresting him, he would undoubtedly resist. And she'd have to shoot him. For some reason she didn't want to shoot him again—because then he might disappear again, like he had that night.

Even now she wasn't certain that he was real, that she wasn't dreaming. Thoughts of him and that night had kept her awake for so many nights that she was beyond exhausted. She was probably just dreaming…

Heat flashed through Warrick James, radiating from where his thigh rubbed against her hip. Only denim and a thin satin sheet separated his skin from hers. The sheet was so thin that it was obvious she wore nothing beneath it. The dark areolae of her full breasts were visible beneath the champagne-colored satin, her nipples peaked on the shapely mounds—probably from the cool breeze blowing through her open window. She couldn't want him…as much as he wanted her.

His body hardened as blood rushed through his veins, hot and heavy. He would have to be crazy to be attracted to her—the woman who had tried to kill him and obviously felt no remorse. "Don't you have a conscience?" he asked. He shouldn't have been surprised that she didn't. Apparently nobody he knew had one.

"Yes, but there's no reason for it to bother me," she murmured, her brow furrowing with genuine confusion. A lock of silky-looking black hair fell across her forehead and skimmed her jaw. Her hair was dark, her skin pale and her eyes a sharp, clear blue.

Hell, maybe he would be crazy if he wasn't attracted to her. But this attraction did nothing to cool his anger with her.

He barely resisted the urge to reach out and shake her. But she was still holding that damn gun. And while she couldn't kill him with it—permanently—the bullets still hurt. He grimaced in remembrance of the pain that had burned so fiercely in his chest that he had actually lost consciousness. "Because you shot me."

"And if the situation was the same, I'd do it again," she replied. "Shooting you was the only way to stop you from killing that man. Even after I identified myself, you wouldn't listen to my commands to let him go. And you had this look on your face…" She shuddered.

"You didn't understand what was going on," he said. "You should have given me a chance to explain." That he had been doing her job for her. He had been protecting and serving *all* the citizens of Zantrax—both human and superhuman—as well as his home village of St. James.

"You were too busy strangling the life from that man," she reminded him.

"Yes," he said, frustration gnawing at him that she had stopped him from doing what had to be done, what apparently should have been done years ago so that other lives wouldn't have been lost and destroyed. Now the bastard, Reagan, had gone underground. He hadn't been easy to find the night Warrick had chased him into that dead-end alley; he would be even harder to track down now. Thanks to Detective Kate Wever.

"Why?" she asked. "I fired the first two shots into your shoulder, but you wouldn't stop. You were in such a murderous rage."

He couldn't deny that he had been. "I had a damn good reason."

"You should have stopped beating him when I told you to," she said, "then I would have taken a report and you could have explained your actions."

But he had been beyond explanations. Beyond reason. All he'd known was his hunger for vengeance,

the exact same hunger he should be feeling for her—
just for vengeance. But, despite the gun she held on
him, another kind of hunger gnawed at him—and
only that thin sheet separated her naked body from
his gaze, from his touch. His fingers itched to reach
for the sheet, to tug it off. But she would undoubtedly
shoot him again.

"Explain the situation to me now. Why were you
trying to kill that man?" she asked. "You called him
a killer."

Reagan was. But Warrick shouldn't have told her
that; it was none of her business. It couldn't be. He
couldn't share his story without disclosing secrets he
would really die if he revealed. That story haunted
him, like he had tried to haunt her. Since she kept staring at him as though he were a ghost, he must have
been successful haunting her. But he didn't bother
correcting her misconception; it was better that she
think him a ghost than what he really was. He lifted
his shoulders in a shrug, but he couldn't shake off the
pain any more than he could the hunger. "Some people just need killing."

She sucked in an audible breath and adjusted her
grip on her gun, steadying the barrel that was still
pointing directly at his chest. "That's not for you to
decide."

"It wasn't for you to decide that he should live and
I should die." Because she had let that bastard live,
more would likely die. Maybe even her...

She drew in a shuddery breath. "You gave me no
choice. I couldn't just stand there and let you kill him."

"So instead you killed me."

"But you're not dead," she murmured, reaching out

the hand not holding the gun toward his face. And as she did, her sheet slipped a little lower and revealed the deep cleft between her breasts.

He sure as hell wasn't dead, not with the way his heart pounded frantically as desire coursed through him. Then her fingers brushed across his face, scraping over the stubble on his cheek until her fingertips covered his lips. Heat sizzled between them. He uttered a gasp of breath, and she shivered.

"You're not a ghost, either."

"No," he admitted, moving his lips against her fingertips.

She shivered again, and her nipples hardened even more, pushing taut against that thin sheet. "If you're not a ghost, what are you?"

"Well, I'm no angel." But if he was, Warrick would be an avenging one. Or he would have been had she not interfered. Because she had, he had lost his chance for vengeance...against his enemy.

Her interference should have made her his enemy, too. He'd told himself that she was. And that was why he couldn't leave her alone even though he no longer had any reason to stay in Zantrax. Except vengeance. Against her.

Liar.

His tense, aching body called him on his lie. He didn't want vengeance on her. He just wanted *her*. Her fingers still pressed against his lips, he didn't have to speak—to explain. All he had to do was lean closer...to her.

Kate's heart hammered against her ribs. He was staring at her mouth with that intense, eerie topaz gaze. He was going to kiss her. And just like she hadn't wanted to shoot him in the alley, she didn't want to stop him.

He had broken into her apartment and had been watching her sleep. And instead of shooting him, she was going to let him kiss her? After all of those sleepless nights, she had totally lost her mind. She had no doubt anymore.

Only desire.

She had touched him to see if he was real or if her fingers would pass right through him like mist. But she couldn't stop touching him, skimming her fingers along his jaw to his lips—which were surprisingly soft and warm. She wanted to taste them, too. She slid her hand to the nape of his neck and tugged him closer so that only a breath separated his lips from hers.

He was breathing. Fast and ragged. And his heart was beating. She could feel the vibrations of it despite the small space that separated his body from hers. His skin radiated warmth to hers, making her tingle in reaction.

He was no ghost. No dream.

"What the hell are you?" she murmured again. "Indestructible?"

"I'm destructible," he replied with a heavy sigh that teased her lips.

"You weren't wearing a bulletproof vest," she said. "I saw the gunshot wound, saw you bleeding." Her trembling fingers skimmed down his neck to the buttons on his shirt. She needed to see the scar, needed to understand how a man could have survived such an injury. If he was a man…

He caught her fingers in his hand. "If you see my scars, I'm going to have to see yours."

Goose bumps lifted along her bare shoulders and arms. She had scars, but hardly anyone knew about them. How could he know? The fear she should have been feeling the minute she'd discovered him in the shadows finally coursed through her. The hand holding the gun tightened on the grip.

"Who are you?"

He chuckled and cupped her cheek in his hand. "Poor Kate, you can't figure out if you want to kiss me or kill me."

She gasped at his arrogance and his perception. And the desire that jolted her with his touch.

"Remember how well that worked out for you last time," he goaded her with a wink, his long thick lashes brushing against his chiseled cheekbones. "You can't kill me."

"You said you're not indestructible."

"Killing someone isn't the only way to destroy them."

She knew that better than most. "Is that what you're trying to do to me?" she asked. "Destroy me?"

Reporting an officer-involved shooting and being unable to produce the body had harmed her career. Seeing glimpses of him everywhere after she thought she'd killed him had harmed her sanity. That had to be why she was so addled, so confused—that she'd asked none of the questions that she should have, that she hadn't fired her gun.

He sighed again, raggedly, and leaned his forehead against hers. Then his hand slid from her cheek, down her neck to clasp her throat. "Like you, I can't figure out if I want to kiss you or kill you."

Chapter 2

The barrel of the gun jammed hard into Warrick's chest. He smiled in anticipation—not of the bullet but of her mouth beneath his, her lips opening for his possession. And he wanted to possess her.

In every way.

A clock chimed, the metallic clang reverberating from the living room beyond her closed bedroom door. He had been out there before, when he had checked out her whole place after coming through her window. The open living area was as big a mess as her clothes-strewn bedroom. But out there newspapers and mail littered the couch, small table and countertop. Only the grandfather clock standing on the wall next to the front door was neat and polished—its wood and brass gleaming. The old clock chimed again.

His skin tightened, tingling and itching. He shouldn't

have made his presence known to her—not this close to midnight. But when she'd awakened with that emotional shout, he hadn't been able to just walk away—no matter how much he should have. He had been watching her…to see if the man she'd let get away that night was also watching her. Or that was what he'd told himself—that she might lead him to Reagan. Or maybe he'd just liked messing with her because of that—because she'd let Reagan go while she'd shot *him*.

The chime clanged again.

He didn't have enough time. Not for what he wanted to do *to* her. And *with* her.

The clock chimed for the fourth time. And another, higher-pitched chime echoed it as someone rang the doorbell. Kate's eyes widened as she glanced from him to her bedroom door.

"You're not going to shoot me," he said.

And the clock chimed again.

"No," she agreed. "I'm going to arrest you."

"Arrest me?" he asked. "For what?"

"Breaking and entering, for one," she said. "And assault."

"I haven't assaulted you," he said, flinching as the clock chimed for the sixth time. His scalp tingled, and his jaw grew tight, his teeth aching from the pressure. He didn't have time to assault her. He had to leave. Now.

He pulled back from the tantalizing closeness of her sensually full lips. And closing his eyes against the sexy temptation of her naked body covered with just that thin sheet, he stood up and stepped back from the bed.

Her doorbell echoed the chime again. And he opened his eyes.

Still clutching that sheet to her body with one hand, she stood up, too, and kept the gun barrel trained on him. "I'm arresting you for the assault of that man in the alley."

He focused on her face, anticipation of another kind winding through him. Maybe Reagan was still here. Maybe she would lead him to his father's killer. "He swore out a complaint against me?"

Her lips thinned, pressed tightly together—refusing to answer him.

He clasped her bare shoulders in his hands. "Did he? Do you know where he is?" Maybe he hadn't completely lost his trail.

She shook her head.

"Then no complainant—no case—no arrest," he said, as that damn clock chimed for the seventh time.

"*I* will swear out a complaint."

"If we hadn't been interrupted," he said, trailing his fingers down the bare skin of her shoulder in a caress, "you would have no complaints." And then, despite the damn chiming clock and doorbell, he leaned down and brushed his mouth across hers.

Damn. Like honey and caramel and all the sweets that had always been his weakness, she tasted just as good as he had known she would. Too good for him to resist deepening the kiss. With gentle pressure, he parted her lips with his and dipped his tongue inside her mouth.

She closed her eyes and pressed her body against his. But he stepped back so that only their lips touched, clinging. He didn't want to break the kiss. Didn't want to leave her. But the damn clock chimed again.

Lips tingling, breath coming in ragged pants, Kate finally opened her eyes. But he was gone. Cool air chilled her skin from the breeze blowing through the open window. Had she left that open? Or had he opened it?

Or had he ever really even been there? She still couldn't believe that the man she had shot, the man she'd watched die, had been in her bedroom. It wasn't possible. But then, his dead body disappearing wasn't possible, either.

Fists pounded at her door, her visitor having abandoned the bell and whatever patience he or she might have possessed.

Kate couldn't blame them; she had kept them waiting for a long time. But hell, it was midnight. Who would visit her so late—except *him*?

Had he actually been there—or had she dreamed it all? *No, impossible.*

She could still taste him on her lips—as dark and dangerous and rich as his eerie topaz gaze and gleaming black hair. Another knock and the twelfth chime of the clock pulled her to her senses.

Still holding the gun, she thrust her arms into the sleeves of the robe draped across the foot of her rumpled bed and one-handedly secured the belt. Then she rushed to the front door before her crazy visitor woke the whole damn apartment complex. "What the hell—"

Palms lifted up, Paige stepped back from the doorway. "Don't shoot."

"Tell me why I shouldn't," Kate challenged her blond-haired friend.

"Because we're your friends," Paige replied. Their other *friends* stood behind her. Brown-haired Elizabeth "Lizzy" Turrell, the red-haired assistant DA Campbell O'Brien, and Dr. Renae Grabill, the trauma resident with her short, dark hair and haunted gaze. Like Kate, Renae saw too much tragedy on the job.

"You woke me up," Kate said. That alone had to be a shooting offense, especially when the dream had been as real and erotic as the one she had been having. But if it had been a dream, it had been the most vivid one she'd ever had.

"Looks like you were having one hell of a night," Campbell perceptively remarked, lifting an auburn brow above one of her green eyes. "Is he still here?"

Lizzy snorted. "When's the last time you saw Kate with a man?"

"Yesterday, but she was handcuffing him," Campbell admitted. "Maybe she's into that kinky stuff, though."

"I'm into getting my sleep after a shift," Kate said and feigned a yawn. "And you know why I was cuffing that guy—I was on duty."

"You're never off duty," Paige said.

"You need to take a break once in a while," Lizzy added.

"That's what I was just trying to do," Kate pointed out, "when I was sleeping."

"Sleep sounds good," Renae agreed. As a trauma surgeon in a crime-ridden city, she never got enough herself. "But you were supposed to meet us at Club

Underground." She had agreed to meet them this Friday since none of them had to work the next day.

Kate shuddered.

Even though Paige owned the place, Kate hated it for so many reasons. When Paige had first bought the club, someone had relentlessly stalked and terrorized her at the place.

That had been years ago. Paige's stalker was gone now, but Kate still didn't know the whole story. She just knew that her friend was safe and happier now than she had ever been. The investigator in her wanted to find out exactly what the hell had gone on at the creepy underground club. But because Paige was her friend, Kate hadn't pressured her for details. She hadn't wanted to disturb Paige's happiness.

Now Kate had her own worries. Her own stalker.

That was another reason she hated Club Underground. Him. She had shot him in the alley behind the building. But she hadn't killed him, like she'd thought. It wasn't his *ghost* haunting her; it was *him*—gaslighting her.

"Hey," Paige said with a chuckle. "That's my place you're disparaging."

"Not disparaging," Kate said.

"Just avoiding?" Paige probed, her blue-eyed gaze narrowed with concern. "You're lucky Sebastian gave up on waiting for you to open the door. He took off when you didn't answer the bell. He'd be quite upset that you're not patronizing the club anymore."

Sebastian, Paige's younger brother and the long-time manager of Club Underground, had talked his sister into buying the place after she'd given up the law profession years ago. With his movie-star good looks, he could talk anyone into anything. Usually he talked women into his bed.

"He probably realized that waking up a detective is not a good idea," Kate said, tapping her lowered gun against her thigh.

"He probably realized that there was somebody more welcoming waiting for him," Campbell said.

"Since you wouldn't come to happy hour, we brought happy hour to you," Lizzy said.

Paige held up a bottle of white wine, and Kate snorted in disgust. Then Campbell raised another bottle, of liquor nearly the same amber as the man's topaz eyes. Whiskey was Kate's drink—when she drank, which wasn't often. Just during happy hour, which was whenever the busy women managed to get together.

"You've been so busy the past couple of months," said Renae who was equally, if not more so, busy but always made time for her friends, "that we've missed you."

"So let us in," Campbell said.

"Sorry," Kate murmured as she stepped back so her friends could enter her messy living room. She had one couch, which was littered with clothes and newspapers, and a coffee table that was buried under plates and fast-food containers. If she'd known she was having visitors…she still wouldn't have had time to clean up. Not with the shifts she worked and not with all the time she spent off duty trying to solve a case nobody believed was a crime—because they hadn't seen the body.

But she'd seen the body. That night and again in her bedroom.

"Kate?" Lizzy asked, her soft voice full of concern. She was the mom of the group—having raised four kids on her own. She tended to mother them, too. "Are you sure everything's all right?"

Kate nodded and lied, "Yeah, I'm fine."

Her place was small, hardly enough room for herself. But she picked up and tossed stuff aside, making room for her friends just as she had made room in her life for these women; their friendships were vital to her sanity. She had never needed them more than now.

Renae and Campbell dropped onto the floor while Paige and Lizzy squeezed together on the couch, making room for her to join them.

"I'm really glad you guys came over," she said with gratitude for their friendship and their concern.

But she dare not tell them about her other late-night visitor, or they might think her as crazy as she already thought herself. He couldn't have really been in her bedroom—in her bed. She couldn't really have kissed him.

He was dead. She'd killed him.

Warrick hit the ground on all fours then glanced over his shoulder at the leap he'd taken off the fire escape outside Kate Wever's fourth-floor apartment. "Damn…"

"You're lucky you didn't kill yourself," a deep voice murmured.

He tensed and cursed. He couldn't be discovered. Not like this…not after he had already turned into the form he took every night from midnight till dawn. But the man was too close for Warrick to disappear, unseen, into the shadows.

"But I already know that you don't die easily."

Finally recognizing the voice, Warrick whirled around, claws drawn—teeth bared as he uttered a warning growl.

"And neither do I," Sebastian Culver reminded him. "So you can put those away."

Warrick had just been messing with the other guy. He felt no hostility—only gratitude. He sheathed his claws and grinned at the dark-haired man. Well, actually, Sebastian wasn't a man—or not *just* a man. Either. "I'm glad to see you again."

"I can't say the same," the vampire replied, his voice and pale blue eyes cool. "I thought you would have left Zantrax by now."

"I have unfinished business here," Warrick said, tensing at the other man's unfriendly tone. Why was the guy hostile toward him now? Had Reagan gotten to him somehow?

"She," Sebastian said as he gestured toward the bedroom window four floors up, "better not be your unfinished business."

Warrick had been in Zantrax long enough to hear the underground gossip. Sebastian Culver was quite the playboy. Had he been involved with Kate? Or did he want to be? Warrick's guts knotted, jealousy twisting them. "Why?"

"Because if she is," Sebastian replied, "it'll make me regret saving your sorry life."

"I appreciate your help that night." Warrick had wanted to thank the man for a while for pulling him into the underground passage to the club when Detective Wever had briefly left the alley after shooting him. Sebastian hadn't brought him into the club but to a secret room between it and the passageway—and to a special surgeon. "But you can't actually save a man who can't die."

"You can die," Sebastian said. "Same as I can die."

"But I wouldn't have died that night." The surgeon, Dr. Ben Davison, had eased his pain, though.

"But your secret would have been discovered," the vampire pointed out. "And to men like us, that's worse than death."

"And will lead to death." Someone's death…

He glanced up to that dimly lit window, too. She hadn't turned on any lights in her bedroom, so she must have left the door open to the living room. What was she doing in there? Maybe someone other than Sebastian had been ringing her bell. Who?

"She's a smart woman," Sebastian said. "She'll figure it out."

"Your secret or mine?"

Sebastian gestured at him—in his changed form. "Your secret is more obvious. You cut it close."

"Cut what close?" he asked, feigning innocence.

"I saw you jump out the window," the other man informed him. "You were with her."

"Jealous?" he couldn't resist goading.

Sebastian uttered a sigh of such weariness that it revealed he was much older than his physical appearance would lead one to believe. "I'm concerned."

"For her or me?"

"I don't know you."

Yet the man had been compelled to help a stranger—a strange creature, no less. Fortunately one legend—the one about vampires and werewolves constantly being at war—was myth.

"How well do you know her?" Warrick asked, that insidious jealousy winding through him again. He hadn't been a jealous man until the people he'd loved the most had betrayed him. But he'd been a fool then. Their betrayal had made him much wiser.

"Kate is a friend," Sebastian replied. "A good friend."

"Does she know your secret?" Warrick asked. "Does she share your secret?" He didn't think so; he had felt no fangs when he'd kissed her—only softness and warmth.

"She's human," Sebastian said. "And unaware of the Secret Vampire Society."

"For now," Warrick said, worry joining his jealousy. "But if she's as smart as you think, she will figure it out."

"You're not one of the society," Sebastian said, his light blue eyes narrowed as he studied Warrick. He must have noticed his concern because he added, "But you know its rules."

"Our pack shares many of those same rules."

"If a human learns of the secret society, she becomes a threat that must be destroyed," the vampire said.

Warrick sighed with regret. "That's one of the rules we share." A rule that was necessary to protect the pack.

"The society has an amendment to that rule," Sebastian admitted. "If a human learns the secret, he or she can avoid death if they become a member of the society."

"A human can only become a member of the pack by mating with one of the wolves…" He swallowed hard, choking down bad memories and a pain he had once thought he would never survive. It had been much worse than the bullets Detective Kate Wever had fired into his shoulder and his heart. "For life." There was more to it than that, like with vampires—biting was involved. But it was more a brand than a feast.

"The society's rule is supposed to be the same," Sebastian said, "but too many exceptions have been made to it for it to be stringently enforced."

"That might be the rule that the pack enforces most stringently," Warrick said. That was why he had lost so much. The love of his life, his family, his pride, his trust...

And now, dallying as he had with Kate Wever, he must have lost his damn sanity, too. He hadn't really wanted vengeance against her; he had only been telling himself that so he'd had a reason to stick around. He'd also told himself that Reagan might not have left. But he wouldn't have known because after she'd shot him, all Warrick had been able to see was Kate.

She was beautiful, but there was something else about her—a strength and an integrity—that attracted him.

But why would Reagan have stayed? If he was as smart as Warrick had always believed he was, he wouldn't have stopped running yet. He was probably far, far away by now.

"You don't have to worry about Kate," Warrick assured the vampire. "I will be leaving Zantrax." There was no reason for him to stay now. But he caught himself sneaking another glance up at her window.

"Going home?"

He shook his head. Just as he had no family, no

mate, no honor—he had no home, either. "I still have unfinished business. I just don't think it's here any longer."

Despite his usually exceptional tracking abilities, he had lost the scent that night. Reagan would have known to put distance—a hell of a lot of distance—between them. And Kate shooting Warrick had given him time to do just that. But his anger with her had cooled. If only his desire could…

Her scent filled him. She didn't smell of flowers or some other cloying odor. She smelled like she tasted: sweet—sugar and vanilla and some spice. How could such a strong, fearless woman be so sweet?

Sebastian sighed, as if giving up a battle he had waged with himself. "You might be wrong about that."

Confusion wrinkled the hair on Warrick's brow. "I thought you warned me off her."

"I did," Sebastian said. "I'm giving you another warning now. The reason you came to Zantrax may not have left yet, either."

"You're saying…" His heart slammed into his ribs. "He's still here?"

"The guy you tried tearing apart in the alley?" Sebastian nodded.

"How do you know?"

The dark-haired man grinned. "In addition to managing Club Underground, I fill in at the bar some nights. A bartender hears things…"

"Your surgeon friend treated him, too?" Warrick guessed. How else would he have known what Warrick had done to him? It had been just the two of them—and Kate—in that alley. Sebastian hadn't come out of the passageway until Kate had left. She'd been getting him help; that was why she had rushed from the alley. But her paramedics wouldn't have been able to help him—not when he had *changed* moments after she'd left him.

Sebastian shook his head, probably trying to protect his surgeon friend from Warrick's wrath, because he wouldn't meet his gaze. For Kate had let the murderer go and then the special surgeon had treated him…

Of course these people had no idea what Reagan had done—what kind of monster he was. Warrick must have injured the son of a bitch, though. Satisfaction filled him. But like Warrick, Reagan wouldn't die easily, either. So he would have to try harder.

"Why do you hate him so much?" Sebastian asked.

"Because he took everything away from me that I ever cared about…" Until then Warrick hadn't hated Reagan; he had actually been foolish enough to care about him, to love and respect him. But he had been an even bigger fool to trust him. It didn't matter that they were brothers—at least, it didn't matter to Reagan.

"Then I was right to warn you," Sebastian said.

"Warn me?" Warrick considered it more good news than bad. He hadn't lost Reagan's trail, like he'd worried he had.

"Yes," the vampire replied with a nod. "Sounds like this man you're trying to find poses quite a threat."

Warrick chuckled. "Hell, no. He can't hurt me anymore."

"But he could hurt someone you care about again."

"There's no one left." And he had nowhere to go—because Warrick couldn't go home again until he'd gotten justice for his father's murder. The son of a bitch had really taken everyone and everything from him.

Sebastian Culver glanced up at Kate Wever's window now. "No one left?"

Warrick chuckled again but this one was hollow. "The woman shot me. Why would I care about her?"

"I was wondering that myself," the vampire said. "What the hell were you doing in her place tonight?"

"She shot me," he repeated. "Her interference allowed him to get away that night." But not again. Reagan would not get away again. Maybe that was why the murderer hadn't left Zantrax, either. Maybe even Reagan knew that it was time to end this.

"So you were going to hurt her?" Sebastian asked, anger flashing in his eyes, as he stepped closer to Warrick.

They might not be able to kill each other. But if they tangled, they could do a lot of damage. Inflict a lot of physical pain…

Warrick uttered a weary sigh and quipped, "I'm all about revenge."

For what felt like so long now…

"She was just doing her job," Sebastian said in her defense and with great respect. It was unusual that vampires respected humans. But then Kate Wever was an exceptional human.

"I know that." Logically he had always known that, yet he hadn't been able to stay away from her. "I'm not going to hurt her."

Sebastian pushed his hand through his long, dark hair. "Maybe you're not the one I should be worrying about…"

Warrick dragged in a deep breath. And as he did,

he caught another scent. Fear. His own. "You think *he* might hurt her?"

"I don't," Sebastian said. "But do you care about her?"

"I don't know her." But he did care—enough that he didn't want her harmed because of him. While he had no future with Kate Wever, he wanted her to have a future of her own.

"Does *he* know that?" Sebastian asked. "If he's been watching you, what might he think?"

He bit off a curse. The vampire was right, but Warrick didn't want him to know it.

Reagan had ruthlessly taken away everyone Warrick had ever cared about. And because Warrick had stayed in Zantrax, because he had stayed near her, *he* might think Warrick cared about her. His obsession with Kate Wever had put her in danger.

How badly had that human detective's bullets wounded Warrick? She hadn't killed him; Reagan knew that or he wouldn't have left the alley that night.

But because he didn't know how badly Warrick had been hurt, he hadn't left the city yet. He should have. No good would come of him and his brother being in the same city—not unless he could make Warrick listen to him. Make him realize that Reagan wasn't the threat to him.

Guilt tugged at him, though, and the sunrise on which he had been so focused blurred before his eyes despite his front-row seat on a rooftop of one of Zantrax's highest buildings. He had hurt his brother—far worse than the female detective's bullets could have. He didn't blame Warrick for wanting to kill him.

But Reagan wasn't the only one who would die. Warrick would die, too. And probably so would *she*.

That was why Reagan hadn't left yet. He had to make his brother listen to him. He had to—or they would lose more than their father and each other. They would lose even more than *their* lives…

Chapter 3

The high-rise buildings cast deep shadows, blocking out whatever glow of the moon that might have illuminated the alley. Kate had only her flashlight, which she gripped tightly in one hand, and her gun, which she gripped in the other. The Glock was still holstered, but the leather strap was unclasped, so it was ready to be drawn.

This place, this *damn alley*, and the club housed in the basement of one of the buildings, creeped her out. Too many strange things happened in this part of Zantrax—around Club Underground. Paige's stalking, Bernie's flying people and now *his* disappearing body...

Last night that strangeness had invaded Kate's bedroom when his body had reappeared there—alive.

Despite the sweater and heavy jacket she wore and

the fact that none of the cool mid-November breeze could blow between the buildings, Kate shivered. She actually would have welcomed a fresh breeze; there was only stagnant, stale air in the alley. It smelled more of the trash in the Dumpster than the crisp scent of burning leaves and roasting pumpkins she usually associated with autumn.

But the ghost that never quite seemed to leave her—he fit in with the season. But he wasn't really a ghost; she didn't believe in them.

He had to be real.

But then who had she shot in the alley?

His twin? If so, what had happened to the body? She shone her flashlight beam around the alley, bouncing it off every brick on every wall of the three buildings that backed up to and blocked off the alley. There was no space between the buildings, no way for a body to squeeze out. None of the doors that opened onto it had been unlocked that night—most of them were walled off inside so that they never opened.

Frustration coursed through Kate and triggered her usually long temper, so that she snapped and kicked out, driving her heel into the corner of the Dumpster. Its rusty legs squeaked as it rolled back a couple of inches.

That squeak echoed one she'd heard before, just as she'd been running from the dark alley to get help for the man she'd shot. She had relived that night so many times that she remembered every sight, every smell and every sound...

The Dumpster must have moved that night, too.

She stepped closer to the rim of the rusted metal bin, gagging on the putrid odors that emanated from it, and shone her flashlight beam inside. The circle of light glanced off boxes and torn bags of garbage, from which coffee grounds, old liquor bottles and other food scraps and papers spilled out.

No homeless man.

Had Bernie been there that night? Was he the one who'd moved the Dumpster and the man? He'd claimed he hadn't been, but Kate knew better than to believe what anyone told her. Too many people lied. Or kept secrets.

But if the vagrant had been there, would he have moved the Dumpster or would he have hidden quietly inside to avoid detection? She had checked the Dumpster that night; she had looked for that body everywhere—except beneath the metal bin. Kate pulled her hand from her holster and shoved her flashlight into her back pocket. She reached out for the Dumpster, pushing at it with both palms.

Her muscles strained in her shoulders, arms and stomach, but the metal crate barely budged, skidding inches across the asphalt. It creaked and squealed in protest of every bit of distance it moved. Gritting her teeth, Kate pushed harder. Then she reached for her flashlight again and shone the beam beneath where the Dumpster had been.

If she could find a trail of blood, she could prove that she hadn't imagined what had happened that night. But a couple of months had passed. The blood could have washed away or degraded enough that she wouldn't be able to find it with a flashlight. She would have to bring in a forensics crew. Would the department authorize it when they'd already gone over the alley once and found nothing but blood they claimed they couldn't even prove was human?

Doubtful. So she had only herself and her own investigative skills to prove what had happened that night. That she had killed a man. She shivered, jiggling the flashlight so that the beam bounced around the asphalt and glinted off the metal of a manhole cover. She hadn't noticed that before.

Could someone, perhaps his twin, have dragged the body down into the sewer? That made more sense than any alternative. Kate always needed to find the sense in even the most senseless of acts. Rationalizing the irrational was the only way she managed to keep her sanity with her career. And with her life...

She had seen and done many irrational, senseless things over the past forty years of her life. And this was probably another—but still she reached for the manhole cover, after setting her flashlight down on the asphalt, its beam directed toward the opening to the sewer.

But when she reached for the cover, the light moved off it. The beam rose, shining into her eyes—blinding her. She squinted against the light. "Who's there?"

She hadn't heard anyone enter the alley. Had felt no other presence. But, like last night in her bedroom, she was suddenly not alone.

"Is it you?" She reached for her holster—and the gun—even though it had done nothing that night. If she believed her late-night visitor, he had survived the bullets she'd fired into him. If she believed him, she couldn't kill him. "What do you want with me?"

But she received no verbal reply. Her only answer was physical, as the beam swung down, and the heavy metal flashlight struck her head. For a moment she glimpsed a shadow behind the beam—tall, broad-shouldered. Dark.

It could have been him.

But then everything else went dark as Kate fell and her body struck the asphalt.

She was going to die. She was actually surprised that she wasn't already dead—especially given what she had done to the pack—the dissension she had caused. But there was a reason they hadn't killed her yet. They intended to use her as bait to draw Warrick and Reagan back to St. James—the village their father had founded in a remote area of the upper peninsula of Michigan.

But to draw them back, one of them would actually have to care about her. She glanced around the log and fieldstone cabin—empty but for her and the memories she had made there. Good and bad.

No. Reagan and Warrick weren't coming back. And she couldn't stay—because once the others realized that she served no purpose, they would kill her.

Sylvia's fingers trembled as she struggled with the zipper on her suitcase. She had to hurry because time was running out. Warrick and Reagan had already been gone too long.

Maybe they had already killed each other, or maybe they had been killed. Grief and guilt struck her like a blow, and her eyes stung from the pain, tearing up. But she had already shed too many tears—of guilt and pain and loss and, if she was to be honest, self-pity. She blinked away the moisture and ignored the sting.

And wouldn't she know if *he* was dead? They'd

had such a strong—almost otherworldly—connection. Their souls had called to each other. But if that connection was real, he wouldn't have left her.

That relationship hadn't been real; it had been only a fantasy. But something real had come of that fantasy.

And so she had to be strong now—because her life wasn't the only life she needed to save. She pressed her shaking hand over her swelling belly. She had to leave before the others figured out that Warrick and Reagan weren't coming back. Dragging the suitcase off the bed, she turned toward the door and finally she realized that she wasn't alone.

And that it was already too late…

Warrick was too late. He could already smell her blood, the scent—so thick and sweet—burned his flaring nostrils. He rushed into the alley. Blind in the darkness until his eyes adjusted to the deep shadows, he could have been jumped—had whoever attacked her still been present.

But he cared less about his own safety than he cared about hers. And with good reason. She was alone in the alley, lying on the asphalt. Her hair tangled across her face, the ends of it falling into the blood pooled beneath her head.

His heart kicked his ribs as fear and concern jolted him. He had once wanted to see her like this—in those moments after she'd shot him and he had writhed in pain on the asphalt. He had wanted to see her lying in her own blood, like he had been. But that killer vengeance had lasted only for those pain-filled moments. As he'd told her vampire friend, he knew she'd only been doing her job that night.

He dropped to his knees beside her and skimmed his fingers across her face, brushing her hair from her eyes. They were closed. Because she was unconscious or dead? Blood oozed from a deep gash on her forehead, staining her skin red on the path it had taken across her face to the asphalt.

"What were you doing here tonight?" he wondered. "Doing your job?" Or looking for him again? But she considered that her job, finding and arresting him for assault. If she only knew the circumstances...

She probably still wouldn't condone his vigilante justice. She wouldn't understand that he had to reclaim his honor to reclaim his position in the pack.

His fingers trembled as they trailed down her cheek to her throat where he felt for her pulse. It stirred beneath his fingertips, faint but steady.

"That's my girl," he murmured. "Hang in there." He glanced around the alley, but unlike the night Sebastian had come to his aid, no one stepped from the shadows—or the sewer—to help. Dare he move her to that secret clinic? Or would moving her hurt her more? It couldn't hurt her any more than leaving her alone and vulnerable in the alley.

If any of the other creatures of the underground caught the scent of her blood...

She wouldn't survive the feeding frenzy.

He slid his arms beneath her and gently lifted her limp body. Her head lolled back, blood dripping from her wound. He grasped her closer and cradled her neck in one hand.

"How the hell did I get to that clinic?" he muttered. He'd blacked out for a while and had just briefly regained consciousness in the passageway beneath the alley.

His attention zeroed in on the manhole cover near where she'd been lying. Was that what she had been investigating when she got attacked?

"Oh, God, you have to let this drop," he implored her—even though she couldn't hear him. But learning about the Secret Vampire Society would get her killed for certain. So if he took her down that manhole, he was risking her life. But if he didn't get her help...

She was human. She would *really* die. And that was something that he couldn't just watch happen. Hopefully, she would not regain consciousness in the sewer. He kicked the cover aside and stepped into the hole, feeling for the rungs with his feet. Careful of her head, he maneuvered her through the opening and descended into the passageway that led from the alley to the basement clinic.

Holding her close, he knocked—using his foot—on the riveted steel door. "Someone's gotta be here..."

She hadn't stirred, hadn't even murmured, and her body was so limp, so lifeless. Maybe it was already too late. Maybe she had already lost too much blood...

He kicked harder at the steel, so that the door vibrated in the jamb. "Come on! I need help!"

The knob rattled as a lock turned and finally the door opened. He breathed a sigh of relief while Dr. Davison cursed. Shoving past the surgeon, Warrick carried Kate to the table.

"What the hell did you do to her?" Dr. Davison asked, his dark eyes hard with suspicion and anger. The doctor wasn't old—at least not by vampire standards—but gray liberally sprinkled his dark hair.

"I didn't do this," Warrick hotly denied. Maybe he'd once considered hurting her, but he wouldn't have been able to bring himself to actually do her harm. Now the person or creature that had hurt her…

Even the special surgeon wouldn't be able to save that animal after Warrick got done with him.

"Then what the hell happened to Kate?" The doctor grabbed up some instruments.

"You know her?"

"She's my wife's best friend," Dr. Davison shared as he leaned over her and examined the gash on her head. Then he checked her neck, too, probably for puncture wounds. "So tell me how she got hurt."

"I don't know," Warrick replied. "I found her like this, lying unconscious in the alley."

"She never came to?"

"No."

The doctor opened her closed lid and shone a light into her eye and then repeated the action on her other eye. "Her pupils aren't blown."

"That's good?"

The doctor nodded as his fingers gently probed her head wound.

"Do you work on humans, too?" Warrick asked, wondering if he had brought her to the right doctor. Maybe he would have been smarter to bring her to the local emergency room, but the clinic had been closer.

Davison nodded again. "I started with humans and still work on more of them than the other creatures."

"So you can help her."

The doctor sighed. "I don't know…if anyone will be able to help her if she regains consciousness *here*."

Warrick shuddered as he worried that in trying to

help her that he might have put her in more danger. But the society's wasn't the only secret he risked exposing as his watch buzzed out a warning that midnight was only minutes away. Already his skin was beginning to itch as hair rushed to the surface. His jaw ached as the bone stretched—his face was changing shape.

"I hope Kate doesn't wind up like me," Davison murmured as he reached for a syringe.

"How's that?" Warrick asked.

"I stumbled onto a secret I wish I had never learned." A muscle twitched in the doctor's cheek. "And it nearly cost me everything…"

"But you learned the secret and lived."

"Extenuating circumstances. They needed me," the surgeon explained. "But now I'm one of them."

Kate as a vampire? It was easier to imagine her as that than as a werewolf, though. His muscles expanded, ripping through his jeans and his shirt, as his body took its other form. This was the only life he had ever known, having been born and raised in the pack.

He had only imagined turning one human into what he was, and he had lost her…just as he had lost everything else that had ever mattered to him.

Just as he might have lost Kate tonight…

But Kate didn't matter to him. She was a stranger, a human who had thwarted his plans. He needed to leave her to the doctor's care and get the hell out of Zantrax.

"You'll be able to help her?" he asked the surgeon for his assurance.

"I won't be able to go home if I don't save Kate,"

Davison replied. "Now get out of here. She can't see you like that."

A moan emanated from Kate's throat as she shifted on the table, reaching for her head.

It was too late for Warrick to hide.

Images flitted through Kate's mind. Bright lights and searing pain and dark alleys and sterile rooms… and a man who wasn't a man. Her head pounded as she tried to sort out those brief images. But they were like old photographs, the colors faded and washed-out, so that she could barely make out the subjects.

Like old dreams that she could barely remember…

Dreaming. She had to be dreaming. Her eyes were closed; the lids so heavy she could barely lift them. After some effort she managed to blink them open and blink away the grit of deep sleep.

Then she focused on the room. Sunlight streaked through the blinds at the window, casting a warm glow onto the hardwood floor where her clothes lay in a heap. She fought against the sheets tangled around her, but as she sat up, the room spun. Her head lightened and the bright glow dimmed.

"Easy," a familiar deep voice murmured. "Not so fast…"

He was back.

Instinct had her reaching under the other pillow but her palm skimmed across the satin sheet to the edge of the bed. The gun was gone.

"You don't need it," he said as he approached the bed. "I'm not going to hurt you."

"Someone hit me…in the alley." That had happened, hadn't it? She'd been in the alley, searching for...*him*. But he must have found her first.

"It wasn't me," he said and just as he had that first night, he settled onto the bed beside her—as if he was familiar with her bedroom. With her.

She snorted. "As if you'd admit it if it was... I would arrest you for assaulting an officer."

"You've tried once to arrest me for assault."

But he had disappeared, like those images from her mind. She couldn't remember now exactly what she'd seen. What had been real and what a dream. Was he a dream?

"How did I get here?" she wondered. Not just in her apartment and in her bed, but naked beneath her sheets. Just how much of the night before had she forgotten? Had he taken off her clothes? What else had he done to her? She shivered as she imagined him touching her and more...

"I found you in the alley," he said. "I got you some medical help then brought you back here. Don't you remember anything?"

She reached a trembling hand toward her head, and her fingers skimmed over a gauze bandage. Stitches tightened the skin beneath it, which throbbed with a dull ache. "No..." she murmured. "I don't remember anything after I got hit." At least she didn't remember anything that seemed real—that could have actually happened.

"You have a concussion," he said as he gently trailed his fingers along the edge of the gauze. "Someone hit you really hard. Did you see who it was?"

"Only the bright light..." And the shadow behind

it. The tall, broad-shouldered shadow. It could have been him.

But then why was there so much concern in his eerie topaz eyes? "Your pulse was so weak…" He shuddered. "I thought you were dead or nearly dead."

"Why would you care?" she asked. After all, she had shot him. Or so she'd thought…

He shrugged those mammothly broad shoulders. "I don't know…"

"You're mad at me for not letting you kill that man," she reminded him. He certainly had seemed more upset about that than her shooting him.

"Yes, I am," he freely admitted.

"Was that really you?" she asked. "That man in the alley?"

"I told you I didn't hit you—"

"Not tonight…" She glanced to the sun-streaked blinds. "Not last night. That night a couple of months ago. The man in the alley—the one that I shot. It couldn't have been you. Was it your twin?"

He reached for the buttons on his shirt, undoing them so that the dark gray material parted and re-vealed the hard muscles of his chest, dusted with silky-looking black hair. But something marred the masculine perfection—a jagged scar over his heart. He shrugged off the shirt and revealed two more puck-ered, nasty-looking scars in one of his broad shoul-ders.

She gasped and reached out, running her finger-tips over first the scars on his shoulder and then the one on his chest. The scars weren't makeup or theat-rics but real skin—so warm that her fingers tingled from the contact. The very air between them heated.

Her breathing slowed and grew shallow, so that she nearly panted. Her pulse raced, pounding harder and faster than that faint ache in her head.

"It was you." She swallowed the rush of emotion and desire. "I shot *you*."

"Yes, you did."

So he'd had every reason to want to hurt her back, every reason to have struck her in the alley. But he touched her gently now, his fingers trailing from her bandage down the side of her face and along her throat. "Are you sorry?"

She shook her head, but pain reverberated inside her skull with the motion and she winced and whimpered.

"Shh…" he said. "Take it easy. Go back to sleep." He reached for his shirt again.

But she grabbed his shoulders. "Don't leave…"

His body tensed, and his topaz eyes dilated. "Kate…?"

"Don't leave without telling me your name."

His mouth, with those sexy sensual lips, curved into a slight grin. "Warrick."

"Warrick?"

"Yes. Warrick James."

"Warrick James," she repeated, loving the sound of it—the feel of his name on her lips.

He leaned closer, as if she'd drawn him nearer. "Yes, Kate?"

"You're under arrest for assault—"

He laughed at her now. "You never quit." He moved to stand up.

But she clutched at him, holding him down on the

bed. Holding him to her. "You're not disappearing again."

She needed to bring him in to the department, needed to prove her sanity to her coworkers. Especially the one who had been most vocal with his disdain for her story about what had happened that night.

"How are you going to stop me, Kate?" he asked. "You have no gun. You're hurt. You're weak."

She winced—not in pain but in self-disgust. "I'm not weak." She wasn't that same scared woman she'd once been. She was older, wiser and stronger now than she had ever been. And to prove it, she launched herself at him, wrestling him down to the mattress.

He sprawled on his back without a fight, his arms wrapped loosely around her waist. Her breasts nestled against his hard, scarred chest. "You're not weak at all," he assured her. "You've overpowered me."

"Because you let me," she suspected.

He nodded. "I don't want to hurt you."

"You did."

"Not anymore," he said, lifting his head to close the distance between his mouth and hers. His lips skimmed across hers. "Now I just want you…"

And she wanted him, her skin heating and tingling everywhere they touched. The sheet had slipped down, so that her breasts were bare against his chest. His hair, which covered his impressive pecs, tickled and teased her nipples, bringing them to tight, sensitive points.

"And I want—" she struggled free of his loose grasp and grabbed up the sheet again, holding it between them like a shield "—to arrest you."

"I'm not a monster, Kate."

One of those dreamlike images rushed back to her mind—of a man that wasn't a man. Of a man who was a monster—a mammoth, heavily muscled, hairy beast.

She didn't believe him; she didn't believe anything Warrick James said. She had been fooled once before and had believed a man to be a hero when he was really a monster.

So what could a monster be…but a monster?

Chapter 4

The human detective hadn't killed Warrick, but what she'd done might have been far worse. She had bewitched him.

"Poor bastard," Reagan murmured to himself as he sat alone at the bar in Club Underground, staring into his drink. He, too, had become besotted with a woman—so besotted that he'd lost himself in her. He had lost his honor and his integrity. He'd also lost his father and his brother.

Even if he could talk to Warrick and could actually get through to him, their relationship was destroyed. Reagan had destroyed it and maybe because of that, he deserved to be destroyed, as well. But Warrick didn't deserve it. He didn't deserve any more pain.

And neither did *she*. Reagan glanced down at the picture he'd set on the bar next to his untouched drink, and he sucked in a breath at her beauty. With her silvery blond hair and mesmerizing green eyes, she was beyond beautiful; she was ethereal. Reagan needed to get back to St. James—to her—before something happened to her. If only he'd had time to bring her with him...

But everything had happened so quickly—had gone so wrong. There hadn't been time. And after what he'd done, he wasn't sure she would have gone with him. Like Warrick, she would probably hate and distrust him, too.

And, he assured himself, nothing would happen to her—until he was dead. Then she would be of no use to the pack anymore. They couldn't bait a dead man.

"You're about to break that glass," the bartender warned.

Reagan hadn't even been aware how tightly he'd been gripping it until Sebastian Culver commented on it. Then he glanced at his hand and noticed how his fingers had gone white. He forced himself to release the glass.

"It's not like you're going to drink it anyway," the vampire bartender remarked. "You just sit here every day until midnight—waiting for him to show up."

And after midnight, he took to the rooftops, so that he could watch the city. So that he could watch Warrick.

The bartender shook his head. "I don't get it..."

"What?" Reagan asked.

"He wants to kill you," Sebastian told him what he already knew. "You should be trying to avoid him. Instead, you're trying to find him."

He had been trying to find him—to make sure that the human detective hadn't wounded him too badly.

But now Reagan knew where to find Warrick—near her. And he'd chosen to avoid a private confrontation that would probably end as badly as the one in the alley had. With them both wounded…

"I want him to find me," Reagan corrected the bartender's misassumption. "Here—in a public place."

"You think that'll stop him from trying to kill you?" Sebastian glanced around the crowded bar and snorted derisively. "Gunshots to his shoulder and his heart didn't stop him from trying to tear you apart. I don't think anything will stop him."

Reagan sighed in resignation and reluctant agreement. "Not even the truth…"

"You're wasting your time here," Sebastian said.

"Not if I can save his life…" Then it would all be worth it. Even leaving Sylvia…

"Then you better find him," Sebastian suggested.

"I know where he is," he said. "With the detective."

Sebastian shook his head. "He's not with Kate." He chuckled. "Maybe she's done what she tried that night. Maybe she arrested him."

Alarm slammed through Reagan. If Warrick was in custody and changed…

More than just his life would be lost.

Warrick stared through the bars, his hands grasping the old brass rungs. "Glad you're here."

"Glad I found you, boy," the old man said. "You've been gone for much too long."

"I can't go back."

"Not until he's dead," Stefan James agreed. His hair was more gray than black, his eyes nearly the same steely gray. But his age didn't indicate weakness; if anything it represented the reverse. The older and wiser Uncle Stefan had grown, the stronger he had become. He was a good leader for the pack, but he wasn't Warrick's father. That was whose advice Warrick really needed, but he could never speak to his father again.

Because of Reagan…

Warrick's hands slid from the rungs and he walked around the partition wall that separated the tellers from the vault area of the former bank. Or it would have had the bank still been operational but it had been deserted…until a few months ago when someone had taken up residence to hide inside the vault. As if that would have prevented Warrick from picking up his scent…

"You tracked him here?" Uncle asked, sniffing the air.

Warrick nodded.

"His scent is old, his trail cold," the old man remarked. "But you're still here. Why?" That steely-gray gaze narrowed as Uncle totally focused on Warrick.

"He'll come back," he claimed. But he wasn't sure. He had only the vampire bartender's word that Reagan hadn't left the city. And why should he trust a vampire who didn't trust him, either?

"You thought he would come back home, too," Uncle Stefan reminded him.

"For her…"

"But he left his *mate* alone," Uncle remarked, watching him closely—probably for that flash of jealousy and rage that Warrick had always exhibited when it came to *her*. "And he keeps running."

"Because he knows I'm chasing him."

"You're not chasing him," Uncle said with a disparaging snort. "You're chasing your honor."

"My honor or vengeance?" Warrick wondered now. And his hunger for vengeance wasn't as overwhelming as it had once been. Probably because his hunger for Kate was greater. He shouldn't have left her...

"Both, in this case," the old man asserted. "You cannot lead the pack if you cannot claim justice for crimes committed against it."

"I'm not leading the pack," Warrick pointed out. "You are."

Stefan shrugged as if the leadership role meant nothing to him. "It was always your father's wish that one of his sons take over for him when he was no longer able to fill the role of leader."

Warrick flinched, remembering how he'd found his father. All that blood spilling from his wounded heart, leaving nothing but the corpse of an old werewolf as, even dead, he turned at midnight. None of his power or intimidation had remained—nothing of the spirit of the fearsome leader and father.

But now another memory haunted Warrick more, of Kate lying alone in that alley in a pool of her own blood.

"Perhaps you are the right one to lead the pack, Uncle," Warrick said of the role he, himself, had wanted to fill since he was just a pup. But as the younger son, he had never been groomed for the role—had never really been considered a possible candidate by anyone but his uncle.

Uncle Stefan shook his head. "I am an old man," he said. "I have no sons now. No one to carry on when I grow too weak to lead. You are the future, Warrick."

"Only if I can reclaim my honor."

"You set off on this quest for justice," Uncle reminded him, his brow furrowing with confusion. "Your belly burned with the desire for it."

Warrick remembered when the heat and hunger of his rage had consumed him. Rage had ruled his life, had blinded him to anything but vengeance. Blinded him so much that he hadn't even noticed the woman in the alley until she'd fired those shots into his shoulder.

It ached still, all these months after the shooting, just as his body ached for hers days after they had touched skin to skin—lips to lips. Now the desire burning in his belly was to possess Kate Wever in every way. She was so beautiful—all silky skin over sleek muscle. As he had once tried to haunt her, she haunted him now.

"What has changed for you?" Uncle asked. "Did *he* get to you?"

He had tried, that night in the alley—had tried to spew his lies and manipulations. That was when Warrick had threatened to rip out his throat, so that he wouldn't have to listen. He shook his head. "Not him."

"But someone has?"

He shook his head again, unwilling to tell his uncle about Kate for fear of sounding like a fickle boy instead of the decisive man necessary to lead a pack. It wasn't as if he and Kate had a future anyway. She wanted to arrest him now for assault. What would she do once he'd committed murder?

He sighed. "Perhaps I am just wearying of the chase."

Maybe Warrick had finally realized that his quest had been more about vengeance and pride than justice. But now, after finding Kate bleeding in the alley those few nights ago, it was less about vengeance and more about Kate.

How could he leave Zantrax when she was in danger, especially when he might be the reason she was in danger?

Blood stained the cement floor of the secret surgical room. Was some of that Kate's blood? Paige shuddered to consider it, to remember that her friend had been that badly hurt. That strong, fierce Kate had been lying unconscious and vulnerable in an alley.

"Are you sure she's all right?" she asked her husband. "She didn't come to happy hour again."

Ben nodded, but there was concern in his dark eyes. "As long as she doesn't remember being here, she should be all right." He poured a bottle of something onto the floor that dissolved the blood and cleaned the cement, but it couldn't remove every trace of the horrors that happened in that room. It was as if screams of pain hung in the air with the pungent scent of the cleanser.

"She doesn't remember," Paige said. "She didn't even mention getting hurt when I called her." And Paige hadn't been able to bring it up for fear that Kate would remember who had treated her injury and where.

"She has to know she was hurt," Ben said. "She has stitches and a bandage."

"Then why didn't she mention it?" Maybe Kate had remembered more than she was willing to admit to Paige.

"Because she's Kate," Ben replied. "She's proud and independent. And she wouldn't want you to worry. And she especially wouldn't want you to fuss over her."

"Or she didn't want me to know what she remembered and warn you," Paige said.

Ben glanced at the security monitor that showed the video feed from the cameras outside both reinforced steel doors. One led to the hallway to the club; the other to the sewer. Both had been reinforced so that vampires—or other *creatures*—couldn't get inside unless Ben let them in. It wasn't just for his protection but for the protection of whatever patient he was treating. She looked at the monitor, too, and breathed a sigh of relief that both the hallway and the sewer were empty.

"She's not out there," Ben said. "And she would be if she had any suspicions about this place."

"She has suspicions," Paige reminded him. Kate had wanted inside this room back when somebody had been stalking Paige. But Sebastian had convinced her that the entrance to the sewer had been sealed off and the door led to nowhere.

If Kate ever found this room, Paige would lose her best friend. The society would order the human's death.

As if he'd read her mind, Ben reached out and wrapped an arm around her shoulders. But because he knew her so well he offered her no false assurances. He only offered his love as he held her closely.

"I don't want to lose her," Paige said.

"Maybe we can talk to the society," Ben said.

She looked up at him and arched a brow. As if the society would listen to her. She had no way to negotiate—not the way the society's special surgeon could.

"Maybe *I* can," he amended his comment, his sexy mouth curving into a slight grin.

"But the society isn't the only danger she's in," Paige said. "What about this other *creature* or *creatures*? You've said there are two of them."

Ben groaned. "I shouldn't have told you about them."

"We promised," she reminded him. "No more secrets." At least not between the two of them. But they kept secrets—the secrets of the society—from all their human friends. "Are they a danger to her?"

"The pack has the same law the society does," Ben reminded her. "But the one she shot—he was the one who brought her here for me to treat."

"You think he cares about her?"

Ben shrugged. "I don't know what to think about Warrick James. The night I treated his gunshot wounds he was furious with her."

"So he could have been the one who attacked her in the alley," Paige said. She wanted to meet this creature who was threatening her best friend.

"I don't know if he attacked her, or if she was attacked because of him," Ben said. "But I feel like he might be more responsible than the society."

Or was that only what he wanted to believe because he and Paige and the child they'd adopted were all members of the society? It could have been a vampire who'd attacked Kate. And if that was the case, she was lucky she had only taken a blow to her head instead of a fang to her throat. But if she kept investigating, Kate was too good a detective to not figure out the secret and get herself killed.

Goose bumps lifted on Kate's skin as she stepped into the thick darkness of the alley. Not even her flashlight beam could chase away the shadows this late at night. The anonymous call, promising to reveal everything she wanted to know, had lured her back to the alley. She had considered that it was just a ploy to get her here—to hurt her again. Yet she hadn't been able to ignore it. Zantrax PD made it a policy to follow up on every silent observer tip. Maybe this tip was even better since it had come into her direct line and had been traced back to a public phone near Club Underground. A real witness could have made that call. Maybe Bernie.

Or the person who'd struck her that night…

She was a detective. Whatever risk it took to learn what she wanted to know was a risk she was willing to take. Of course she wasn't usually foolish enough to go into a potentially dangerous situation without backup. But this was the second night she had taken that risk. Third, if she counted that first night when she'd chased Warrick James into the alley. But then she hadn't wanted to risk his killing that man.

And now, she hadn't requested backup because she didn't want to risk her reputation. Her "missing" body case had undone the respect she'd fought for years to gain in the department. *He* had ridiculed her the most. Not the man she'd shot but the man from her past, the man she wished she could leave in her past— forgotten only to surface in rare nightmares to remind her to never make that mistake again.

To never trust.

But they worked together. He worked nights, though, and she worked days. Except now when she was off the clock but not really off duty.

Tonight she was more prepared, though. Her gun

wasn't in her holster but clasped tightly in her right hand while her left grasped the flashlight. She shone the beam around the alley, illuminating only one small circle of darkness at a time. Nothing moved in the shadows, though.

Well, nothing human. Small feet scurried across the asphalt. Confident she was alone, Kate gave in to a shudder of revulsion over the nearness of the rats.

"Hello?" she called out. "Anyone here?"

Why call her if the person had no intention of showing up? He or she had gone to the trouble of disguising his or her voice so that it was unrecognizable. Maybe it was just a joke. Since that night when they had all searched for a body no one had been able to find, her coworkers had subjected her to many jokes. Like the bloody dummy left in her desk chair. And her locker and even her car…

If only she had been able to arrest Warrick the other night…to bring him in to the department and show his scars. She could have proved that she hadn't imagined it all. That she hadn't imagined him. He was real.

But too strong for her to have overpowered without her gun. Hell, when she'd had her gun she hadn't been able to stop him. At least not permanently. He had survived injuries that would have killed anyone else.

Was he real?

He had disappeared from her bedroom just as quickly as he had the first night she'd discovered him there. One minute he had been there, almost as if he'd been watching over and protecting her after her concussion. Then the next minute he'd been gone…before she'd been able to find her gun or her cuffs. Before she'd been able to arrest him.

Or make love with him…

She wasn't sure which she'd wanted more. Or at least she wasn't willing to admit which she'd wanted more.

"Warrick?" Could he have been her caller? Somehow she doubted he would have gone to the trouble of altering his voice, though.

Who would have gone to the trouble of luring her here only to not show up? It had to be a joke. She sighed over her wasted time. But it didn't have to be wasted. She could finish the investigation a concussion had ended those few nights ago. Instead of putting away her gun and putting down the flashlight, she leaned her shoulder against the Dumpster and shoved.

The metal creaked and squeaked as it edged slightly across the asphalt. Hell, she hadn't entirely gained back her strength after the concussion. But the Dumpster seemed heavier tonight. It certainly smelled as if it was full since mingled putrid odors wafted out and overwhelmed her.

One scent—sweet and metallic—was new.

She rose up on tiptoe and shone the flashlight inside the Dumpster. The beam illuminated a man's face, his skin pale but for the dirt and grease smeared across it and his beard.

"Bernie!" She recognized the homeless man from whom she had taken the statement about the people he had seen flying from the alley.

Maybe that was how Warrick disappeared so quickly from place to place. Usually she would never consider such a fantastic explanation, but at least it was an explanation. And that was more than she had managed to discover on her own.

She waved the flashlight in the homeless man's face. "Bernie!"

The vagrant's eyes were closed. Had he passed out drunk? She could smell the liquor, too, that saturated his clothes and oozed from his pores. The beam of light shining in his face didn't even stir him.

Her pulse quickened and she moved the flashlight down. Horror, over what she saw, rushed up to gag her. But she choked it down just enough to scream.

He had already been tracking her scent, not surprised that it was leading him to the alley, when he heard her scream. The sound of the terror in her voice raised all the hair on Warrick's body. She needed him.

But could he come to her like this?

It was after midnight, so he had taken his other form—the form he was from midnight to dawn every night. The form that might frighten her more than what was already in the alley with her. Unless…

He ran to her, legs straining to close the distance between them before she could be hurt again. Before *he* could hurt her…

But when he burst into the alley, he found her alone, staring into the Dumpster. What had she discovered this time that she shouldn't have?

Then she turned and discovered…him. Fear had already drained her face of all color, leaving her skin deathly pale in the dark. Now her eyes widened, and another scream rose to her open lips. But she bit it back, as if afraid of startling him. "Stay away," she murmured, cowering from him.

But the Dumpster was at her back, and he stood between her and the only exit. He was down on all fours, hoping to resemble more dog than werewolf. But dogs weren't this big, this powerful, and she knew it.

"What are you…?" she asked the question, but he doubted she expected an answer.

She did not know that he could speak in the same voice he used in his human form. She didn't know anything about werewolves, and she could never learn because the rules of the pack were as strict as the rules of the Secret Vampire Society. Perhaps stricter, because no exceptions were ever made within the pack.

At least they hadn't been when his father had been the leader. His uncle was unlikely to make exceptions, either, as his pride demanded he be as fearsome a leader as his brother had been—even though he was not nearly as ruthless.

"Get back," she said, her voice soft but the command unmistakable. "I'm not going to let you finish him off."

Finish him off? Who? Just what the hell was inside the Dumpster?

He moved closer, hoping to catch a glimpse. But on all fours, he could not see inside the metal bin. He wanted to talk to her, wanted to ease the fear that had her gripping her gun and flashlight tightly as if she was ready to use either as a weapon. But his speaking to her, in his present form, would only scare her more—and put her in more danger.

"Get away!" she said, her voice rising and cracking with her panic. "Leave me alone!"

If only he could…

Every time he left her, trouble found her. Usually

here in this damn alley. He moved closer to the Dumpster, needing to know what she had found this time. He needed to know which secret she was at greater risk of discovering.

But in moving closer to the Dumpster, he also moved closer to her. The gun shook as she trained the barrel on him. "I know you can't understand me," she said, "but I'm begging you to just leave me—and him—alone."

Just as he had that first night they'd met, he ignored her commands. And he surged up on his hind legs. With his front ones braced on the edge of the Dumpster, he peered inside. And now he understood her horror and the scream she had probably involuntarily uttered.

He didn't recognize the man, but he recognized the wound. Someone had torn out the throat of the victim—as he had threatened to do to his enemy. But this man was not his enemy. Neither was Kate.

But she didn't realize that. Trembling with fear, she stared at him—her eyes wide as if she was afraid to blink in case he attacked.

He wanted to say her name, wanted to soothe her fears. But she probably thought he'd done this—either in his present form or his other one. She had been there the night he'd made this threat to Reagan; that was why she'd shot him.

She looked about to shoot him again. But instead of backing away from her, of leaving her alone, he stepped closer. If only she could see that he was no threat to her...

That he wanted to soothe her fears.

But she breathed fast, in frantic pants. "Please, don't make me do this…"

He wasn't growling, wasn't snarling—wasn't doing anything to intimidate her but being. And that, with his mammoth size, was intimidating enough.

"Please…" The plea slipped through her lips with a whimper.

She didn't want to shoot him tonight any more than she had that first night when she'd broken up his fight in this very alley. He understood that now. That he had left her no choice.

He had a choice—he could speak to her, could explain what he was. He wasn't sure that she would understand, but he was sure that knowing the pack's secret would put her in danger. No, he had no choice, either. He would rather endure whatever pain she might inflict on him than put Kate's life at risk. But that urge to comfort and protect her had him moving closer to her.

"Stay back," she yelled at him, as if raising her voice might make him understand—if he really was just the creature she thought he was.

He had moved too close to her—so close that he'd backed her right up against the Dumpster behind her—the Dumpster she thought held his last victim. And she was scared that she would be his next.

If only he could assure her…

But he had no choice. And neither did she.

She'd shot him once to protect another man. Tonight she lifted the gun and she shot him to protect herself.

The bullet seared through his pelt and then his skin,

burying deep in his flesh. He dropped to the asphalt as blood gushed from his wound.

And he heard her scream again…

Chapter 5

His blood had been spilled again. Even in his human form, Reagan's sense of smell was extrasensory. It was past dawn now, but no light shone into the alley. If his vision wasn't extrasensory, too, he might not have noticed the crime scene tape cordoning off the entrance. He'd seen it as he'd stepped right over it.

Warrick had been hurt here. Again. Why the hell wouldn't he just leave Zantrax? Did he realize that Reagan was still here? Or was it because of the woman that Warrick stayed?

The human detective had shot him once already. Had she shot him again? Warrick was lucky she had no silver bullets. But she wasn't lucky. She would need at least one silver bullet. Because Reagan picked up someone else's scent in the alley and he knew that no one was safe now.

The real danger had arrived in Zantrax.

* * *

"You look like hell."

Kate flinched at the man's voice, but she wouldn't let him see her fear. Not anymore. She didn't even glance up from her computer screen. Keeping her focus on the report she had to write up about the body—poor, drunk Bernie—she had found in the alley last night, she offhandedly replied, "You always did know how to sweet-talk me."

Occasionally he had talked with his fists, too. That was why their marriage had been brief. And painful. So painful that it wasn't a mistake she had ever dared to make again.

Detective Dwight Beckenridge was a decorated officer with Zantrax PD. He had taken a bullet meant for his partner. He had saved a teenage girl from her kidnapper. He had been everyone's hero…but hers.

But how could she have known? How could she have seen the dark side that no one else ever had?

With his light blond hair and light blue eyes, he appeared more angel than devil. Only she knew the evil that lurked within him.

"Kate?" he called her name now with concern. Probably because they were in a public place, in the detective bull pen with only short cubicle walls separating their desks, he acted as if he actually gave a damn about her. "Are you okay?"

She nodded. "Fine. Just busy." And she wished he was, too, at his desk across the room, instead of standing next to hers.

He reached out, but she jerked her head back before he made contact with the bandage on her forehead. "You're not fine. How'd you get this?"

She met his gaze then, hers full of the resentment she had never overcome. "Walked into a door."

That was what she used to tell people when he'd left bruises on her. But that had only happened twice. The first time she had accepted his apologies and explanations. No one understood the stress and frustration of their job better than another officer. But the second time...

She had packed her bags and filed divorce papers. She wasn't about to become one of the statistics whose domestic abuse reports she had taken for years. She should have reported him, too. She knew that, but other officers would have been more willing to believe that humans that weren't human flew out of the alley than that their hero was really a monster.

"Kate, are you involved with someone?"

His image came to her mind—all that long black hair and those eerie topaz eyes. The dog—or wolf— or whatever that thing had been in the alley had reminded her of Warrick. They both had those same eerie eyes.

Maybe that was why she had called her friend Paige's husband before she'd called the police. She'd wanted him to help that *thing*.

"Is he violent?" Dwight asked, his voice thick with emotion and concern that actually seemed real.

She shook her head. "I'm not involved with anyone. And if I was, I would know better than to get mixed up with another violent man."

Dwight flinched now, as if she'd hit him. She had tried once, but he hadn't even felt her punch. Like Warrick, he'd seemed superhumanly strong. Invincible.

Too bad the vagrant hadn't been.

Remembering how violently poor Bernie had died, she shuddered.

"Something's going on, Kate," Dwight persisted. He planted his palms on the edge of her desk and leaned close. "I know you'll never forgive me for what happened between us. Hell, I'll never forgive myself. But please know that I still care about you. I want to help you."

God, he was good at spewing all those pretty lies, at inspiring confidence and admiration and forgiveness. That was why there had been a second time—because he was that good. She had never hated him more.

"I don't need your help," she said. "I don't need anything from you but for you to keep your distance." That had been their agreement. She wouldn't report what he'd done to her as long as he didn't contest the divorce and he stayed the hell away from her. Despite nearly ten years passing since they had made that agreement, Kate wasn't about to let him renege on the terms of it.

"You do need my help," he said. "You're just too damn proud to admit it." He sighed, his breath stirring her hair. "You're getting mixed up in something too dangerous for you to handle alone."

She turned to him now and studied his handsome face through narrowed eyes. "What do you know about it?"

His voice hard, he adamantly told her, "I know that you need to stay far away from Club Underground."

She could have informed him that her best friend

owned the place, but she shared nothing of her personal life with her ex. So she just asked, "Why?"

"You saw what happened to that homeless man," he reminded her. "You don't want to be next."

He hadn't come to the scene—which was good since she had been distraught after shooting that... *thing.* So how did he know what had happened to Bernie? Sure, someone else in the department might have said something to him. But he acted as if he had *seen* the horrific scene himself—not just heard about it.

"Is that a threat?" she asked.

He shrugged. "Just some friendly advice."

"We're not friends," she coldly informed him.

"We could be," he offered, his eyes gleaming with hope, "if you could find a way to forgive me."

Her resentment bubbled up, gagging her. "When hell freezes over."

"You're making a mistake, Kate," he warned her. "You could use my help."

"I could use your honesty," she said. "Tell me what you know about what happened in that alley last night." It was clear he knew more about Bernie's death than he was willing to admit.

"I don't know anything about last night," he said, but his pale blue eyes shuttered, hiding other secrets—just as he had during their brief marriage.

"But you know something about other nights." Maybe the night she had shot Warrick even though Dwight had acted as if she had gone crazy and hallucinated the whole experience. Then he'd taunted her about it.

"And you know something about Club Underground," she surmised.

"Just leave it alone," he advised her. "Forget about everything you've seen."

"I can't."

"Why not?"

"A man died," she reminded him. But she suspected her determination had less to do with Bernie's violent death than with Warrick James. "And you need to stop bothering me so I can get back to work solving his murder." She reached for the phone.

But Dwight caught her hand, his touch chilling instead of warming her. "Kate, I don't want to see you get hurt again. And you will…if you don't let this go."

She didn't have to ask him again. She knew without a doubt that that was a threat.

"That was Kate," Dr. Davison said as he slid his cell phone back into his pocket. "The two of you have been keeping me busy lately."

"Do you think she remembers being here, Ben?" Warrick asked the underground surgeon. Tonight had brought him and Dr. Davison to a first-name basis— when Kate had called her friend's husband to the alley to help him. "Do you think that's why she called *you* tonight?"

Ben tensed. "I don't know why but I'm damn glad that she did."

"Me, too," Warrick said. If she had called someone else…

But why had she called Ben earlier to the alley and again now?

"What about that call?" he asked. "Was she checking on me?"

Ben nodded. "She also wants me to make a cast of your teeth."

"Why?"

"To see if your teeth will match the wounds on the victim she found in the alley."

Of course she didn't know that, when the sun had risen an hour ago, he had turned back into his human form. He no longer had his canine teeth or the bullet she had fired into him. He lifted his hand to the bandage on his shoulder. The flesh beneath was raw and tender from where the surgeon had dug out the bullet and stitched up the skin.

"Was he your victim?" Ben asked.

Offended, Warrick sucked in a breath of surprise. "No."

"That first night Kate shot you because you were trying to tear some man apart."

"It wasn't the man she found in the Dumpster tonight." He had never seen that man before, and he wished like hell that Kate hadn't seen the guy, either. Not like that...

"Then who were you fighting with that night?"

Sebastian had already let slip that Ben had treated Warrick's enemy, too. So the doctor knew—he probably just wanted Warrick's side of the story he would rather not share. So he vaguely replied, "Someone I used to know."

At least he'd thought he had known him until Reagan had betrayed him. Apparently Warrick had never really known him at all. "I didn't know the man in the Dumpster," he said. "I'd never seen him before."

"I knew him. Kate knew him. She said she thought

he was a witness," Ben remarked as he checked the tape securing the bandage to Warrick's skin.

"A witness to what?"

The older man shrugged. "Considering his condition, I don't think she had a chance to find out. She did say that someone called her to the alley—promised to give her information."

"And she thought it was the homeless man?"

Ben shrugged. "I don't know if she recognized his voice or not."

"And this information?" he asked. "What was that supposed to be about?" Him? Reagan?

The surgeon shrugged again. "Obviously one of her investigations."

"Kate and her damn investigations."

"She's a detective," Ben said with a sigh of resignation. "It's her job."

"I know." Frustration gnawed at him, hurting more than the ache in his wounded shoulder. "But it's going to get her killed."

"Kate's not your concern," Ben pointed out. "In fact, if I were you, I'd stay away from her. Every time you two are together one of you winds up getting hurt."

He tensed with indignation. "*I* would never hurt Kate."

"She can't say the same about you. She's shot you twice now." Amusement lightened the doctor's dark eyes.

"Only because she doesn't understand…"

"And you can't explain," Ben reminded him. "You have to keep your secrets." He tossed a shirt at Warrick to go with the jeans he'd already loaned him.

"And you have to keep your distance. You should probably leave Zantrax before anyone else gets hurt."

Warrick shook his head. "Not now. That man was attacked right where Kate had been just a few days before." And she had been called to that alley. By the vagrant? Or by whoever had killed the vagrant?

"He was brutally murdered from what I saw of his body," Ben agreed. He had arrived before the coroner and crime scene units. "It looked like a werewolf attack."

"It wasn't me," Warrick maintained. And since it wasn't him, it had to mean that his enemy had not yet left the city. The homeless man could have seen something he shouldn't have, and Reagan had been forced to kill him. Perhaps Reagan was as sick of running as Warrick was sick of chasing him.

"Someone—or *something*—attacked him," Ben said.

But had the man been the intended victim or had Kate?

She was a victim, perhaps of her own selfishness. If only she hadn't made such a mess of her life and of theirs. Even if Reagan and Warrick were still alive, why would either of them return for her? She had caused so much trouble.

And now she was paying for what she'd done, imprisoned inside the house where once she had envisioned living happily ever after. That would have never been her fate, though—only a fantasy. Especially after the rift she'd caused between the St. James brothers.

Her baby—or babies—moved inside her belly,

kicking her. Sylvia had needed that kick—that urging to fight for them. For herself. She wasn't a victim. She would not be a victim.

She pulled open drawers in the kitchen, looking for tools—for something that would help her break the heavy locks at the doors and the windows. She needed to escape. And then instead of waiting for them to return to her, she needed to find Reagan and Warrick. She needed to warn them—that the danger wasn't from each other.

The true danger was coming from someone they would never suspect. One of those chains holding the doors shut rattled, as a key turned in the lock. She tensed as fear overwhelmed her. And once again it was too late for her to escape. Too late for her to save herself or the man she loved.

While their relationship had been a fantasy, her feelings hadn't been. She'd felt that connection to him—that had drawn her to him as if their souls had called to each other. She could still feel him—could sometimes feel his frustration, his guilt, his torment...

She had caused him that pain—him and his brother. But she hadn't meant to hurt anyone. The same could not be said for the person—the monster—holding her hostage. Had a ransom been demanded?

Their lives for hers?

Tears of exhaustion and frustration burned Kate's eyes. She had been up all night writing that damn report. It was full of gruesome details but no conclusions. No explanations. Because she hadn't reported what else she'd found in that alley besides Bernie's mutilated body...

Her hand trembled as she shoved the key in the lock of her apartment. She turned it and the knob, nearly falling inside the door. The sleepless night wasn't the reason for her exhaustion. Not even the frustration really.

It was that damn dog—or whatever the mammoth, muscular beast had been. When she had called Ben earlier, he had given her the news: the dog hadn't made it. While she was pretty certain that it had probably been what had attacked Bernie the homeless man, she hadn't wanted to shoot the animal.

But it had just kept coming at her. She lifted her fingers to her throat. And she hadn't wanted to be next. So she'd done the only thing she could do, but just as Warrick had, she suspected that beast would haunt her, too.

She fought to keep her lids open, but they were so heavy, her eyes and body so tired. No matter what she might see when she closed them, she had to sleep. Or at least try.

While it was close to noon, she had all the drapes drawn in the apartment. So she moved through the shadows to the bedroom, kicked off her shoes, unclasped and stepped out of her pants. Buttons freed, she shrugged off her coat and shirt. The panties and bra she dropped beside the bed, wanting nothing between her skin and the satin sheets.

But when she crawled into her bed, she found something between her and the sheets. She found a hard, warm male body.

Strong arms closed around her, a hair-covered chest rose and fell beneath her breasts—as his breathing came fast and hard. He wasn't sleeping. He was tense, every muscle taut as her body moved over his.

"You're here," she murmured. She'd hoped he would be and not because she wanted to arrest him and prove his existence to the department. She didn't care anymore what anyone thought. Not even herself because she was beyond thinking—because all she'd thought about was his kiss and how much she wanted him.

She could only feel now. And he felt so good beneath her. So very strong and male. His erection nudged her hip. The warm flesh throbbed with desire. For her?

He wanted her as much as she wanted him. That surprised her. She was forty, probably ten or twelve years older than he was since barely any lines marred the masculine perfection of his handsome face. His unusual topaz eyes didn't even crease at the corners.

But even if she wasn't older than him, she still wouldn't have thought he would consider her that desirable. Except for her breasts, she had few curves: skinny hips, long, skinny legs—all lean muscle instead of voluptuous softness.

But his hands slid over her as if he had to touch every inch of skin. With a fingertip, he traced the line of her spine down to the small of her back. She shivered and arched against him, pushing her breasts into his chest and her hips into his. His erection pulsated, and a rough groan slipped through his lips.

"Woman, you feel so good in my arms…"

She smiled as whatever insecurities she'd briefly entertained drained away along with all her stress and worries. If this was a dream, then she hoped she never woke up.

He ran his hands up her back and tangled his fingers in her hair. Then he tugged her down so that her mouth met his. He kissed her hungrily, nibbling at her lips before parting them. He invaded her—with his tongue and his flavor—so rich and seductive.

She moaned as passion consumed her, heating her blood and her skin and accelerating her pulse. Tension gathered deep inside her, building another kind of frustration apart from what she'd been feeling when she had unlocked her door.

The door had been locked. Dead-bolted even. Like it had been all those other times she'd found him in her bedroom. She pulled back to ask, "How do you always manage to get inside?"

"I'm not," he said. "Not yet. But I want to be inside you—buried deep inside so that we don't know where one of us begins and the other ends."

She shivered at the image his words invoked. Then, like a cat, she rubbed against him.

"If you do that again, I won't be able to wait," he warned her.

"What are you waiting for?"

She wasn't going to stop him this time; she wasn't going to pull her gun and shoot him. She didn't want to think about violence tonight. Not anymore. She didn't want to think at all. She only wanted to feel—as out of control with desire as only he had ever made her feel.

He wrapped his arms around her again and flipped her over so that she lay sprawled on her back beneath him.

She lifted her legs and arched, so ready to take him then—if he thrust inside her. But he kissed her again. Touching just his lips to hers. He didn't deepen the kiss. Instead, he skimmed his lips down her chin, along her neck to the curve of her collarbone.

Finally his hands—those big, slightly rough, calloused hands—touched her again, sliding over her skin. He ran them up her sides, tracing the slight curve of her hips to the indent of her waist. Then he moved his palms up her rib cage until he cupped her breasts.

"So damn beautiful…" he murmured and lowered his head to the slope of the mound. He pressed kisses to the sensitive skin before closing his lips around a nipple. He tugged gently with his lips and his teeth.

She arched off the bed, whimpering as the sensation spiraled through her. "Oooh…" Heat and moisture rushed between her legs as the orgasm peaked.

He eased back with a grin. "*This* is what I'm waiting for…"

"*This* is good," she agreed. Had she ever come so easily before? It had been so long since she'd made love with anyone that she couldn't remember. She'd been focused on her job and her friends. She hadn't focused on herself and her needs in a long time.

"Just good?" he asked, those topaz eyes igniting with a playful challenge. And he lowered his head again, lapping at one nipple with the tip of his tongue while teasing the other with his thumb.

She writhed beneath him, greedy for more of the pleasure that somersaulted through her. The pressure built again, winding tightly inside her, and she wrapped her legs around his waist, trying to pull him toward her.

But he eased back again. A wicked grin curved his naughty mouth. Then he lowered his head, and that naughty mouth moved down her body. His tongue flicked into her navel before tracing a path lower to the very core of her.

She arched up and cried out. He pulled her tight against him, driving his tongue deep inside her. And his thumb teased her there, stroking over her most sensitive spot until the unbearable pressure broke. And she came with a cry of intense pleasure.

"Was that just good?" he asked, a dark brow arched over one eye. Cords stood out on his neck and along his muscled arms, as if he was holding himself tightly in rein.

Unable to speak as she panted for breath with her heart pounding out of her chest, she managed a nonchalant shrug—to challenge him more.

He uttered a soft growl of frustration. "What's it going to take to satisfy you, woman?"

She reached between them and wrapped her fingers around the thick muscle of his erection. The sleek flesh pulsed in her grasp, so she slid her hand up and down the impressive length of him. Then she summoned the energy to lift herself up, so that her mouth could reach his chest. She moved her lips through the soft, velvety hair until she found a tight male nipple. And she teased him as he'd teased her, sliding the tip of her tongue over it.

He tangled his fingers in her hair again and tugged her head up so that he kissed her again, thrusting his tongue between her lips—deep inside her mouth.

Kate stroked him faster, and a bead of desire spilled from the end of his cock and into her palm. He pulled his mouth from hers, and they both panted for breath.

"No more waiting," he warned, his voice rough

with passion and impatience. His control snapped, and he pushed her back onto the bed.

He parted her legs and pressed his hips against hers. With her hand still wrapped around him, she guided his erection inside her. He was so big that she had to stretch and arch her hips, but he eased in, inch by tantalizing inch. But before he could fill her completely, he pulled out.

A protest—half moan, half growl—slipped from her throat. And she dug her nails into his back, then his butt—pulling him back.

He thrust hard. Deep.

And she screamed.

He tensed, sweat beading on his brow and upper lip. His muscles quivered as he struggled for control. His voice gruff with passion and concern, he asked, "Did I hurt you?"

"No! I want more...of you. I want all of you." His body, his passion and his secrets.

He thrust hard and deep again. She locked her legs around his waist and held on, arching into him. Then as the tension built again, the pressure was unbearable, and she lost all control. Desperate for release, she clawed at his back and bit the side of his jaw and his neck.

He growled and thrust harder and faster, winding the tension so tightly inside her that when it finally broke she nearly lost consciousness. The orgasm crashed over her with an intensity she had never felt before. Her body shuddered and spasmed and clutched him tightly and pulled him even deeper inside her.

Some primal, guttural roar emanated from him and his passion spilled, filling her. He clutched her tightly, his arms—muscles bulging—locked around her as if he never intended to let her go.

"God, woman…" He panted for breath, his chest rising and falling with the same frantic rhythm of hers. "You're going to be the death of me."

Kate was afraid that the reverse would actually come true. He would be the death of her. Because he had given her his body and his passion but not his secrets. While two out of three usually wasn't bad, she suspected that in this case—with his secrets—it might prove fatal.

For her.

She didn't regret making love with him, though, because she had never known such passion before. Or such completeness. She curled up in his arms and laid her head on his chest as exhaustion again overpowered her. She drifted off to sleep with no regrets but with many, many fears…

Chapter 6

"She shot him again?" Sebastian asked.

In the human world, Ben would have had to worry about violating HIPAA laws. But in the Secret Vampire Society, the only secret that couldn't be shared was with humans. Neither Sebastian nor he were human anymore. Ben just for years while for Sebastian it had been centuries.

With a sigh, Ben nodded. "Yes, she did, but Warrick was in his other form." As a man Warrick James was damned intimidating; as a werewolf he was terrifying—especially to a human who wasn't aware of the creatures of the underground.

The vampire bartender cursed and glanced around the secret surgical room as if looking for Warrick. "Where the hell is he?"

"She didn't shoot him with a silver bullet," Ben

said. If she had, he wouldn't have been able to patch him up again.

"But she shot him," Sebastian repeated. "The last time she did—he was furious with her. She could be in danger."

Ben shook his head now. "I saw his face when he brought her here after he found her hurt in the alley."

"He could have done that to—"

"No," Ben said. But he didn't expect Sebastian, the playboy, to understand. Ben, as a man madly in love with his wife, recognized another man taking the fall. Sure, Warrick James was stubborn and trying to fight his feelings, but no matter how strong the werewolf was, love could make *any* creature powerless. "He was ready to tear apart whoever had hurt her. It wasn't him."

"But she shot him again…"

"And he didn't care," Ben assured him. "She's not in any danger from him…"

Sebastian uttered a ragged sigh. "I don't know who the hell is the danger anymore. Reagan James swears it's not him."

"There is someone else," Ben said. While he'd been able to patch up Warrick, there had been nothing he could do for poor Bernie. Someone—*something*—had torn out the vagrant's throat.

"If it isn't Warrick…"

Ben hoped like hell that it wasn't. If Kate was in danger and he had done nothing to protect her, Paige would never forgive him. She couldn't lose her best friend.

But even if he was right about Warrick, that didn't mean that Kate wasn't in danger. That image of poor

Bernie lying among the trash in the Dumpster flashed through his mind. Kate had told him that someone had called her to that alley to meet them. Had Bernie been the intended victim? Or had Kate?

Warrick barely resisted the urge to press a kiss to her forehead, near where the bandage covered her wound. But her thick lashes lay against her pale cheeks, and he didn't want to wake her. He wanted, instead, to slip from her bed and leave her with only memories—the same ones he would carry with him for the rest of his lonely life. His muscles quivered yet in reaction to the passion that had consumed him... when she had consumed him.

He had never known as sensual or responsive a lover, and he suspected he would never know another woman like Detective Kate Wever. She had overwhelmed and humbled him. His body protested leaving her bed, his erection throbbing against his thigh—begging for another release. She had blown his mind, but after watching her sleep for several minutes, he had finally gathered his wits about him again.

He had to leave. For her sake more than his. Feeling his heart heavy with regret, he sat up and reached for the shirt he'd left beside the bed. But before he could shove his arms into the sleeves, soft fingertips glided across his back to his wounded shoulder. He'd torn off the bandage when he'd undressed, leaving the skin, puckered with stitches, open to the air. The wound would heal quicker that way—like his other wounds had healed.

She gasped and asked, "Did you find him again? Did he do this to you?"

"No, it wasn't him."

"Then who did this to you?" she asked. "Who hurt you?"

She had done this…again, but he couldn't tell her that without revealing a secret that would cost her her life. He had been crazy to come to her apartment—even crazier to undress and climb into her bed. But he had been tired—tired of fighting his desire for her. And he'd been worried about her. He'd needed to see her—to make certain that she was all right, that she wasn't in danger.

But by being near her, he was putting her in danger. He'd already lost everyone else he'd cared about…

And despite his best efforts to fight his feelings, he cared about her. Too much.

He shrugged off her fingers and her concern. But he could still feel her touch on his skin. "Zantrax is a dangerous city," he said. "People get hurt here."

She had been hurt the night she'd been struck down in the alley. And she was still determined to be a detective here, where she wasn't even aware of all the dangers—of all the creatures. If she became aware of those dangers, she would wind up as dead as the homeless man in the alley.

"People get hurt around *you*," she said, her tone chilling as suspicion crept into her voice. And even though he hadn't turned toward her, he felt her pulling away from him—at least emotionally.

Apparently, even in his human form, he was a suspect for the vagrant's murder.

"I'm not the one who hurts people," he said. She was. And Reagan.

"But that man in the alley…"

"I was trying to stop him from hurting anyone else," he explained.

"You keep calling him a killer," she said, the suspicion replaced with a trace of hope. "If he's killed before…" Previously she had seemed skeptical of his claim. Now she seemed almost eager to believe him.

He flinched as the image flashed through his mind of Reagan standing over their father's body, blood pumping from the hole the silver bullet had blown through his dying heart. "He's killed."

"Are you still looking for him?"

He jerked his head in a quick nod. But it was a lie. He had let her distract him from his quest. He had used revenge against her as an excuse but now, after making love with her, he realized his obsession with her had nothing to do with vengeance and everything with attraction. He hadn't wanted revenge; he'd just wanted her. But he shouldn't have acted on that attraction. He shouldn't have stayed in Zantrax because he had only put her in danger.

Now Reagan had another way to hurt him because now he had someone else he could take from Warrick.

"Do you have any idea where to find him?" she asked. "Where will you be looking?"

He glanced over his shoulder at her and grinned in amusement at her serious face. She'd pulled up the thin sheet that did little to hide her nakedness. She was no longer his lover; she was a detective interviewing a suspect—or a source that could possibly lead her to a suspect. He would rather be her source than her suspect. Hell, he would rather be her lover.

But he had already endangered her and had lost his

focus. He had to find Reagan before he hurt anyone else. Before he hurt Kate...

"I'll be looking everywhere," he replied. "I have to find him."

"Why?" she asked, and the suspicion was back in her voice.

But no matter how tough an interrogator Detective Wever might be, she wouldn't crack him—for her own protection. "I have my reasons," was all he told her. He didn't want to talk anymore. He wanted to reach for her or for that damn sheet and drag it off her delectable body. But he couldn't—at least he shouldn't—stay any longer.

"What are your reasons?" she persisted, her voice vibrating with frustration. "What has he done?"

"Nothing that concerns you." At least he hoped like hell it didn't and that his enemy hadn't turned his focus on her. Warrick did reach out for her. But he just touched his fingertips to the bandage on her forehead. If Reagan had hurt her...there would be no place he could hide from Warrick this time.

Either her wound was still sensitive or she had seen the rage flash in his eyes, because she flinched and leaned back—out of his reach. "If he really killed someone, it would concern me," she said. "If he's broken any law, it would concern me."

He expelled a ragged sigh and let his hand drop to the bed. "He's broken just about every one of them—just not here in Zantrax." That Warrick could prove, anyway. Reagan could have killed that homeless man. Maybe the vagrant had seen him strike Kate that night Warrick had found her bleeding and unconscious in the alley.

"But there are police looking for him, too, then," she said, and some of the tension drained from her tense shoulders. "There must be a warrant for his arrest."

He shook his head. "The police aren't involved."

"Why not?"

"Because I don't want them involved." Like the Secret Vampire Society, the pack had their own laws—and their own law enforcers.

"Warrick—"

He leaned toward her and pressed his mouth over hers, shutting off her incessant questions. But then passion ignited, and the kiss became less about silencing her and more about savoring her. She tasted so sweet—so sexy. Her silky lips moved under his, parting for his possession. But then her tongue slid out, the tip teasing his lips before slipping inside his mouth.

He groaned as desire overwhelmed him. His muscles tensed, his shaft hardened. He had intended to leave without waking her—without giving in to desire again. He'd thought he'd had enough memories—perfect memories—to carry him through however long his life lasted. But now he was greedy for more.

He was greedy for her.

He slid his mouth from hers, across her cheek to her neck. Then he moved it lower, along her throat to her collarbone. The sheet slipped down, baring her breasts. But he quickly covered them—with his hands. Cupping the soft weight in his palms, he stroked his thumbs over her turgid nipples.

A moan slipped through her lips as she arched into his touch. She was greedy for more, too.

So he obliged. He lowered his head. Closing his lips around one of those nipples, he tugged gently.

She cried out—not in pain but desire. Her hands clutched his back, pulling him closer. But he was too big for her to move easily.

And he wanted to take his time, teasing her nipples—teasing her.

But then her hand closed around his shaft and her thumb flicked back and forth over the tip of it. "Kate…" he growled her name as a warning. He had a tenuous hold on his control at best. If she kept touching him…

She wriggled away from him, moving around until her lips replaced her hand. And she slid her mouth up and down his shaft, taking him deep in her throat.

He was too big for her. And she was still too fragile with her concussion for him to take advantage of what she offered him. Heaven…

So he reached for her, lifting her in his arms. She squealed and clutched at his shoulders. "What are you doing?" she asked. "Let me please you—"

"You please me," he assured her. Then he shifted her back onto the mattress, so that her head settled back into the pillows. "But I want to please you first…"

He lowered his head again, spreading kisses down the length of her gorgeous body. She was all sleek, silky skin. He kissed every inch of her and laved her nipples with his tongue before moving lower.

She squirmed and shifted against the pillows as he tasted her—intimately. His tongue flicked over her clit before sliding inside her.

She clutched at the pillows and screamed as an orgasm claimed her. The evidence of her pleasure and the sweet taste of it in his mouth snapped his control. He needed to take his own pleasure. He needed her.

Pressure wound tight inside him. His cock throbbed and pulsed, needing to be buried deep inside her. He could deny his base urges no more. He lifted her in his arms again and rose up on his knees. She wrapped her legs around his waist as he slid her down onto the length of his pulsing shaft.

She shifted to take him deeper inside her wet heat. Her inner muscles gripped his cock, holding him tightly inside her. They moved together, him thrusting—her arching. Her nails clawed at his back and his shoulders as she fought to get even closer to him. As the pressure gripped her again, she moved frantically against him, and he matched her frenzy as the madness overtook him. Tension filled him; he had never needed anyone more.

She rose up in his arms and pressed her mouth to his. They kissed—deeply—their tongues tangling like their bodies as he continued to thrust inside her.

She tensed, and her inner muscles tightened, pulling him deeper as her body contracted and her orgasm—so hot and wet—broke over him. She screamed his name, "Warrick!"

And it was the sound of his name on her lips that snapped the unbearable tension gripping his body and his mind and his soul. A low growl tore from his throat along with his release. He shuddered as his orgasm pumped fast and hard from his cock, filling her.

Her body had gone limp in his arms, so he eased her gently back against the pillows. He hadn't meant to take her again and not as passionately as he already had.

But the woman was dangerous even without her gun. She hadn't fired any shots at him, but still his heart constricted, aching as feelings flooded it. As crazy as he had been to come to her, he was even crazier to care about her when he knew so well—so painfully—what happened to anyone he cared about.

She wrapped her arms around him, pulling him down on top of her. "Don't stop," she murmured, and she arched her hips up, rubbing against him. Her legs tangled around his, silky skin sliding against his hair-roughened limbs.

Despite the soul-shattering orgasm he'd just had, his cock hardened again—ready to take her. Panting for breath and struggling for control, he pulled back. "Kate, you need your rest."

She had stumbled into her bedroom just past noon—beyond exhausted. And he had let her get very little sleep yet. But she needed more than rest; she needed his protection. And he would protect her best by keeping his distance and finding the man who posed a danger to her.

"I need you to let this rest," she said.

"This?" With his body already tense and ready to take hers again, he couldn't focus on what she meant.

"Your vendetta against that man," she said. "You need to report what laws he's broken, and let the authorities handle him."

He shook his head. The authority in the pack, his uncle, had given him that assignment—to save his honor. But he couldn't explain any of that to her. "You don't know what you're talking about—"

"Because you won't tell me," she said.

"I can't."

She clutched his arms, her fingers tight against his biceps and urged, "Let him go, Warrick."

"I can't do that."

Disappointment dimmed the brightness of her light blue eyes. "So when you find him again, you'll kill him?"

"I have to." For her now, for her safety. She mattered more now than anything that had happened in the past.

Darkness had fallen—providing cover for him and for the other watchers who lurked in the shadows on the Zantrax street. Reagan knew they were there. But Warrick must not have sensed them—or *his* presence—as he dropped onto the asphalt from the fire escape outside the human detective's bedroom window. Instead of glancing around to survey his surroundings, he gazed up at that darkened window. There was a longing on his face—a longing that Reagan had felt himself—that he still felt.

The female detective had distracted his brother—dangerously so. Just like Sylvia had distracted him. Lives had been destroyed and lost because of his distraction. What would Warrick's distraction cost him?

Reagan tensed, readying himself in the shadows—not for a confrontation with his brother. Warrick was completely unaware of his presence. But he was unaware of the others watching him, too.

The man was a tracker; Warrick James was known in their pack, and all other packs, for being able to pick up the coldest of trails. But tonight the only scent in his head was hers.

Couldn't he feel the hostility of the others?

Reagan could.

That was why he was ready to rush to his brother's defense. He knew Warrick wouldn't welcome his help. He'd probably attack him instead. So Reagan held back, waiting to see if he was needed.

Finally, Warrick tore his gaze from that window and slipped off into the shadows on the street as he walked away. Reagan waited to see if the others followed him. But they stayed behind—beneath her window.

Maybe Warrick wasn't the one in danger. Maybe it was the human detective.

What had she learned? Enough to get her killed?

Paige closed the door as the bar manager/relief bartender stepped inside her office.

"I'm needed at the bar," Sebastian said. "It's getting busy out there."

She didn't care about Club Underground, at least not tonight. "Not as busy as it's been back there," she said, gesturing to the room at the end of the hall—that secret room where her surgeon husband helped the creatures of the underground.

Sebastian shrugged. "I wouldn't know."

"Ben and I have no secrets anymore," she reminded the man who most people thought was her brother. He was actually her father. But he looked younger than her and he always would because of when he had been turned so many centuries ago.

"Then you already know…" He stepped closer to the door.

"I know what Ben knows," she said. "That Kate found poor Bernie dead in the alley. And that she shot that…" She'd only gotten used to the vampires—to being one herself. She couldn't bring herself to consider what other creatures were out there. "And Ben saved him."

"He wouldn't have died from her bullet," Sebastian assured her.

"Then Kate's in danger from him," she said, "if she can't defend herself from him." But there were very few creatures of the underground that Kate could kill with her gun. It would take a stake or…

Sebastian said nothing.

"You told Ben that Kate is in danger from him," she prodded her father.

Sebastian cursed, but there was a twinkle of amusement and approval in his blue eyes. "You two really don't have any secrets anymore."

They'd had too many secrets for too long. Those secrets had destroyed their first marriage. But not their love for each other. That had survived their divorce and would now endure for eternity.

"No, we don't," Paige confirmed. "Ben doesn't think he would hurt her."

Sebastian shrugged. "Maybe he knows Warrick James better than I do. They've spent more time together."

"With Ben patching him up," Paige said. "Someone hurt Kate, too, though."

A muscle twitched along Sebastian's tightly clenched jaw, and dread filled Paige as she recognized the tension and the fear in her father.

"You know something…"

He shrugged again. "I've talked to Warrick's brother a few times."

"And you don't think he's a danger, either," she said. He'd admitted as much to Ben, which her husband had also shared with her.

Sebastian cursed again as he realized she already knew what he was willing to admit. It was what he was holding back that she really wanted to learn—that she had to learn.

"So who is a danger to Kate?" she asked. "What have you heard?"

"Paige, it's better if—"

She slapped his shoulder—albeit gently. "Stop trying to protect me." He had done that for too long and his *protection* had inadvertently put her in danger instead. "Just tell me what you know."

He uttered a ragged sigh of resignation and concern. "Certain members of the society are getting concerned about Kate."

Fear coursed through Paige, making her gasp. She could imagine who—the vampire who'd nearly taken her life. "Why? Kate isn't aware of the Secret Vampire Society."

At least she hoped her friend wasn't aware of them. It did feel as if she had been avoiding her and their other happy-hour friends, though. Had she discovered the secret and realized that it was Paige's secret, too?

Was Kate afraid of her?

She nearly chuckled at her ridiculous thought. Kate feared no one, and that fearlessness was what would put her in the most danger.

Sebastian tilted his head in consideration and replied, "She has been investigating more—"

"Because of that werewolf," Paige said. "Her investigation has nothing to do with the society."

"But if she learns about him…"

Paige's fear increased instead of abating. "She'll be in danger from the pack." Ben had told her that they had the same rule as the society.

"Not just the pack," Sebastian said. "She's poking around. She's going to see or learn something that she can't know…"

"And live," Paige finished for him. She had always worried about Kate finding out too much. Knowing Kate and her inquisitiveness and her determination, Paige should have realized that it was only a matter of time before her friend learned the secret.

That muscle twitched in Sebastian's cheek again. He knew how much Paige loved her friends. She had inadvertently put them all at risk, like he had with her. Maybe she would have been a better friend if she'd ended their friendship—if she'd found a way to keep Kate away from Club Underground.

"Is there anything we can do?" she asked. "If she finds out…"

Sebastian arched his brows above his blue eyes, and she corrected herself, "*When* she finds out…"

He shrugged. "You know what the options are," he said. "What do you think Kate will choose?"

When Paige had found it, the choice for her hadn't been between death and becoming a vampire. Her choice had been between love and death. Because becoming a vampire had meant that she was able to spend eternity with the man she loved.

But Kate didn't have that choice. She wasn't in love with a vampire.

"What do you think is going on between her and the werewolf?" she asked.

Sebastian shook his head. "I am not the person you should be asking," he said. "She's your friend."

"So why don't I know?" Paige wondered and worried.

Why was Kate keeping secrets? Was she falling for the werewolf and too scared to admit to her feelings? Knowing Kate, she would probably refuse to admit them even to herself let alone her friends.

Paige had known her long enough to know that her friend feared love. She had no idea that there were far greater dangers out there for her. She need not worry about losing her heart; she needed to worry about losing her life.

Chapter 7

She pried her lids open and peered around, but her vision was blurred. Wood and prints blended into a kaleidoscope of colors, and it took her a few moments to recognize her surroundings. She was still in the cabin. She didn't have to try the doors or windows to confirm that she was still chained inside—still imprisoned like a criminal. A guard had brought her food last night. She shouldn't have eaten it; it had obviously been drugged.

Sylvia blinked hard and trembled, trying to fight off the grogginess. Her hands slid over her swollen belly. Had whatever drug she'd been given harmed her baby or babies? Tears stung her eyes, welling in them so that she no longer saw the cabin. She no longer saw anything but pain.

If she lost her baby, she would have lost *every-*

thing. But her belly shifted beneath her palms as a tiny foot kicked out. A sigh of relief slipped through her lips. More kicks and punches followed; she didn't care about the discomfort. She only cared that her child or children—there were so many kicks and punches that it felt like more than one set of feet and hands—were alive inside her.

A giggle bubbled out. But her happiness was short-lived because she knew that her children might not survive—if she couldn't escape. She couldn't eat the food again. She had to take the opportunity instead to overpower the guard and escape. It was her and her children's only hope.

And Reagan...

Was he beyond hope? No. She could still feel his emotions—his frustration and guilt and fear. He was worried about someone.

She doubted it was her, though, or he would have come back for her. He wouldn't have left her alone for so long...

But if he and Warrick were dead, she would be dead, too. She was only useful while one or both of them were still alive. The day before she'd searched for a tool to escape; now she searched for a weapon.

She would do whatever was necessary to protect the ones she loved—like Reagan had done. It was just too bad that he hadn't really loved her.

With her hand close to the holster hidden beneath her jacket, Kate moved through the crowd at Club Underground. The dimly lit bar, with its exposed brick, dark wood and polished brass was always crowded—with the most unusual patrons. Most were young, with flawless pale skin and lean bodies. They looked as if they belonged in a club in Hollywood instead of an urban city in western Michigan. It didn't matter where Club Underground was; Kate didn't want to be there.

Not because her ex-husband had warned her away from the place but because her own instincts warned her away from Club Underground. But she had no choice tonight. So she maneuvered to the table in the back and settled onto an empty chair.

"Glad you could make happy hour," Lizzy welcomed her. The dark-eyed brunette clasped her arm around Kate's shoulders and squeezed.

She relaxed into her friend's embrace, appreciating her warmth. They were the same age, but Lizzy reminded Kate of her mom, who had always been so loving and supportive. Too bad she and Kate's dad had died a decade ago when their small plane had crashed into Lake Michigan. The only thing Kate had left of them now was that grandfather clock Kate's father had bought her mom for their anniversary. It had been his way of telling her that they had all the time in the world. But they hadn't.

That was why Kate knew how important it was to spend as much time as possible with the people you loved.

"You don't look very happy, though," Campbell observed. The assistant district attorney studied Kate through narrowed green eyes.

"What happened to your head?" Renae asked. The bandage was gone now, the wound nearly healed, but of course the trauma surgeon would notice the injury.

Kate touched it. "It's nothing," she lied, "just more banging my head against the wall." That was what it had been like trying to get through to Warrick, to let the authorities handle justice instead of his seeking his own vigilante brand of an eye for an eye, a life for a life. Whose life had the man taken that Warrick was so determined to avenge the death?

The surgeon's eyes narrowed in skepticism. "Looks like blunt-force trauma to me."

Lizzy sighed. "Dr. Grabill, it's happy hour. Let's talk about *happy* things." Considering she spent most of her day with clients bickering over their divorce settlement and most of her night with teenagers bickering over the remote and the computer, Lizzy really needed happy hour.

Tonight, so did Kate.

She had done it again. Despite knowing better, she had gotten involved with another violent man. Warrick wasn't just into assault and battery, though. He was determined to kill. And no matter what she said to him, she couldn't stop him.

She should have arrested him instead of making love with him. Why hadn't she? Sure, she'd been both physically and mentally exhausted, but she had summoned the energy to move over him and beneath him, to meet his thrusts, to spiral out of control with passion.

"Looks like you all can use a drink," Paige said as the club owner, clad in a slinky red dress, approached their table. The blonde looked younger and happier every time Kate saw her. Paige had many reasons for her happiness: her successful business, the reunion with her ex-husband and their adoption of an orphaned patient of Ben's. Finally, Paige had everything she deserved.

Would Kate look like Paige, that happy and care-free, if she fell that deeply in love? Kate knew only the painful side of love: the loss and helplessness. It was no wonder that she never chose the right men.

"Make mine a double," she murmured. No matter how much she drank, though, she wouldn't be able to forget what she'd done and what she'd felt…with Warrick James.

"You better order fast," Paige suggested. "Sebastian's pouring tonight, and the place is filling up."

Lizzy glanced toward the bar. "With pretty girls. We'll be lucky to get our drinks at all."

"Come on," Campbell said with a wink. "He'll serve us. We're the prettiest girls in the club."

Kate chuckled. "I haven't been a girl in a while."

"Me, either," Lizzy added with a laugh. "But that man at the bar has me blushing like one, and I'm not even the one he's staring at…"

Campbell followed their friend's gaze and whistled in appreciation. "I haven't seen him around before."

"There are always strangers in this place," Kate remarked. That was partly what made her so suspicious of the club. If she didn't know Paige better, she might have considered that it was a front for drugs or something even more nefarious. But Paige, as a former attorney, was all about law and order, too.

"He's not looking at *you* like you're a stranger," the assistant district attorney told Kate, her voice rising with excitement and curiosity.

Finally, Kate turned toward the bar, and her heart constricted as she met that eerie topaz gaze. He stared at her for several moments, and it was as if everyone else disappeared from the overcrowded club—

leaving just the two of them. Alone and naked like they had been just a couple of days before—all tangled up in her bed.

All tangled up in each other.

It was as if she could feel him moving inside her, filling her. Heat rushed through her, and her skin tingled as if he was touching her again. And he was but with just his gaze. She wanted his big hands on her again—cupping her breasts, stroking her nipples and her clit...making her scream his name as she came apart in his arms. She was burning up and it wasn't because the club was crowded. It was because of him and that intensity of the passion he brought out in her—a passion she hadn't even known she possessed.

"Who is he?" Campbell asked. She pressed a meticulously manicured hand to her chest. "And if you tell me a suspect, it's going to break my heart."

Kate was more worried about Warrick breaking hers. She drew in a deep, shaky breath, bracing herself before she shook her head and severed that strange connection between them. Then she turned back to her friends and lied. "I don't know who he is."

Maybe that wasn't a lie, though.

While she knew his name, it was pretty much all she knew about him and that was only if he had actually given her his true identity. He hadn't shown her any proof that he was who he claimed: no driver's license or passport. She hadn't been able to run his prints. Maybe she should have dusted her bedroom or her body and processed him that way, but she hadn't.

Even if he had told her the truth about his identity, it was really all he'd told her. He kept too many other secrets for her to really know him at all.

"If I were you, I'd get to know him," Campbell said with a lustful sigh. "That is some good-looking man."

And her friend hadn't even seen him naked like Kate had. He was better than good-looking; he was magnificent. Lust filled Kate now with the urge to see him that way again—to pull off his black sweater and his jeans and expose all that hair-roughened skin stretched taut over hard muscles.

"Kate's all about work," Renae said.

"You are two of a kind," Lizzy teased the surgeon.

No. Renae was too smart to make the mistakes that Kate had. The young surgeon had never been married and seemed to focus only on her job.

If only Kate had done the same…

She would have missed out on the most exciting sexual experience of her life.

"What are you working on now?" Paige asked.

Something in her tone drew Kate's attention. She was more than curious; she was worried. But then she and Paige had always been close. That was why Kate had been keeping her distance—because Paige knew her too well to miss all the conflicting feelings Kate was fighting. Instead of drinking with her friends and ignoring Warrick, she should be arresting him. But no one had sworn out a complaint against him.

"No," Campbell said, waving her hands like a referee at a fight. "No shop talk. You know the rule, Paige."

Yes, she knew the rule. She'd made it herself. So why had she asked? What did she know?

Warrick forced himself to look away from Kate. She had already turned away from him, just as she had at her apartment after they'd made love those couple of long days ago. He hadn't slept since then. He hadn't been able to get her taste and touch from his lips or his skin. Not even when he turned at midnight. Hell, it had seemed to intensify then, especially when he stood vigil outside her apartment—making sure no one tried to hurt her again.

Someone had been there—that night he'd left her bed and dropped from her fire escape. Various scents had assaulted him when he'd wanted only hers in his head, on his skin. But he'd smelled others.

Reagan.

His hadn't been the only scent. There had been others. But it hadn't been the scents as much as the intensity of the emotion emanating from them. Hatred. And so he'd led them away from her—or he had tried. When he hadn't caught anyone following him, he'd sought out Sebastian instead. He'd asked him to protect her, so that she didn't wind up like that homeless man in the alley.

But he hadn't trusted Sebastian with her protection every night. He'd had to make certain for himself that nothing happened to Kate.

His Kate…

He started at his possessive thought and at a sharp noise. His watch alarm sounded the warning that midnight was nearing. The pitch was at a frequency he could hear despite the heavy throb of the low bass of the live band and the loud rumble of conversation. He had adjusted the alarm to give him a fifteen-minute warning.

Sebastian leaned across the bar and told him, "You should go now."

Warrick doubted the vampire had heard the alarm; he just wanted him gone because Kate was here. The bartender kept staring at her table, too.

As if he'd read his mind and picked up on the jealousy, Sebastian lifted his hands to ward him off. "Hey, you told me to watch her."

So maybe Sebastian had an excuse. But every other man in the place stared at her table, too; she was so beautiful. Her silky black hair skimmed her delicate jaw. Thick lashes fringed her eyes, which shone that startling, pale blue even in the dim lighting of the club. She wore a jacket over a sweater, but her breasts strained beneath them, as if begging him to free them.

Kate ignored him, never turning toward him again, while her friends continued to stare at him. They were all attractive women of various ages and coloring, but Kate was the one who held all of his attention. And they all knew it. He forced himself to look away—because they might not have been the only ones who'd noticed his interest in Detective Wever.

Although if Reagan was the one who'd attacked her the night Warrick had found her in the alley, then he already knew that Warrick was interested in her. That must have been his reason for hurting her—to hurt Warrick. Reagan actually owed her; if not for her shooting Warrick that night, he would have torn his brother apart.

"So you can leave," the bartender told him.

"I will leave," he assured Sebastian, "once you tell me what else you've heard about *him*."

The vampire bartender shook his head. "Nothing about *him*. Nobody's talking about anything but that body that Kate found in the alley behind here."

Was that why she had come to the club tonight—to continue her damn investigation? If she wouldn't let it go, she might wind up like that body in the Dumpster. He had to make certain that didn't happen, though. And there was only one way to do that—by eliminating the threat against her.

"Come on," Warrick persisted, suspecting that Sebastian was holding something back, "you've had to have heard something else…"

"Just speculation," Sebastian admitted.

"About him?"

"About you," he replied. "A lot of people think that, given his particular wounds, you're responsible for that poor man's death."

"That's bullshit," Warrick said, irritation fraying his nerves. He didn't have time for this—not with Reagan still out there—ready to kill again. "Until that night, I'd never seen the man before. I had no reason to kill him."

Sebastian shrugged. "Some members of packs have been known to go rogue and attack innocent humans."

He couldn't deny that happened. He'd had rogue cousins; ones whose hunger for humans had endangered the whole pack. His father had dealt with them… like Warrick needed to deal with his father's killer.

"I wouldn't attack an innocent," he assured him. And he would deal with the other members of his pack who had or would. Now that his father was gone the responsibility to enforce justice had fallen on Warrick.

"You came to Zantrax to kill a man," Sebastian reminded him. "And a man has died."

"I didn't kill that man," he insisted. "I haven't killed either man." Yet.

Sebastian glanced toward Kate's table again. "Maybe you should just leave it at that. And leave."

The second alarm sounded its warning; he had no choice anymore. He had to leave. The bar. Not Zantrax. He couldn't leave the city yet. But he rushed from the club, jostling patrons as he hurried out.

On the concrete stairwell leading from the basement to the street above, he began to turn. Hair poked through his skin as his bones shifted and changed shape, tearing his clothes. He reached the street on all fours, his face close to the ground. And, carried on the cool midnight breeze, he picked up the scent he'd been trying so hard to track. He had caught only the faintest trace of it that night outside Kate's apartment. And intermingled with the other scents, he wasn't able to fully distinguish it like he was now.

His nostrils flared as he tracked it from the door of the club to the alley behind it. His enemy had been here. Perhaps the night that Kate had found the body. Warrick had been too concerned about her that night, after her terrified scream, to notice if Reagan had been there then.

Given the strength of his enemy's scent, Warrick suspected Reagan had been to the club even more recently, though. Maybe tonight. Maybe he had been one of those men who'd watched Kate or who had watched Warrick watch Kate.

Either way, he'd been too close to her. Stalking her before he attacked again?

Kate had interrogated this man before and like then, she suspected he wasn't being entirely truthful with her. If only she could have brought him down to the department…

But since he was her best friend's husband, Paige's office in the back of the club had to do. With no windows and brick walls, it was similar to an interrogation room except for the flowers on Paige's desk and the sophisticated oak-and-leather furniture. Kate perched on the corner of her friend's antique oak desk while Dr. Benjamin Davison sprawled over the leather couch.

The last time she had questioned him had been in his office at the hospital and in regards to his ex-wife being stalked. Paige had insisted he hadn't been responsible, and apparently she'd been right. But still Kate thought he'd known more than he had shared with her then.

She suspected the same now.

"So you had already destroyed the animal's remains when I called that night?" she asked.

He nodded. "I didn't realize that the dog could have been evidence, so I tossed its carcass in the medical waste incinerator at the hospital."

She bit the inside of her cheek to hold her temper in check over his wanton destruction of evidence. "But when you met me in the alley that night, you saw the body in the Dumpster. You didn't think that—" she couldn't keep calling it a dog; it had been so much more than that. And Ben knew it, too, increasing her frustration with him "—that *thing* could have inflicted that fatal wound?"

"I'm not a coroner, Kate."

No, he was a brilliant cardiologist—world-renowned even, but instead of referring her to a vet, he had chosen to work on the animal himself. That was one of the reasons she'd cornered him when he had showed up at the club with his and Paige's adoptive daughter, Addi. After Paige had taken the child home, Kate had asked to speak privately with Ben.

"It's too bad you're not," she said. "The coroner's having trouble figuring out just what is responsible for the wounds on Bernie Wilson's body. Dr. Peterson's never seen anything like that before."

"Well, that's a good thing," Ben said with an involuntary shudder of revulsion.

Goose bumps of unease lifted on her skin. "How is it a good thing that the doctor can't figure out who or what killed that man?"

"I mean it's a good thing he's never seen anything like it before," Ben clarified. "Then no one else must have died that way."

She shuddered over the gruesome, painful death poor Bernie had suffered. "Fortunately not yet," she replied. "But if we can't figure out what killed Mr. Wilson, we won't be able to stop him—or *it*—from killing again."

"No other bodies have been found?" he asked.

She shook her head.

"So maybe that thing did kill him," Dr. Davison concluded, as if her case could be solved that easily. With no evidence. If anyone had known she'd tried to get help for that thing after shooting it, they would have teased and harassed her for being too sensitive—or for being crazy. And they'd already been treating her as if she was crazy over shooting Warrick.

But she had wanted to save that thing, so she had called Ben before she'd called in to report finding the body. She'd figured if anyone could save the thing, he could, and she'd trusted him to help her. After all, he was her best friend's husband. But because he'd also once been Paige's *ex*-husband, Kate didn't particularly like the man. She should have known better than to trust him. After Dwight, she should have known better than to trust any man. Maybe it was more Dwight's fault than Ben's that Kate suspected he was lying. Because why would he bother to lie about some animal?

"What breed was it?" she asked. "I've never seen anything like it before." She shuddered, remembering its eerie, glowing eyes and its enormous size. It wasn't like any dog she had ever seen before. Hell, it had been bigger even than the wolves at the zoo— maybe bigger than the grizzly bear, too.

His broad shoulders lifted and fell in a slight shrug. "I don't know, Kate," he said. "I'm not a vet, either."

"I should have taken the thing to one," she conceded. But she hadn't known where to bring it, and she had wanted it to have immediate medical attention. So she'd called Ben. But it had died anyway...

Or had it? Ben had conveniently destroyed the body so that there was nothing left to prove it had ever existed or that she had ever shot it. Just like after she'd shot Warrick and he had disappeared...

But she knew he was real.

And tonight her friends had seen him, too, at the bar. He hadn't stayed, though. Despite trying to ignore his presence, she had known exactly when he'd left—when he had slipped out right before midnight.

"It wouldn't have mattered if a vet had worked on it," Ben assured her. "The animal still wouldn't have made it—not with that GSW. It was fatal."

"All gunshot wounds aren't fatal though," she said, thinking of the scars on Warrick's chest and the old and new ones on his shoulder.

"Fortunately not."

She wholeheartedly agreed or she would have never known the intensity of the passion she'd felt with Warrick James. But how had that beast died from a bullet to its flank and Warrick had survived a bullet to the heart?

She narrowed her eyes and studied the cardiologist. "In the past few months have you operated on anyone with multiple gunshot wounds?"

He nodded. "Zantrax can be a dangerous city. You know that better than most. You investigate all those reports about shootings."

"Just the major case ones," she said. "So I see more of the fatalities than the survivors."

"Thankfully there are more survivors than casualties," he remarked with the arrogance of a man—of a surgeon—who was good at what he did and knew it.

She was good at her job, too. Or at least she had been until she'd shot Warrick James and his body had disappeared. "You have to report all gunshot wounds, though," she reminded him. "Fatal or not."

"The hospital calls Zantrax PD over anyone who comes into the emergency room with a GSW," he said. "Just ask your friend Renae."

The morning after Kate had shot Warrick in the alley, she had asked Renae about any gunshot victims, but the trauma surgeon hadn't treated any the previous evening. That was another reason Kate had been so convinced he hadn't survived and another reason her coworkers had been convinced she was crazy.

They hadn't found him at any of the area hospitals or clinics. How could someone have been shot as many times as she'd claimed to have shot him and not seek medical attention?

"I'm asking you, Ben," she said. "Do you remember treating anyone, a couple of months ago, who had two bullets in his shoulder and another in his heart?"

He whistled as if stunned, but no actual surprise flashed through his dark eyes. And his handsome face remained tense and guarded. "I would have remembered treating someone with those injuries," he replied—which wasn't a real response. "I always remember the ones who don't make it."

"You're saying a man couldn't have survived those wounds?" But she had seen the scars on Warrick's shoulder and chest from the bullets she'd shot into him. He even had a new wound on his shoulder... where she had shot that beast—in his right front flank or shoulder.

She tensed as shock gripped her.

No. It couldn't have been...

It wasn't possible.

But then, according to Ben, it wasn't possible that Warrick was still alive—that he had survived his injuries. She had been wondering who Warrick James really was.

Now she began to wonder *what* he really was...

Chapter 8

Warrick rubbed his jaw, the bones aching as he returned to his human form. While outside dawn had broken, here the blinds were drawn, blocking out those first streaks of sunlight. He had been out all night, following the scent of his enemy to every place Reagan had been.

And he had been all around Zantrax. Back in the bank vault. In the alley behind the club. Under the city in the secret passageways. Outside Kate's apartment. Everywhere that Warrick had been. But never in the same place at the same damn time that Warrick was.

Except for that night Kate had shot him. If only she had known what Reagan had done...

He grinned. It wouldn't have mattered to Kate; she still would have shot him.

"Damn you, Kate," he whispered, not wanting

to awaken her—just wanting to protect her. "If you would have let me kill him, you wouldn't be in danger right now."

"She was right to stop you," a deep voice spoke from the shadows of Kate's bedroom. "You would have regretted killing an innocent man."

His heart hammering against his ribs, Warrick vaulted toward the bed, but it was empty—the sheets left in a tangled heap. Had there been a struggle? Or were the sheets like that because it was how he and Kate had left the bed days ago and she hadn't made it?

Kate was a slob. But she was also a fighter. She wouldn't willingly have let this man in her bedroom. Unless…

No, not Kate.

"Where is she?" He turned to the man who remained in the shadows. "What have you done with her?"

"Nothing," Reagan replied.

"If you've hurt her—" Emotion rushed up and choked him, so that he couldn't spit out the rest of the threat.

"I haven't even seen her," Reagan claimed.

"Then why are you here? In her apartment?" In her *bedroom*? And where the hell was Kate?

"I'm here because I need to talk to you."

Warrick shook his head in disbelief. "How did you know to find me here?"

"Just the same as you've been tracking me, I've been tracking you," Reagan replied. "I know everywhere you've been and everyone you've seen."

Sebastian had been right about his enemy being a danger to Kate. Reagan had figured out how much

Warrick cared about her—more than he wanted to—more than he'd thought he could.

"I knew you would come back here," Reagan said, confirming all his fears. "To her."

"I came back here to protect her from *you*." But he probably would have protected her more if he'd kept his resolution to stay away from her. But no matter how much he knew he should, he couldn't. She drew him as if there was some invisible cable connecting them. He could get only so far before it retracted and pulled him back to her.

"I am no threat to her," the killer insisted. But his muscular build and empty soul reeked of danger. "I am no threat to you, either."

Warrick snorted in disgust. "You really have no respect for me—to think I'm stupid enough to fall for your lies." He leaped across the distance separating them and clasped his hand to the man's throat. "Now tell me what you've done with Kate."

Fingers clawed at his hand, loosening his grip. "I'm telling you the truth. I haven't even seen her—well, she hasn't seen me," he corrected himself, "since the night that she shot you in the alley."

"If you are really no threat to me, why did you run off that night?" Warrick asked. "Why did you leave me lying there, bleeding?"

Reagan shuddered. "I knew you would not die. She didn't have silver bullets."

"But I did." After a fruitless night spent tracking Reagan, Warrick had left the gun in a safety deposit box at the abandoned bank. He kicked himself now for locking it away when he needed it and those silver bullets now. But he'd figured he would meet up with his brother there and have the key handy to unlock the box and fire that gun.

"It's gone," Reagan said.

"What?" He silently cursed himself for slipping up and revealing that he didn't have the weapon on him.

"They're gone now. The gun and the bullets. You won't find them when you go back to the place you're staying," Reagan matter-of-factly informed him, "the place I was staying when you first tracked me to Zantrax."

While Warrick still carried the key to that box, Reagan was so strong that he probably hadn't needed it to tear apart even the reinforced metal.

"You took the gun?" Warrick tensed, bracing himself for the bullet that would end his life.

But Reagan brandished no weapon. "I threw it out," he claimed. "I only kept the bullets."

Warrick readjusted his fingers, tightening his grip on Reagan's throat.

Nearly choking, the man gasped, "I—I just want to talk to you."

"I don't want to hear anything you have to say." He'd had enough of his excuses and lies.

"You need to listen to me," Reagan insisted. "You need to let me explain…*everything.*"

"You think I believe you came here to talk?" God, he really did think Warrick was an idiot—with good reason. He had been one because he'd once trusted this man. "You're stalling while something happens to Kate."

"I wouldn't hurt her. I wouldn't hurt you," Reagan insisted. "I'm not your enemy. I'm your—"

"Don't say it!" Warrick shouted. "Don't even think

it. You and I are nothing to each other." But they had once been more; Warrick had once idolized him. He had loved him. Now nothing but hatred filled him. "You're not going to get away this time."

Because Kate wasn't there to stop him. Where the hell was Kate?

"This time I'm going to kill you."

Reagan shook his head, trying to break Warrick's hold. "That's why I took the gun. You can't kill me like this. Not with your bare hands."

"I can tear you apart, so you can't run away again. I'll find another gun. I'll get more bullets." He would have to call Uncle Stefan again, and the pack leader would think him a fool for not always having the weapon on him. But he hadn't dared to carry it around Kate, hadn't wanted to give her a reason to shoot him again. And while he'd wanted to protect her, he didn't need the gun to stop Reagan from hurting her.

He only needed it to kill him.

"Then you'll shoot me?" Reagan asked. And the pain that flashed in his dark eyes wasn't physical.

But Warrick hadn't considered that he could hurt him emotionally—not the way that Reagan had hurt him. He hadn't thought his brother cared. Had he been wrong?

He closed his eyes, and that image replayed in his mind—of Reagan standing over their father's body. The man was a soulless killer. He couldn't be hurt; he could only hurt.

"I have to kill you," Warrick insisted.

"For justice for the pack?" Reagan asked. "Or for vengeance?"

Warrick wanted neither now. "Because I can't let you do any more damage."

Reagan gasped for breath then lifted his arms and broke Warrick's hold on his neck. The man was a formidable fighter; until that night in the alley Warrick had never overpowered him before. Reagan outweighed him and outmuscled him.

But he didn't strike out; instead, he kept his hands raised, as if Warrick held a gun. "You need to let me explain—"

But Warrick was beyond explanations. He was too worried about Kate. So he launched himself at Reagan. The man deflected his blows, but like that night in the alley, he didn't fight back.

What the hell game was he playing? He didn't want to physically hurt Warrick—just emotionally destroy him by taking away everything and everyone that mattered to him? How could Reagan have known—before Warrick had even realized it himself—that Kate mattered most?

More than his pride and his honor—Kate mattered.

"Where the hell is she?" he growled. She should have been home by now...unless someone had done to her what had been done to that homeless man. Mauled her and tossed her body into a Dumpster. He shouldn't have trusted that damn playboy vampire to protect her. He should have protected her himself. "What have you done with Kate?"

A shot fired. And both men turned to where she stood in her bedroom doorway, the gun clasped in her hand. "Break it up!" she yelled.

"Kate..." Relief shuddered through Warrick. But it

was short-lived because now she was here. With Reagan. And that put her in too much danger.

He turned back to his enemy. He might not be able to kill the man, but he could stop him from hurting Kate. So he launched himself at Reagan again. But before he could connect, another shot rang out—stopping him.

Kate cursed. She hadn't wanted to shoot him. But she'd reacted out of instinct.

Warrick turned to her, his topaz eyes wide with surprise...until she screamed at him. "He's getting away!"

The man, whoever he was, vaulted out the window—heedless of the bullet wound in his shoulder. Heedless of the fact that her apartment was four floors up from the ground. Just like her first shot into Warrick hadn't fazed him, her shooting his enemy hadn't fazed him, either.

Instead of chasing after the man he had vowed to kill, Warrick grabbed Kate and covered her mouth with his.

It was a quick, hard kiss, but heat and passion filled her at just that brief touch of his lips to hers. Before she could open her mouth, before she could return his kiss, he pulled back. But he didn't release her; his hands still clutched her shoulders, holding her closely.

He stared down at her, his eyes alight with passion, too—and relief. "Thank God you're all right."

"I'm fine," she assured him even though she felt a little shaky now—more from his kiss than from finding two men fighting in her bedroom. "But I'm confused." Partly about how much she wanted a man she couldn't even trust. She shook her head, trying to clear the desire from it. "I need to know what the hell is going on. Why did you bring that man *here*?"

Had he changed his mind about involving the police? Had he wanted her help? Had he reported finding the man? Sirens wailed in the distance as patrol cars approached. She doubted Warrick had called them. Someone in the building must have reported hearing the gun fired in her apartment.

Now Kate would have to report the shooting and explain what had happened. At least she would finally be able to prove that she hadn't been hallucinating that night in the alley: Warrick really did exist.

But he heard the sirens, too, and stepped back, his hands dropping from her shoulders. He turned and headed toward the window his enemy had gone out just moments ago.

"No!" she protested and she reached for him with the hand not holding her gun. She clutched at his arm, pulling him back around to face her. "You can't leave!"

"I have to," he said. "You're okay. And he's not. I can track him now. I can catch up with him."

And kill him.

"Warrick, don't—"

His broad shoulders slumped for a moment before straightening as his body tensed with determination. And he easily tugged free from her grasp. "I have to."

"You have to stop." She lifted her gun now. "Or I'll shoot you, too!"

He grinned. "No, you won't."

She moved her finger toward the trigger, but she couldn't pull it. She couldn't hurt him again. Even though he had somehow miraculously survived gun-shot wounds a surgeon had declared fatal, he had nearly died that night in the alley. He'd stopped breathing. His heart had appeared to stop beating. She couldn't risk that he might not survive again. So she lowered her weapon.

But he didn't see that she did. He had already turned away from her. He wedged his broad shoulders through the window. This was the same window through which his enemy had gone. It didn't open onto the fire escape; there was nothing beyond it but cold air. Unconcerned or blindly focused, Warrick leaped through it to the street below—far below. Four stories.

"No!" she yelled.

She rushed to the window and leaned out, staring down. But she could see no bodies sprawled on the asphalt. The fall hadn't hurt either man badly enough to stop them. So were they only men? Or were they something else—something Bernie had warned her about before he'd been so brutally murdered?

She shivered and not just because of the cold autumn air rushing over her. She shivered because of the thoughts rushing through her mind and the fear rushing through her heart.

What the hell was Warrick James?

The sirens grew louder as the cars pulled up in front of the apartment building. Moments later fists pounded at her front door. She hurried from her bedroom, but before she could cross the living room to the door, it swung open—the door and jamb splintering from the force. Uniformed officers were not who burst into her home, though. It was her ex-husband, clad in one of his dark suits and brightly patterned ties.

Old fears replaced new ones. Dwight had been superhumanly strong, too; she had had no defense against his blows. Her grip reflexively tightened on her gun. But then the uniforms followed him inside and she relaxed. He wasn't here alone. She holstered her gun.

Dwight, his face tense with concern, asked, "What the hell happened here, Kate?"

She wished she knew. "I came home to find an intruder in my bedroom."

"So you fired your weapon?"

She nodded and waited for the ridicule. After Warrick had disappeared from that alley, Dwight had taunted her about shooting at shadows.

But now he breathed a sigh of relief. "Good. Did you hit him?"

"If I did, I only grazed him because he managed to get away," she admitted.

"What did he look like?"

She shook her head and answered honestly. "I don't know. It was very dark in my bedroom. I didn't get a good look at him. I just know he was big." Even bigger than Warrick. That was why she had fired because the guy could have hurt him. Or worse.

Or could he have? Could either man actually die— when gunshots and four-story falls didn't harm them?

Dwight turned toward the uniforms and shouted orders at them. "Search outside for an injured man." They hastened to obey him, rushing off before they'd even secured the apartment.

But maybe they'd trusted her to do that—despite what the past couple of months had done to her reputation as a detective. What Warrick had done to it...

But he'd done more than affect her career. He had affected her heart and now her mind. What she was actually considering…

No, it just wasn't possible.

Alone again with her ex, she reached for her holster—settling her hand on her weapon in case she needed to draw it. In case she needed to defend herself…like she probably should have when they were married. "They won't find him."

"You think he disappeared again?"

"Again?" She was more surprised over his question than his kicking down her door. "So you do believe there was someone in the alley that night?"

"I've always believed in you, Kate," Dwight replied, and his voice and the steady gaze of his eyes conveyed sincerity. But it was a lie.

Anger gripped her. She really hated him, hated when he acted the magnanimous hero. "You didn't support me," she reminded him. He never had—even when they had been married. "You were the one who first started calling me crazy, saying I was imagining things. That I was overwrought."

"I'm sorry," he said—as he had so many times before. But just like then, she didn't believe him.

"I took advantage of the situation for a little payback," he admitted.

His confession shocked and confused her. "What do you owe me besides a lifetime of groveling?" she wondered.

"You can frustrate a man, Kate, with your stubborn independence," he said, and that frustration darkened his eyes. "You're always so strong and so sure of yourself. I guess it was kind of nice to see you…"

"Weak?" she asked. That explained a lot of their marriage, most especially how it had ended.

"Uncertain."

She'd doubted herself and her sanity and he had enjoyed that? "Get out!"

"I should stay here with you to make sure that he doesn't come back."

She pulled her weapon from her holster and hoped he gave her an excuse to use it. "I'll be fine. I can take care of myself."

And that was probably what he resented about her. But he gave up arguing and left. Her too-small, over-cluttered apartment suddenly felt big and empty with everyone gone.

She actually did want one of the men to come back. Warrick. And not just for that explanation he'd been denying her. When she had found him fighting again with the man he swore was dangerous, she had acted out of instinct and fired her gun to protect the man with whom she had such an uncanny connection.

And it wasn't just physical. There was more between them than that. But how could she be falling for a man that she wasn't even certain was a man—or at least not *just* a man?

Pain gripped her, doubling her over with its intensity. She grabbed for her belly—for her babies. But the pain wasn't in her stomach. The pain struck her heart, clutching it in a tight fist.

Reagan...

Her pain was his. He had been hurt.

Now she pressed her hands to her chest. He had been shot. With a silver bullet?

Was his life ebbing away?

The pain overwhelmed her. But now it was all hers. She couldn't lose him like this. His children couldn't lose him before they'd even been born. Before he even knew they existed…

She had been afraid to tell him that she was pregnant. And then he'd taken off, abandoning her. If he'd known, maybe he wouldn't have left her behind.

Or maybe he would have come back for her.

But no, it would have been for them. Not for her…

If he'd really wanted her—if he'd really loved her, he would have already returned. And now he might never have that chance.

"Let me in!" Warrick demanded, hammering at the steel door between the secret passageway and that damn secret clinic where the special surgeon saved lives. But some of those lives didn't deserve to be saved.

Didn't he know that? In the underground did it really matter that Dr. Davison had taken the Hippocratic oath?

"Do you need medical attention?" a voice asked from behind him.

He whirled toward Sebastian, who stood in the middle of the passageway—as if blocking his way back or trapping him. "I'm not hurt." Just very, very pissed. And if the vampire tried anything, he would be the one getting hurt.

"Then you don't need to get inside," Sebastian said. "And you'll need to wait if you want to talk to Ben. Dr. Davison is working on a patient."

"I know what patient he's working on," Warrick

said, "and that's why I have to get in there." He turned back toward the door, hammering at it. "Stop! Don't help him!"

A hand—a surprisingly strong hand—gripped his shoulder and turned him back around. But then vampires were strong—superhumanly strong. And Warrick was still in his human form. Could he overpower the vampire?

As if he'd read his mind, Sebastian shook his head. "Sorry," he said but his tone was not at all apologetic.

"Son of a bitch," Warrick cursed him.

Sebastian shrugged off the insult. "You can't compromise the sterile environment."

"You don't want to let the doctor save that man." Not with Kate's life at risk. The man had been in her home, in her bedroom. The red haze of fury blinded him. "And you sure as hell don't want to leave your brother-in-law alone with him."

Sebastian grinned in amusement. "Ben can take care of himself."

"So it is Reagan," Warrick said, his heart beating faster with anticipation. If only he had a gun and silver bullets, he could end this now.

Forever.

He could keep Kate safe. She was his first concern. Avenging his father's murder was an afterthought.

"Reagan?" Sebastian's light blue eyes widened in innocence. "Who's that?"

"The guy I've been chasing down for the past few months. The man who must be responsible for the murder of that Kate found dead in the alley." He swallowed hard, choking on that murderous rage, and added, "The man I found in Kate's bedroom tonight."

Sebastian's grin slipped away completely as he tensed. "Did he hurt her?"

Pride had Warrick flashing the grin now. "No. *She* hurt *him*. She shot him."

The vampire expelled a shuddery sigh. "So she's okay?"

Warrick nodded. "For now." He turned back to the door and rattled the handle. If he could tear the door from its hinges, he would, but it had been reinforced. "You have to let me in there."

"I don't know if that's who Ben's working on," Sebastian insisted.

"Then let me check." He had to know. He didn't care about Reagan's well-being. He just wanted to make sure he was in that room and not back with Kate.

Sebastian shook his head. "I can't."

"Then you do it," Warrick said. "You check for me." But he wasn't sure if he could trust the vampire. What if Reagan had conned him like he had so many others? Their father had thought Reagan was the good son. If he'd only known...

"I can't," the vampire repeated with a ragged sigh. "Only Ben can unlock the door from the inside."

"Then I'll wait here until he does," Warrick said. He didn't care that the passageway was really just a tunnel of the sewer system and that it was dank and smelled as putrid as the Dumpster in the alley. He would wait however long it was necessary. Reagan wouldn't slip away from him again.

"What if it's not him?" Sebastian posed the question as if he was just wondering aloud.

Warrick tensed now, apprehension lifting the short hair on his nape. "If what's not him?"

Had Reagan been talking to the residents of Zantrax, lying to them as he'd wanted to lie to Warrick? Trying to deny culpability for all the evil he'd done? Was that why Sebastian was protecting him? Because he didn't believe Reagan was a killer?

He hadn't witnessed what Warrick had—what he had witnessed every time he'd shut his eyes until he'd met Kate. Now, when he closed his eyes, he saw her—her beautiful face, her pale blue eyes, her sexy as hell body naked and flushed with passion…

"Ben's patient, the person in the surgery room with him," Sebastian clarified. "What if it's not your guy?"

Concern clutched Warrick's heart. "Then he'd still be out there…"

"And he already knows where Kate lives," Sebastian reminded him. "And neither of us are watching her right now—we're both here."

"Damn it!" And what if, like Warrick, Reagan had gone back to her to extract vengeance for her shooting him?

"I'll wait here," Sebastian offered. "You go—"

To her. The vampire didn't have time to finish what he'd been about to say because Warrick was gone. He only hoped that he could get back to her in time. Because she could shoot Reagan over and over and over again. But she wouldn't be able to stop him…

Not unless she had a silver bullet. And she didn't know she needed silver bullets. She didn't know what Reagan—what he—was. And she probably wouldn't until it was too late…

Chapter 9

He hoped he wasn't too late.

Fear—fear for *her*—gripped Warrick as he ran as fast as his human legs could carry him through the underground passages to the ladder that led up to the manhole cover outside her apartment building. Once through the hole, he scaled the brick wall to the fourth floor and vaulted through her window. He landed on his feet, as he always did. But then something struck him across the stomach, dropping him to his knees.

Pain gripped his guts as he groaned but rolled, trying to regain his feet. Reagan would not get the jump on him again.

"You're lucky I didn't shoot you," Kate remarked as she tossed the bat she'd swung at him onto the floor.

He flinched and finally managed to stand straight again as relief and pride filled him. Kate was fine;

hell, she was better than fine. "God, woman, you're dangerous."

Heat warmed her blue eyes, and he remembered the last time he'd called her woman—when he was making love to her. Kissing and caressing every inch of her. And now doing that all over again was all he could think about—kissing her, caressing her, thrusting inside her...filling her.

"Thank God you didn't hit me any lower," he murmured as he wrapped his arms around her. He lowered his mouth to hers.

But she pressed her palms against his chest and pushed him back. "No. We're not doing that..."

"We're not?" His body ached for hers, every muscle taut with desire. It had been too long since he'd touched her, since he'd been inside her.

He saw the longing on her face, too—felt the way her hands trembled against his chest as awareness tingled between them. His skin heated as passion filled him. He wanted her so damn badly.

She shook her head. "Not until you tell me what that man has done and why you hate him so much."

He dropped his arms and stepped back, turning toward the window. Was Reagan out there or locked up in Dr. Davison's damn secret clinic?

"Warrick, he was here—in my bedroom," she said, as if he needed the reminder of his mortal enemy being so close to her. "I need to know how dangerous he is."

"He's a killer."

She touched him now—gently, her hands on his back. "Who did he kill? Someone you loved very much, wasn't it?"

Loved or feared? He had never been able to separate the emotions when it came to the late leader of the pack. "My father..."

"I am so sorry," she said, her hands stroking comfortingly over his back to his shoulders. "I lost my dad...and mom...years ago, but I still miss them."

"My father was killed just a few months ago." But already the pain that had once been so sharp was beginning to dull. She had dulled it for him.

"But if that man murdered him—"

"He did." He could handle Sebastian and the others doubting him and falling for Reagan's lies. He couldn't accept *her* doubting him. He turned back to her, to focus on her face—her beautiful face when he told her. "I *witnessed* the murder myself." Because he had been too late to save his father—too late to stop that damn silver bullet from being fired. "He killed him."

Kate's brow furrowed in confusion. "Then I don't understand why the police aren't involved."

"Because he was *my* father." And his father never would have forgiven him if someone outside the pack brought his killer to justice. If he'd been able to speak as the blood had pumped from the bullet wound in his chest, he would have made Warrick promise to avenge his murder.

"Warrick, you can't take justice into your own hands like this," she said, her voice soft with sympathy. "I'm sure that's not what your father would want."

He laughed. "That just proves that you never met my father. He would want me to—he would *demand* on his honor and mine—that I take justice into my own hands."

Sadness dimmed the brightness of her blue eyes. "Your father sounds like a difficult man."

He laughed again but with bitterness instead of humor. "You have no idea."

"You don't have to do this," she said. "You can let the police take over now." She lifted her hands to his face, cupping his jaw in her palms. Her hands were soft but strong. "You can let *me* take over now."

"You are fierce," he replied. The strongest woman he had ever known. "My father would have liked you. He would have admired your guts and spirit and my father admired few—if any—people." And no humans. But he would have respected her. He would have considered her a worthy mate.

But he had never considered Warrick a worthy son. That was why Warrick needed to be the one to bring his killer to justice—even though he appreciated Kate's offer. Involving her would only put her in danger. And he couldn't handle the thought of putting her in danger, of risking her life…

He cared too much.

"I'm sorry you lost him," she said, "but I don't think I would have liked your father."

"Probably not," he agreed. Kate would have had problems with the rules of the pack, and his father had created most of those rules. That was why they could have no future. He could never tell her what he was because she would never want to join the pack. And if she didn't, she would have to die.

"Is it possible that that man was acting in self-defense?" she asked.

Warrick shook his head. "No. My father would have never hurt *him*."

"Then why would he hurt your father?" the detective—and she was once again the detective interviewing a witness—asked. She was looking for a motive—for a reason why Reagan had done what he had.

But he'd had no reason.

"Some people are just evil," he remarked. "My father isn't the only person he hurt."

"Who else?"

He shook his head. "I don't want to talk anymore."

"I have more questions—"

He swung her up in his arms and headed toward the bed. "Your interrogation is over, Detective Wever."

"Warrick—"

He tossed her down so that she bounced on the mattress. "I'm not making love with Detective Wever. I'm making love with the woman—"

"The woman?" she prodded when he stopped.

The woman I love. But he couldn't say those words, not when he had nothing to offer her but secrets. Because he couldn't give her the truth without risking her life. And he had already risked that enough just by falling for her.

"The woman who drives me crazy," he replied as he dragged off his shirt and unsnapped his jeans. He undressed as quickly as when he changed form—which would happen again in an hour. He had spent too long looking for Reagan—too long away from her. He kicked off his jeans and briefs and joined her on the bed.

"Warrick…"

"You have on too many clothes," he protested. And he began to undress her, tugging off her sweater so that her hair tangled across her face. Next he shucked her out of her pants and dropped them onto the floor where she always left her clothes. She was always so focused on law and order that she didn't even notice how very little order she actually had in her own life—or at least in her own apartment.

When she lay naked beneath him, he lowered his body to hers, so that her breasts cushioned his chest and her hips cradled his straining erection. He groaned at the exquisite sensation of her silky skin rubbing against his.

She moaned and wrapped her arms around his back, clutching him close. Then she lifted her mouth for his kiss, their lips moving hungrily over each other's. But kisses wouldn't be enough to feed his hunger. Or hers.

Her hands ran all over him, her fingers kneading muscles while her nails raked his skin. Then she reached between them and closed her hand around his erection. His cock throbbed and pulsated within her silky grasp.

He jerked back and groaned. "I can't…you can't…" Or it would all be over too soon. Just her touch could shatter his control. His muscles shuddered as he struggled for breath. Then he pulled back and lowered his mouth, sliding it down her throat. He nibbled at her collarbone before moving his lips lower, closing them around a tight nipple.

She rose off the mattress, arching up to him. He pulled her nipple deeper into his mouth, suckling. She shifted beneath him, rubbing her hips against his erection. And a low moan of pleasure emanated from her throat.

He moved his hands over her body, sliding them down her sides and over her hips. He lifted her hips in his hands and lowered his mouth to taste the very essence of her. She was so sweet—so wet.

Her fingers tangled in his hair but instead of pulling him away, she clutched him to her. Her body tensed and she screamed his name as an orgasm shuddered through her.

He didn't give her a second to regain her breath before he thrust inside her, driving deep and hard. Over and over again.

She clutched at his shoulders and wrapped her limbs around him, matching his rhythm. She found his mouth, kissing him with all the passion that flowed over him as she came again.

Sweat beaded his brow while the tension wound so tightly inside him that his body ached with the need for release. Finally, it slammed through him— so intense that he uttered a primal cry. His heart pounded hard, his breath coming in pants so harsh that he barely heard the warning beep of his watch. But her clock echoed the beep as the chimes began. He couldn't hold her like he wanted until dawn broke.

He had to leave…or risk her discovering the secret that would destroy her.

Reagan winced as he rolled his wounded shoulder.

"You have to take it easy," the surgeon cautioned him. "You're going to pull the stitches I just put in."

Reagan glanced at his watch. "In about thirty minutes, I'm going to pull them all out anyway." It was almost midnight. He would be changing soon.

"And if he doesn't get the hell out of here before Warrick comes back," the vampire bartender said, "you're going to have to do more than just stitch him up again."

Dr. Davison held up a bloodstained bullet. "I did more than stitch him up. I had to fish this out of his shoulder. It wasn't a through and through."

Reagan flinched at the sight of the lead. But he was damned lucky it had been lead and not silver. If she'd shot him with a silver bullet, he never would have seen…

"Who's Sylvia?" the doctor asked.

Reagan tensed. "Why do you ask?"

What had Warrick said about her?

Reagan had thought that his brother was falling for the human detective. But was she just a diversion for the woman he really wanted?

"You kept saying her name," Dr. Davison replied, "when you were out of it."

He knew he shouldn't have let the doctor sedate him. It would have been better if he'd just endured the pain. Hell, he'd been enduring pain for months now. But the surgeon had insisted that he couldn't extract the bullet unless Reagan was unconscious.

Apparently, he hadn't been entirely unconscious, or he wouldn't have been able to say her name. But he could have been dead and still wouldn't have been able to think of anything but her.

"That's the woman in the picture," Sebastian answered for him. "The one you carry with you."

He had it on him now. Pain clutched his heart that it was probably the only way he would see her again—in that photo. And maybe that was for the best.

If he saw her in person after what he'd done, he would be afraid of what he might see on her beautiful face: fear, revulsion, regret…

"That's her name," Reagan admitted.

"That's her name," Ben repeated. "But who is she?"

Sebastian snorted. "You want him to talk about his love life? There's a guy out there who hates him so much he wants to kill him. Don't you think it would be smarter to talk about that? What the hell is the deal with you and Warrick? Why does he hate you so much?"

"Because I destroyed his life," Reagan admitted regretfully. Warrick was too proud to have explained himself to the vampires, so they would have thought the worst of him—would have thought him an out-of-control hothead like their father had. Reagan always came across as the more reasonable and responsible brother, but Warrick had proven to be the more honorable one. Just no one knew it but the two of them. "And I nearly cost him his life…"

Sebastian's mouth fell open in surprise, his lip lifting enough to reveal the hint of his fangs. "I didn't think…"

"You didn't think he had a reason?" Reagan surmised. "Warrick isn't the kind of man who would hate someone unless he had just cause."

"He doesn't just hate you," Sebastian said. "He wants to kill you."

"And he has a good reason for that, too." If he didn't avenge their father, the pack would have to step in. Then they would kill Reagan and Warrick—because he'd failed to honor their father.

Sebastian and the surgeon exchanged a look. They obviously realized they shouldn't have helped him. "You need to leave," Dr. Davison said.

"Of course," Reagan agreed. "I'll get out of your way. Thank you for your help—" He held out his hand but the surgeon shook his head, refusing to take it.

"You don't need to just leave this room," Dr. Davison said. "You need to leave Zantrax."

"But Warrick is here," Reagan said.

"He'll leave when you do," Sebastian said. "He'll follow you."

Reagan shook his head, not just in denial but in pity for the vampire. He had no idea what it felt like to love someone. "He won't leave her."

Davison pushed a slightly shaking hand through his salt-and-pepper hair and murmured, "Kate…"

"You need to go back to your pack," Sebastian advised. "You and Warrick both need to return to your pack."

"If we do that, we're both dead," Reagan admitted. But they would not be the only ones to die. Sylvia would die, too.

"If you stay here, you'll probably both wind up dead, too," Sebastian said. And that might have been a threat. Then he added, "But I'm afraid someone else will wind up dead, too."

"Kate…" Davison murmured again.

Reagan gestured to his shoulder. "I think Kate can take care of herself."

Could Sylvia? Left alone with the hostility and resentment, could she survive?

"Kate's human," Davison said. And he held up that chunk of lead again. "And she doesn't have silver bullets."

She was at risk. If Warrick lost her, too…

Happiness rushed through Kate with the afterglow of the most incredible lovemaking she had ever experienced. The other time they'd been together hadn't been a dream. Only a taste of the passion that could burn between them.

She loved him.

Would her love be enough reason for him to set aside his quest for vengeance? Because that was what he really wanted. Not justice or he would have reported his father's killer to the authorities. He would have had the police arrest him, and all he would have done was testify at the man's trial.

"Warrick," she began, ready to share her feelings. But when she turned, she found him pulling on his clothes. "Where are you going?"

He wouldn't look at her, so she could only see the profile of his handsome face where a muscle twitched just above his jaw. "I—I have to leave, Kate."

Had he been as overwhelmed as she was? Was that why he was so anxious to bolt?

"We need to talk," she said. She wanted to tell him how she felt in the hopes that it might change his mind about his mission—about killing a man. But her love hadn't changed her ex—if anything, he had only become violent after their marriage.

The chimes of the clock echoed throughout the apartment. "I don't have time, Kate."

She reached for him, but he pulled easily from her grasp and stepped away from the bed. "You can't just leave—"

Before she could even finish speaking, he did. He leaped out that damn window as quickly and carelessly as he had earlier that day. Then he had been in pursuit of his father's killer; now she suspected that he was the one running.

And she wasn't about to let him get away as he had

every other time he had disappeared from her life. She dressed quickly and slammed out of her apartment just as the final chime announced midnight.

As she ran down the steps and pushed open the door to the dark street, she reached for her holster, but the straps didn't hang from her shoulders. She had left it and her Glock upstairs. He was already so far ahead of her that she didn't dare take time to retrieve her weapon. With Warrick she wouldn't need it anyways. He wouldn't hurt her.

Then again she had never thought Dwight would hurt her, either. And she already knew that Warrick was a violent man, full of rage over his father's murder. She hesitated. But a dark head in the shadows drew her attention down the street. Glass crunched beneath her feet from a broken lamp.

Goose bumps lifted on her skin. It was too dark. And cold. She needed to turn back for her weapon and her common sense. She had lost Warrick again. Had she ever actually had him?

Despite the passion they shared, maybe that was for the best. He was bent on revenge, and he was going to become the very thing he hated.

A killer…

With a sigh of resignation and a shiver of cold, she spun on her heel and headed back to her apartment. It had gotten so dark, and the chill in the air penetrated her thin clothes to her skin and deeper. To her soul.

She shivered again, fear and foreboding joining the cold. She needed to get back to her apartment, to the warmth and her weapon. But a dark shadow loomed between her and the entrance, blocking her way home.

"Who's there?" she asked.

The lights by the door had been broken, too, or the bulbs had burned out. She could see nothing but the eerie glow of eyes in the night.

"Who's there?"

Something uttered a low, menacing growl. Oh, God, the thing wasn't dead. Ben had lied to her. She backed up slowly, not wanting to startle it.

But the thing—the enormous, hairy beast—leaped from the darkness, his teeth snarling and snapping as he attacked her. She screamed. Not for help—she suspected that wouldn't come in time to save her.

She screamed in terror.

Chapter 10

"What the hell are you doing back here?" Sebastian demanded, slamming his fists into Warrick's chest.

Unprepared for the attack and the vampire's strength, he staggered back against the cement wall of the passageway. "What's wrong with you? I came to check on the doctor's patient."

"You son of a bitch, how dare you!" the vampire said, lashing out again with his fists.

Ready this time, Warrick caught the guy's wrists and shoved him back. "What the hell are you talking about?"

He had been gone for hours, first making love with Kate and then waiting in the abandoned vault until dawn to come back to Club Underground. He must have been gone too long because Reagan had managed to manipulate Sebastian into thinking Warrick was the villain. "What's he told you?"

"This isn't about him and you damn well know it. I thought you were going to protect her. If I knew you were going to do this…" Sebastian's light blue eyes gleamed with rage. "I would have killed you myself."

"Her?" His heart slammed into his chest. "Kate? What's happened to Kate?"

Sebastian pushed a shaking hand through his hair as if grappling for control.

Oh, God, it was bad…

Warrick's stomach lurched as fear overwhelmed him. "What is it?"

"Something attacked her," Sebastian replied.

"Something?" he gasped the word, fear choking him. "A werewolf?"

Sebastian nodded. "Ben thinks so." Then he fixed Warrick with an intense stare and asked, "Was it you?"

"Hell, no!" He shoved against Sebastian, knocking him away from that damn reinforced door. "Let me in! I have to see her!" He pounded at the steel, ignoring the pain as his knuckles cracked and bled.

Sebastian pulled him back. "You're not going to see her until I'm convinced you're not responsible."

"I would die before I would hurt her," Warrick replied, his voice gruff with the emotion that overwhelmed him now. He couldn't admit it—because he had no right to feel it after putting her in danger. He would die, too, if she didn't survive the attack.

The vampire nodded. "That's what I thought. But the injuries…"

"What injuries? How badly is she hurt?" Desperation to see her, mixed with the frustration that she was being kept from him, twisted his guts into knots.

He attacked the door again. "Let me in! Let me the hell inside!"

Sebastian shoved him back and stepped between him and the door. Then he nodded up at a camera lens nearly concealed in the cement wall of the tunnel. "You have to prepare yourself," he warned him.

"Oh, God…" She had been hurt that badly? That she was disfigured? Hanging on to life? Pain clutched his heart, making it feel as if it was being ripped apart. "Not Kate…"

The door opened to that sterile stainless-steel clinic—except it didn't look very sterile. Blood had spilled onto the cement floor and sprayed across some of the stainless-steel walls and surfaces. Panic and pain nearly paralyzed him, but he walked inside toward where the doctor bent over his operating table.

Why wasn't he concerned about keeping the place sterile now? Was it too late for Kate?

"Is she…?" He cleared his throat. "Is she…?"

Ben whirled toward him, a scalpel held like a weapon. "Sebastian, you're sure…?"

"He didn't do this."

"A werewolf is responsible for her wounds," Ben said. "The marks on her skin indicate teeth bigger than canine."

"Marks on her skin?" He moved closer to peer over the doctor's shoulder. She lay back, her lashes dark against her pale cheeks. Her sweater was torn and bloodstained but only the sleeves were pushed up to reveal stitched wounds on both forearms.

"She fought him off," Ben said, his voice catching with emotion and pride, "she fought until someone or something scared him away."

Of course she fought him off. She was Kate. A human woman against a supernatural beast. The beast hadn't stood a chance. Tears of relief and pride stung his eyes, but he blinked them back. "She's going to be okay?"

"For now," Ben said. "But she was awake when Sebastian brought her here. I don't know if she'll forget this time."

But he'd drugged her again. That must have been why she was unconscious—that or fear over what she'd seen. God, she must have been so scared.

"And she won't believe that it was a dog again." Ben sighed. "Hell, she didn't really believe it last time."

So even though the attack hadn't killed her, what she had learned because of it would. "Damn it…"

"Warrick," the doctor began with the tone he probably used to deliver bad news to his patients, "I don't think it was him, either."

Warrick had been right. Reagan had gotten to them with his manipulations and mind games. No one knew better than he did just how damn charming Reagan could be. "But you had no problem thinking it was me—that I would do this to *her*."

"I'm sorry."

"Hell, it doesn't really matter that it wasn't me," he said, his hand shaking as he reached out to her, skimming his fingers down her pale cheek. How much blood had she lost? Not as much as would have had the beast gotten to her throat. He shuddered at the thought of Kate being brutalized like that homeless man in the alley. "I'm still responsible."

Sebastian clasped his shoulder with belated support. "It's not your fault."

"You warned me what could happen to someone I came to care about…" He could admit to caring about her but his feelings went so much deeper than caring. Reagan had to know—that was why he had attacked her. She had fought him off, but she wasn't safe.

While she wasn't dead yet, she would be soon. Because of him.

Distress clutched at Kate. But it wasn't hers. She fought her way through the grogginess that clouded her mind and paralyzed her muscles. That concern tugged at her, reaching her through the mist of unconsciousness. She felt trembling fingers on her cheek. And she opened her eyes to his face.

His topaz eyes were filled with fear and regret and that concern she'd felt.

"Shh," she murmured. "I'm okay…"

His sexy mouth curved into a slight grin. "Of course you are. You're fierce."

She glanced around him, at Ben's and Sebastian's worried faces. And at the stainless-steel walls of the strange room. Blood spattered them. It wasn't her blood. Just what the hell had gone on inside this room?

She knew where it was. That door at the back of Club Underground that was always locked and that Sebastian had once claimed there was no key to anymore because it had been sealed off. He'd said that it had once led to the sewers. Of course he'd said nothing about the room in between and what the hell went on in that room.

"Go back to sleep," Warrick urged her. "You need your rest to recover."

She shook her head, her hair moving against the cool surface of the metal table on which she lay. "No. I need to go find that *thing*…"

All hair and muscle and teeth.

The concern fled Warrick's topaz eyes; rage replaced it with that murderous intent she had seen the first time she'd bumped into him. "I will take care of that," he vowed. "Once and for all."

"No." Ignoring the dull throbbing in her arms, she reached out to him. "It wasn't that man. It wasn't a *man* that attacked me." She shuddered as she remembered the growling and snarling and the snapping teeth of that horrific beast as it had attacked her, tearing at her flesh. "It wasn't even a dog. It was a *monster*."

He leaned down and kissed her forehead and promised her, "I will take care of it. I'm going to make sure it never hurts you again."

When he tried to straighten up, she clutched at his shoulders, holding him close. "Don't go after it. That thing will tear you up."

That intense gleam hardened his topaz eyes, and he shook his head. "No. It won't."

The animal in the alley, the one she'd shot had had those same eyes. And it had not snarled or snapped at her. The one outside her apartment had been different—its gaze pale and cold. Were those beasts really animals?

Or…

"Warrick, what's really going on?" she asked. "*What* are you really?"

"I'm sorry," he said, and he stepped back—free of her weak hold on him. "I'm so sorry you got mixed up in the middle of something that has nothing to do with you."

She lifted her bandaged arms again; they felt heavy, awkward and, fortunately, almost numb but for that dull throb. "It has everything to do with me now."

If only she'd had her gun on her…she could have shot the monster. Next time she would make certain she was armed. Hell, she would make certain that she was always armed.

Warrick shook his head again. "No. You need to forget about it. Forget about all of it."

"All of what?" she asked. Just what the hell was going on and why was she the only one who didn't know?

He gestured around them. "This place."

She glanced at the blood-spattered walls and shuddered. She wouldn't mind forgetting this room. But now that she knew about it…

"Forget what happened tonight," he continued, and a muscle twitched along his tightly clenched jaw as he looked down at her heavily bandaged arms.

If only she could…

She could still hear the echo of that sinister growl and the snapping of those teeth…

She flinched at the too-recent memory of the pain those teeth had inflicted. Whatever drugs Ben had given her had dulled the present pain, but she wouldn't forget what it had initially felt like. She couldn't—no matter what Warrick wanted.

"And most of all, Kate," he continued, his deep

voice even gruffer with emotion and finality, "forget about me."

"No," she murmured as she suddenly felt weaker—dazed. Maybe she'd lost a lot of blood. She couldn't remember anything but the initial attack. "Don't go…"

But he stepped away from her—only a short distance but it felt like miles already. He had already emotionally left her.

"Protect her," he told her friends, who were apparently his friends, too, since they cautioned him to be careful as he left the room and stepped through the door that led to the tunnels to the sewer. They knew he was going off to commit murder, yet they didn't seem to care that he was going to become a killer. Or was he already one?

The grogginess crept back into her brain, probably along with whatever drug Ben shot into her IV, and consciousness began to slip away from her.

Maybe Warrick was right; maybe she needed to forget it all but most especially him.

He had disappeared. For Warrick's sake. So he didn't do something crazy—something he would regret when he learned the truth.

Reagan only hoped he didn't learn the truth too late. He knew the detective had been hurt. Reagan had been too late to save her from any harm. But her attacker hadn't meant to kill her. Only to hurt her.

And infuriate Warrick.

The plan had obviously worked because Reagan could feel his brother's rage. It echoed inside his own heart when he saw his cabin—the windows and doors secured with heavy chains and padlocks. Even if Sylvia had wanted to leave, she would have been unable.

And she had no doubt wanted to leave—especially after she'd learned what he had done. Unless she had been waiting for Warrick to reclaim her...

Did she regret choosing him over his brother? Did she think Warrick was the better man?

Reagan pushed his hand through his already disheveled hair. Hell, Warrick was the better man. He wouldn't have put her in the situation that Reagan had.

She wouldn't have become a prisoner because of his brother. He lingered in the shadows of the woods surrounding his cabin. He could have broken the links in those chains; they weren't too heavy for him.

But it wasn't just the locks holding her inside; there were guards, too, patrolling the perimeter of the cabin. They were guys he knew with whom he'd grown up. But he knew that they would kill him on sight—and shortly after that, Sylvia would probably die, too.

He couldn't see her, couldn't touch her, couldn't talk to her and try to make her understand why he'd done what he had. He had to try to get through to Warrick, though—before it was too late for all of them.

Sylvia awakened with a gasp. But it wasn't because the babies had kicked her. For once they were sleeping, too. She awakened because she could feel *him*.

He wasn't just alive. He was *close*. Heat rushed through her, warming her blood and making her skin tingle with awareness—that awareness she'd felt the moment they'd met.

Had he come to rescue her?

But the locks were still at the doors and windows,

the guards still pacing around outside. It was too dangerous. If he made his presence known, they would kill him. And her...

The babies shifted now, coming awake with kicks and punches. They were fighters—like their father. But he was only one; he couldn't fend off the entire pack.

They would kill him if they saw him, if he stayed. "Please leave..." she murmured even though she didn't expect him to hear her.

But then her blood chilled as the heat rushed away. He was gone. Had he heard her? Had he left?

Or had the guards discovered him and killed him? She gasped again—this time in pain and fear.

"I need your help," he told Uncle Stefan. Fortunately his uncle was such a good leader for the pack that he didn't have to be in St. James to rule. The pack respected him enough to follow his rules even when he wasn't present. "I need another weapon. And more silver bullets."

His uncle glanced around the vault, as if hoping to find the stolen gun. "It's gone?"

"He took it."

"Then you are at great risk," Uncle Stefan warned him. "He could kill you."

He could have, but he hadn't. Instead, the coward had gone after Kate. "I don't care what he does to me. I just have to stop him." Not only had he lost the gun but he also had to admit, "I've lost his scent. I can't pick up his trail."

"Maybe he's left Zantrax."

Remembering Kate's wounds, he shook his head.

"No. He's still here. And close. You have to get me the gun and bullets so that when I pick up his trail again, I will be ready for him. I have to end this now."

"You needed to end this the day he killed your father," Uncle Stefan remarked. "Before that even, the day he stole your fiancée."

But if Reagan hadn't stole Sylvia away, Warrick would have never met Kate. He felt no rage over that anymore—only disappointment and pain over the betrayal of the people he'd thought he could trust the most.

"Reagan is my brother," he remarked. "Why does he hate me so much?"

"Just because you share blood doesn't mean you share anything else," Uncle Stefan replied. "Your father and I had very little in common."

"But you didn't try to destroy him," Warrick said. If anything, it might have been the reverse, but Uncle Stefan had always been patient and understanding with his older brother's leadership.

"Your father was invincible."

As he remembered the blood pumping from the hole in his father's heart, Warrick sadly shook his head. "No. He wasn't." But like Uncle, he had once believed the same of his father—that nothing and no one would ever hurt him—least of all Reagan.

Uncle Stefan uttered a weary-sounding sigh. "He never considered Reagan a threat, so he didn't see the ultimate betrayal coming."

"Neither did I," Warrick admitted, "until he took away Sylvia. But even then I never suspected what he would do to our father."

He would forever remember the image of his

brother, armed with a gun, standing over their father's dead body. Reagan hadn't denied firing the silver bullet into the old man's heart. He hadn't been upset at all—not guilt-ridden, just resigned and almost relieved.

"I guess he could not wait for his turn to become leader," Uncle Stefan mused.

"He said he did it because of me," Warrick shared. He shuddered. "But that makes no sense. How could anything he's done be for my benefit?" But taking away Sylvia had led Warrick to Kate and a deep and genuine connection.

"I think Reagan feels threatened by you," Uncle Stefan replied. "Even though you are the younger brother, you were always more alpha than he was. You were more capable of leading the pack than he would ever be."

"Were?"

"Until you avenge the loss of your fiancée and your father's death, you cannot reclaim your rightful place in the pack. A man without honor cannot lead."

A man without honor could not live, either. That was one of his father's rules.

"You need to take back your honor," Uncle Stefan urged him.

"My honor be damned." He cared nothing for it anymore. Or for revenge. He cared only for Kate. "I just want Reagan stopped. Now, before he takes away anything else I care about."

"What do you care about, nephew?" Uncle Stefan asked, his pale gray eyes narrowed with suspicion. "Or should I ask whom?"

"Someone special," Warrick said, his heart aching over just how special she was. "Someone I respect."

"Someone you love?"

"Someone I don't want getting hurt because of me." Not anymore. She had already been terrorized and hurt because of him.

Uncle Stefan nodded, accepting his explanation. "I will help you stop Reagan. Permanently."

"So you can get me another gun and more silver bullets?"

Uncle nodded again. "Yes. I will make sure you are prepared when you find him again."

"I better find him soon." Before Kate was hurt again.

Until they found Reagan, Warrick would have to stick close to her. To protect her—not just from his brother but perhaps from the whole Secret Vampire Society, as well. Now that she knew about the secret surgery room and had seen all the blood, the vampires would consider her a threat, too.

She was in so much danger.

While she knew that the beast that had attacked her was more than a dog, she had no idea what other creatures lived with her in Zantrax.

Chapter 11

"Are you sure it's okay for you to come home?" Paige asked as she flipped on the lights in Kate's apartment.

"I couldn't stay in that place any longer." Kate shuddered as she picked some newspapers off the couch so she could sit down. The walk up those four flights had drained what little energy she'd had left after last night. "What the hell kind of clinic is that? And what's it doing in the back of Club Underground?"

"There are some things that can't be explained," Paige evaded the question. She plumped up a pillow and shoved it behind Kate's back. "Some secrets that are safer kept."

"There are too many secrets and too many unusual things happening in Zantrax." The most unusual ones had happened since Warrick had turned up in the city. "I need to know what you know, Paige. I'm your friend. You can tell me."

Paige settled onto the couch beside her. "It's because you're my friend that I can't tell you."

Tears of frustration threatened, but Kate blinked them back—too stubborn and too proud to shed them. She had been through too much to cry now, and she was afraid that once she started she might not stop. "I hate that everyone I care about is keeping secrets from me."

"Everyone?" Paige asked, arching a blond brow. "Who is everyone?"

"You…"

"And who else?" Paige persisted. "The man from the bar—the one you denied knowing? It was obvious he knew you—the way he kept staring at you."

Undressing her with his eyes because he knew exactly what she looked like with no clothes.

Kate sighed. "That's not why you know about him. What have Sebastian and Ben told you about Warrick?"

"That you're involved with him," Paige said, her blue eyes filling with concern. "And that you shouldn't be."

"I shouldn't," Kate agreed, "because he's keeping secrets from me. Dangerous secrets." Incredible secrets because what she had considered in the clinic wasn't even possible; the beast that had attacked her hadn't been human. Ever. It couldn't have been.

"It sounds like getting involved with him has put you at risk," Paige said.

"I put myself at risk every day," Kate said, "when I do my job. And even when I'm off duty, I'm still on the job." That was how she had met him in the first place—trying to stop him from committing murder.

"Don't I know it," Paige said with a chuckle. "You never stop interrogating me."

"Because you never answer my questions. Neither does Ben. Or Sebastian." They were all keeping secrets from her. Frustration tired her, and she uttered a weary sigh. "Or Warrick."

"It's not because we don't want to give you answers," Paige said. "It's because we *can't*."

Kate squeezed her eyes shut, holding in those tears of frustration and exhaustion. "I need to know."

"You need some rest," Paige said. "You should have come home with me, so I could take care of you."

"You have Addi to take care of," Kate said.

"She's fully recovered from her heart surgery," Paige said with a heartfelt smile of relief. "She would love to help me take care of you."

Kate held up her bandaged forearms. "They're just scratches."

"They're bites," Paige reminded her even though Kate was unlikely to ever forget how she had sustained these injuries, "and bites can get infected."

"Your husband gave me IV antibiotics." Among other drugs, she suspected, since her memory was fuzzy again but not gone. Had he not dared to give her as high a dose as the last time she suspected she had been inside that god-awful clinic, the night someone had struck her in the head? "I'm fine."

"But are you safe here?" Paige asked, her eyes glistening with tears of fear. She was not too proud or too stubborn to shed them. "You got attacked right outside your apartment building."

"I was unarmed and unprepared. Now I have my gun and my bat. I'm safe here," Kate assured her. Nothing—and no one—would get the jump on her again.

"But you're tired." Something else Paige didn't need to remind her of. "You need someone to look after you while you rest. I can stay."

And how would Paige protect her? She didn't know how to shoot a gun or wield a bat. Or did she? What secrets was Paige keeping from her? Was she like Dwight and Warrick and that man he pursued— superhumanly strong?

"If you stay, we'll keep talking and I won't rest," Kate said with a smile so that she would not offend her friend. "I really just need to be alone."

Paige studied her for a moment before nodding and then rising from the couch. "Okay."

"I'll be fine," Kate assured her as Paige walked to the door.

Her friend turned back, her beautiful face tense with worry and regret. She didn't believe Kate would be fine. What damn secret did she know that affected Kate's safety?

Before she could ask, Paige was gone. Moments later, though, a knock rattled the door. Kate leaped to her feet and threw open the door. "I'm glad you came back."

Hope brightened in the light-colored eyes of the man on her threshold. "I'm glad you're glad."

She shook her head at Dwight. "I thought you were someone else."

"A man?" he asked and stepped inside the apartment and looked around as if trying to find one in her living room among the discarded newspaper and junk mail.

"A friend." Not that she owed him any explanations. "What are you doing here?"

"I wanted to make sure you're all right," he said, staring at her bandages. "I heard you were attacked."

"It wasn't the first time," she reminded him with the bitterness she had never quite overcome.

"And it probably won't be the last unless you learn to be more careful," he warned her.

She'd been outside her own damn apartment building—not meeting strange callers in dark alleys. She shouldn't have had to be careful.

"You have no idea what you're risking," he continued.

"What are you talking about?" Did he know the secrets, too? Did everyone know but her?

He stepped closer and reminded her, "I told you to stay away from Club Underground."

"I wasn't attacked there." But she had been brought there after the attack. Why? "And my best friend owns the place, so I won't be staying away from it."

His face that she'd once thought handsome distorted with a grimace. He obviously didn't like Paige. "Your best friend is not who you think she is."

"What are you talking about?" Damn him—he knew. Just like everyone else, he knew.

"Nothing." He shook his head. "I can't tell you anything except that you need to let all of this go. You can't dig any deeper."

"Why not?"

"Because if you find out anything else," he said, his voice deep with warning, "it's going to kill you."

"So you didn't come here to check on me at all," she pointed out his lie. "You came here to threaten me."

"I came here because I still care about you."

"Still? When did you ever care about me?" she asked, incredulous that he could claim that he had after how he'd treated her.

"I loved you," he insisted. "I still do, Kate. But I lead a life that I can't share with you."

"We're both detectives," she pointed out. "You and I lead the same life."

He uttered a heavy sigh. "No. We don't."

"I don't understand…" Anything. But then she'd never really understood Dwight, like how he could go from being a hero to being a monster so quickly.

"Just promise me you'll be careful."

Was that actual sincerity in his voice for once? Or a veiled threat? Kate was too tired to discern the difference and too weak to fight Dwight if it was actually a threat.

"She's not the only one who needs to be careful."

Warrick, unable to hide his presence any longer, stepped into the room. He'd kept out of sight while Paige had been warning Kate away from him. But this man was different—his very presence lifted the hair on Warrick's nape. If he'd been in his other form, his hackles would have been raised and his teeth bared.

Kate glanced toward him in surprise. "You're here?"

"Of course," he replied. "Where else would I be?" Reagan was still out there and posing a threat to her safety. But Reagan wasn't the only threat. He turned back to the visitor.

The man's eyes were narrowed with anger and jealousy. "Who is this, Kate?" He didn't ask; he demanded to know.

"I'm—"

"He's none of your business," Kate interrupted. "You need to leave."

The detective shook his head. "Not until he explains his comment."

"Well, where else would I be," Warrick said, "but with Kate?"

"That brings up a lot of other questions," the man said. "But I'm more curious about who else needs to be careful? Were you referring to yourself? Or me?"

"I'm always careful," Warrick replied. He'd learned the hard way to trust no one.

"So you're threatening me?" the blond guy asked with a laugh, as if Warrick posed no threat to him.

"Just advising you to do the same," Warrick replied. "This is a dangerous city."

"Didn't used to be," the man remarked. "So how long have you been in town?"

"How do you know I'm not from Zantrax?" He wondered how much the detective knew about him. He suspected more than Kate knew.

"You're not," the man replied with absolute certainty. "So how long?"

"Not long enough." He hadn't killed Reagan yet. And if this guy kept threatening Kate, he might need to add him to the hit list.

"And here I was thinking that it was too long," the blond guy sarcastically remarked.

"You're the one who's stayed too long," Kate said. "Please leave."

"Kate—" he protested.

She shook her head. "Remember our agreement."

Without another word, the man turned and left, slamming the door behind him.

"What agreement?" Warrick asked, jealousy twisting his guts.

"Divorce agreement," she replied. "Not that it's any of your business."

"You're my business," he insisted. "Why would you marry a guy like him?" Not that Warrick couldn't understand a woman falling for his slick good looks. Just not Kate. She was far shrewder than that. "Better yet, why did you divorce him?"

Her lips twisted into a sexy sneer of disgust. "So you expect me to share all of my secrets but you intend to keep all of yours."

"What makes you think I have secrets?" he asked. What did she remember?

"I know when a man's keeping things from me."

"So that's why you divorced your ex?"

"No. He didn't keep enough from me." She flinched as if the memory was physically painful.

Warrick realized why it was and rage consumed him. "He hurt you?" And then he had the balls to tell her to be careful? Had that been a threat of more violence?

"It was a long time ago," she said. "And he's not the only one I've cared about who has hurt me."

"I would never hurt you, Kate," he promised and reached out for her.

But she stepped back, as if she truly feared him.

"Kate!"

"You're hurting me with your secrets," she said.

"And you're hurting me with your single-minded quest for revenge. You're just as violent a man as Dwight— maybe more so because he's never killed anyone, not even in the line of duty."

"That you know of," he muttered, suspecting that the detective had secrets of his own.

"What?"

He lifted his shoulders in a slight shrug. "I just don't trust him."

She chuckled. "That's quite ironic coming from you."

"You don't think *he* should trust me?"

"I don't think *I* should trust you," she said.

"Kate, I would never hurt you." He caught her fingers in his and tugged her close. But he was careful of her bandages, of the injuries she never would have incurred had it not been for her involvement with him.

Her friend Paige was right and so was she. He was too dangerous for her. Yet he couldn't resist lowering his head and brushing his mouth across hers. Gently. Tenderly. With all the emotion churning inside him.

She clutched at him and a little moan slipped through her lips. He moved to deepen the kiss, to part her lips so that he could taste her fully. But then he tasted something else: the salt of the tears streaking down her face.

He pulled back, his heart twisting in his chest as he wiped away her tears. He had never met a stronger woman than Detective Wever; seeing her cry proved just how much she'd been hurt. Because of him? Or by him? "Kate?"

"I can't handle this," she said.

Old insecurities and jealousies rushed over him,

and he asked, "Because of him? Are you thinking about your ex?"

Her eyes widened in surprise. "What are you talking about?"

He shook his head. "Nothing. You must be tired—you've been through so much…" Whether she'd been hurt because of or by him, it didn't matter—the blame was all his.

"I'm supposed to forget about that," she said. "Did you forget that you told me to?"

Ben apparently hadn't drugged her as much as he had last time. Damn. She remembered. Too much…

"Kate…"

"You told me to forget about you," she reminded him. "And yet here you are." She lifted one of her bandaged arms to touch his face. "Are you really here?"

"I'm here, Kate," he confirmed. But he shouldn't have been. If he'd been able to find Reagan, he wouldn't have been.

Hell, if that smarmy detective hadn't been in her apartment, he probably wouldn't have made his presence known to her. He would have just watched over—protected her.

She touched her head now, and her already pale face grew paler. "I'm not sure what's real or what's not anymore…"

"You're exhausted." And too close to the truth but the truth was so surreal it was no wonder she struggled with reality. "Let me put you to bed."

Her lips curved into a tremulous smile. "If you put me to bed, I won't get any sleep."

"I can control myself."

Her smile widened as she admitted, "Maybe I'm the one who can't control myself."

"Then don't," he tempted her.

Her smile faded as the muscles in her delicate face tensed. "I really do need some rest, though."

"You're trying to get rid of me," he realized. Rationally he understood why, but he didn't react rationally to her rejection. Because her rejection reminded him of another, but Kate's hurt far worse than Sylvia's had. But like his ex, did Kate prefer another man to him? "What—you'd rather your ex had stayed and I'd left?"

"I threw him out," she reminded Warrick. "And now I'm throwing you out for acting like him."

Offended, he lifted his chin. "What do you mean? I'm nothing like him."

"You're a violent man, just like he is," she said. "And you're acting jealous and possessive now."

"Kate—"

"And you have no right to act jealous or possessive," she pointed out. "You told me to forget about you—so let me forget. Just leave me the hell alone!"

"Fine." She was too tired and had been through too much for him to argue with her. Like she'd accused him, he had been acting like a jealous ass. And maybe she would be safer if he left anyway.

"And don't come back until you're ready to tell me the truth," she warned him. "About everything. I don't want you here—I don't want you—if you intend to keep secrets from me."

He paused at the door and turned back. "The truth about what, Kate?"

"It was you in the alley that night."

"We already established it was," he agreed. "You shot me."

"I'm not talking about that night," she said. "I'm talking about the second time I shot you—when you weren't you. But you were…"

"Kate." Oh, God, she had figured it out. "You don't know what you're talking about."

"You had a fresh wound on your shoulder—it was from where I shot you when you weren't you. I knew Ben was lying to me about that…that thing. But I didn't realize that you were lying to me, too." Hurt filled her eyes, which glistened with more tears. "You've been lying to me all along."

"Kate…" He couldn't lie to her now—not with her looking so wounded and raw and exhausted. So, instead of denying her allegations, he just kept walking. Right out the door, closing it quietly behind him. And now he knew that he could never come back.

Kate's head pounded as fiercely as her heart. He hadn't called her crazy; he hadn't even seemed all that surprised that she had figured out his secret.

But was that really his secret? That he wasn't just a man—that at some time during the night, perhaps midnight, he turned into a beast?

How was that even possible?

None of it made sense. Not those beasts. Not that secret room behind the club where Ben did clandestine operations. But then maybe it all defied logic. Maybe there were explanations that, as a detective, she had always been too practical to consider.

Hell, maybe it was whatever drugs Ben had given her that had inspired these crazy thoughts. She'd once thought she had been hallucinating and dreaming up Warrick, though, and he had proved to be real.

She needed to go after him—to get him to explain everything to her. But she didn't have any energy left. She needed rest, time to regroup, and after some sleep, she would be ready to discover all the secrets in Zantrax. Fighting a yawn, she stumbled into her bedroom—already reaching for the zipper on the sweatshirt she wore over a tank top and jeans. Paige had brought her the clothes, her other ones too bloody and torn to wear home.

Her heart felt like her clothes—too bloody and torn.

She was too exhausted to deal with her feelings for Warrick. She loved him; she couldn't deny that she'd fallen for him. But she also feared him and for him. His life was far more dangerous than even hers as a major case detective.

"Don't take off anything else," a deep voice advised. "You're not alone." The man stepped from the shadows, his eerie topaz eyes gleaming in the faint light.

He looked like Warrick but he wasn't Warrick. How had she not noticed their resemblance before? Maybe because when Warrick was around, he was all she could see. Not the man he'd been attacking...

"Warrick doesn't know you're here," she surmised.

He shook his head. "I would already be dead if he knew I'd come back here."

"Why would you risk death then to come back to my apartment?" To her?

Because he intended to kill her just as Warrick had warned her, as he had feared? Apparently he had been right about this man; he was dangerous.

Chapter 12

If Warrick had gone out the window, as he usually did, the man wouldn't have gotten the jump on him. But as he stepped out of the front doors of Kate's building—where she had been attacked just the night before—a fist slammed into his face, knocking him back against the brick wall. His lip split, blood trailing down his jaw. He swiped it away with his hand and met the angry gaze of the man who'd struck him.

But like him, this man wasn't just a man. He had more than regular human strength. "Who are you?"

"I'm the reason you need to stay the hell away from Kate!" He swung again.

But Warrick was ready this time. He ducked and charged forward, shoving his shoulder into the man's chest. Instead of knocking him down, as he would have a human, Kate's ex only stumbled back before regaining his footing.

"You have no claim on Kate anymore," Warrick reminded the man.

Dwight shook his head. "I will always have a claim on Kate."

"A divorce decree says otherwise."

"I don't give a damn about the divorce!" the man shouted, his pale blue eyes gleaming with an obsession that had Warrick's nape tingling again. "I only care about Kate."

"If that were true, you would respect the terms of your divorce because you're the one who needs to stay away from her," Warrick said. "If you ever hurt her again—" He swung out, catching the man across the jaw and knocking him back.

Dwight shuffled his feet again and caught himself from falling when the blow would have dropped a human. He just shook his head, as if shaking off an insignificant slap. "I'm not the reason Kate's getting hurt. You are."

Just as he had suspected, this man definitely knew the secrets Kate wanted so desperately to learn. Or had she already figured everything out?

She suspected what Warrick was. Did she also have suspicions about the Secret Vampire Society? He wouldn't doubt it; she was that good a detective. And she had seen too much—too much of that secret underground surgical room.

"You've hurt Kate before," Warrick reminded the man.

Her ex flinched, as if he actually felt remorse. "We're not talking about the past. We're talking about the danger that Kate's in now. Because of you."

Warrick narrowed his eyes and studied this man

who wasn't just a man or a detective. He was something else entirely—maybe a member of another pack. Because of his obsession with his ex, he could be the biggest threat to Kate's safety. "Where were you when she was attacked?"

"Not where I needed to be," Dwight replied with a glance up at the fourth-floor apartment, "to protect her from whatever one of you mangy animals attacked her last night."

"So you know…"

"That you're a freakin' werewolf?" He curled his lip in revulsion, and Warrick caught a glimpse of fangs. "Everyone in the Secret Vampire Society has been warned about you and the other members of your pack that are in Zantrax."

"You're one of the vampires." That explained his strength. "The first time she was attacked in the alley behind Club Underground, it could have been you." Protecting that damn secret society of theirs.

Dwight flinched. "The bandage on her forehead. Someone hit her in the head?"

"Yes."

"I—I wouldn't have done that," he said.

"But you have attacked her before." Warrick swung again, and it was as if Dwight wanted to be hit because he didn't dodge the blow—just took it to his chin. So that his lip split and swelled.

He wiped away the blood with his tongue and admitted, "I hurt Kate in the past. Back when I was first turned into one of the society after getting bitten during a bust. I didn't know how to deal with all her questions and suspicions without putting her in danger."

Anger and revulsion coursed through Warrick. "So

your way of dealing with her questions was to beat her?" He wanted to do more than hit the vampire detective now; he wanted to rip him apart.

"She's a stubborn woman and smart," Dwight told him what he already knew. "It was the only way to get her to back off."

"You wanted her to leave you," Warrick realized.

"I had to hurt her in order to protect her," the detective explained. "I wanted to keep her alive. What about you? Do you care enough about Kate to let her go to protect her?"

He had tried. He had tried so many times to walk away from her. But he kept coming back. He told himself it was to protect her. But maybe it was just because he was too damn selfish to let her go.

"I'm not going to hurt you," the man assured Kate, his arms lifted as if to prove he had no weapons.

But Kate already knew that a man didn't need a weapon to hurt a woman—especially if he wasn't just a man. She edged closer to the bed, to where she had left her holster and her gun before rushing out after Warrick last night.

"Who are you?" Maybe she should have asked *what* he was although she suspected he would evade her question just like Warrick had. And Paige. And Ben. And Dwight…

They all knew. Why wouldn't they tell her? Was it that awful—that unimaginable?

She was afraid that it was. And if she knew, she would never be safe again. But she wasn't safe now. And she had always believed that knowledge was power. They all had the power, and she was weak.

"My name is Reagan James," the man answered her.

"James? So you are related to Warrick?" She wasn't surprised—not with how alike they looked.

"I'm his brother."

She was surprised now—so much so that she gasped. "But he said you killed his father. That would have been your father, too."

Poor Warrick. No wonder he was so angry. But he was also conflicted; that was probably why he hadn't reported to authorities what this man had done. He was his brother.

Despite Warrick's claim that he had witnessed the murder, she waited for Reagan James to deny the allegation—to claim his innocence as most criminals did.

Instead, he nodded again but grimly, his jaw clenched so tightly that a muscle twitched in his unshaven cheek.

His honesty shocked her. If only the perps that she arrested were as honest... But then he knew there was an eyewitness to his crime. His own brother.

"I had my reasons," he said.

"Self-defense?" Their father sounded as if he had been a horrible man.

Reagan shook his head this time. "Father never would have hurt *me*."

Realization dawned, sickening her, as she suddenly understood why a man would kill his father. To protect someone else he loved.

That she loved, too.

"You did it for Warrick then?" She stepped closer, forgetting that he might be dangerous—uncaring that he was a killer—if he'd done it for his brother's sake. "He was in danger?"

Reagan was back to nodding. "Yes, and he's still in danger."

"You're going to hurt him?" Warrick was a witness to the man's crime. Did he intend to eliminate him? But if he'd committed the crime in order to protect him...

"I don't want to hurt him," Reagan said.

But they both knew that Warrick might not give him a choice.

It wouldn't matter if he was only acting out of self-preservation—she would stop Reagan from hurting Warrick, just like she had tried the night she'd shot him here in her bedroom.

But her bullets hadn't stopped him any more effectively than they had his brother.

"I'm not the threat," Reagan insisted. "But he won't let me explain anything to him. He won't let me warn him, so I'm going to warn you."

She shivered, her blood chilling over receiving yet another warning. But this one worried her more—because it was for Warrick.

"I may not see him again," she said, the words echoing hollowly in her hurting heart. "I told him not to come back until he was ready to tell me the truth about himself."

Reagan sighed. "He *can't* tell you the truth."

"He just *won't*," she said, frustration and bitterness welling in her aching heart.

"No, he can't," Reagan insisted and with brotherly pride added, "Warrick takes the rules very seriously and follows them."

"What rules?" She knew he didn't care about the

law or he wouldn't be so hell-bent on his vigilante justice.

Reagan's jaw clenched again then he replied, "My father's rules."

What kind of man had their father been? If he was the monster Kate was beginning to suspect he was, why was Warrick so devoted to him?

"That's why he's trying to kill you?" she asked.

Sadness and regret darkened Reagan's topaz eyes. "My father would have ordered my death."

"But your father is dead." Had the man been so powerful that he was able to manipulate his survivors from the grave?

Reagan explained, "There's a new leader to enforce his rules."

"Leader of what? I don't understand…" But she was afraid that she was beginning to; that she knew why Warrick and this man had survived her gunshots and why Warrick had a wound where she'd shot that creature that hadn't been a dog but hadn't been…

She was beginning to understand.

And Reagan must have realized that she had because he nodded in reply to her unspoken question. "I can't tell you, either. But I can make sure that you're prepared."

"I told you that he might not come back," she reminded him and herself. "And if he doesn't I won't be able to warn him for you."

"You're in danger, too," he said, gesturing toward her bandaged arms and the fading bruise and scar on her forehead. "You need protection."

"I can take care of myself." She reached for her gun but the holster was empty.

"Looking for this?" he asked, holding up her Glock. The metal glinted in the darkness.

The clock in the living room began to toll the chimes for the approach of midnight.

"You are dangerous," Kate murmured. Warrick had been right to warn her against this man. He had manipulated her into believing him—into trusting him. And he'd had her weapon the entire time.

She lifted her hands—as she had that night against her feral attacker—as if she could fend off a bullet. She wasn't like him and Warrick; if someone shot her in the heart, she wouldn't survive her wounds. Her mind whirred with fear as she tried to think of how to overpower him, but he was even bigger than Warrick.

Warrick…

She'd told him to leave. If only she'd had him stay with her…

"Don't worry," he said. "I'm not going to fire it."

But she kept her hands raised, unwilling to trust him again. She should have heeded Warrick's warning.

"I will not shoot a gun again," he said, shuddering as he handled the weapon. "I'm only going to load it for you." He opened his palm to bullets that gleamed much more brightly than the metal of the gun.

"I have bullets," she assured him. In fact, she was pretty sure it was loaded now. Her weapon was always loaded and ready to go.

He emptied her cartridge, dropping her ammunition onto the floor. Each bullet pinged as it struck the hardwood and rolled away.

Panic filled her. He hadn't just taken her gun; he

was taking her ammunition, too. Even if she managed to get it back from him somehow…

"What are you doing?" she asked.

"Preparing you." He loaded the gun with those shiny bullets.

"What are they?"

"Silver." The gun loaded, he held it out to her— the handle pointed toward her, the barrel pointed toward his chest. "This is the only real way to protect yourself."

"I don't understand…"

The clock chimed again.

"I think you do," he said. "And I'm sorry that you learned the secret."

"You told her?" Warrick asked, his deep voice gruff with shock. He stepped through the window she hadn't realized was open until she shivered with cold. But maybe it was the anger and rage in his voice that chilled her more than the night breeze.

Warrick stalked toward his brother—his muscular body vibrating with that anger. "Why the hell would you do that?" he demanded to know. "You've just ordered her death!"

"She already knew," Reagan said. "She was attacked by one of the pack—she knows what it was."

"It was you! You attacked her!" Warrick shouted the accusation. But then his voice lowered and cracked with emotion when he asked, "Why do you have to take away everything and everyone I care about?"

But just as Reagan had said, Warrick didn't give his brother a chance to explain or defend himself. Murderous rage gleaming in his eyes, he launched himself at Reagan.

But this wasn't a fight between two men. For one, Reagan wasn't really fighting back—just as he hadn't that night in the alley. And for another, something strange began to happen with every chime of her clock. Kate's heart pounded furiously as she watched—fear and shock overwhelming her.

The men began to change—their limbs and faces contorting into different dimensions. Their clothes tore, their expanding muscles and shape shredding the material. They didn't stop—even as their bodies changed. They rolled around the floor; Warrick swinging what was once a fist that turned into something else.

A claw?

Reagan deflected the blow but instead of lifting an arm—it had become a leg.

Kate covered her mouth, holding in a scream of terror at what she was witnessing. The fight was horrible enough, but it grew worse when the men turned from men into beasts. She trembled as they growled and snarled and snapped at each other—reminding her of her own attack the night before.

Pain throbbed in her arms; she knew what it felt like for those teeth to tear flesh. She knew—intimately—the pain they were inflicting on each other.

She found her voice and screamed, "Stop!"

But they continued to grapple, clawing at each other. Maybe Reagan was only trying to stop Warrick—or maybe he had gone on the attack, too. She still wasn't sure she could trust him. She only knew that she couldn't stand by and watch him hurt the man she loved.

Blood was everywhere. It dripped from teeth and

wounds, staining silver and raven pelts red, spilling onto her floor—spattering her walls. She had to stop them.

And Reagan had given her the means. She lifted the weapon. But her hands trembled—not from her injuries but with doubt. If she could believe Reagan, neither of them would survive one of these bullets. With as much as they looked alike as humans, they looked more alike as beasts. She couldn't tell who was who—or what was what.

She couldn't risk shooting Warrick with one of those silver bullets his brother had loaded into her gun. Maybe that had been his plan all along—that she killed Warrick for him.

She couldn't risk it; she couldn't risk Warrick's life. She lowered her weapon and screamed again, "Stop!"

Sirens wailed in the distance. One of the wolves scrambled up off the floor and vaulted through that open window. The other lay on the hardwood, bleeding profusely. He was changed, but from the look of pain and concern and something else—something deeper—in his topaz gaze, she was able to recognize him.

Alarm clutched her heart. "Warrick!"

He hadn't intended to come back to her apartment. It wasn't as if he could give her the answers she had demanded from him earlier. But when he'd gone back to the abandoned bank, he had found Uncle Stefan waiting for him. His uncle had picked up Reagan's scent for him, and Warrick had followed his brother's trail back to Kate.

Why would the son of a bitch not leave her alone?

Because Reagan knew—as everyone did—that Warrick cared about her. Too much.

That was why Warrick needed to come back—to make sure that she was okay. Not to tell her what she wanted to know. But she had learned his secret now.

Reagan had told her.

Warrick might have been able to claim his brother had lied to her. But then she'd watched them change before her own eyes. She wasn't drugged. She wasn't concussed. She wouldn't doubt what she had witnessed with her own eyes—just like Warrick couldn't doubt that his brother had killed their father. Because he'd seen it himself.

If he'd only held on to his temper...

But the thought of Kate being attacked had incensed him. He'd wanted to tear Reagan apart when he should have shoved him out the window and gone with him. But the clock had already been chiming; they'd already started to change.

The sirens grew louder. Kate might not be the only one to see him like this if he didn't leave now. He tried to stand up, but his brother's teeth had torn the flesh of his shoulder, which was already weak from earlier injuries. From the bullets Kate had fired into him. He growled at the pain that radiated from his wound throughout his battered body.

Kate gasped, her eyes wide with fear as she leaned over him.

He had frightened her again. "I won't hurt you," he promised. "I would never hurt *you*."

Not purposely. But he had hurt her—because he hadn't left her alone. Instead, he'd acted on his attraction to her. And he'd fallen for her.

She gasped. "You can talk."

"I'm still *me*," he said. Born a werewolf, it was all he'd ever known. It was two parts of him—the human and the wolf—that made him whole, that made him who he was. Would she ever be able to understand and accept that?

Would she ever consider changing herself? It would be the only way he could save her now.

"You didn't say anything in the alley that night," she reminded him. "And I shot you." She reached toward his shoulder now. Blood oozed from the wound and spread across the fur on his chest. "Reagan reopened your injury."

The pain increased despite the gentleness of Kate's fingers as she examined him. Consciousness began to fade, everything was turning black. He couldn't see her now. He couldn't see if Reagan was still here or if he'd fled the room.

Warrick could see nothing of the present; he could see only the future. If he left Kate unprotected, she would be too vulnerable. That was why he had come back to her—to keep her safe. But he was too weak—just as his father had called him when he'd lost Sylvia to Reagan.

Now he might lose Kate to him, too. Not as a mate but as a meal for his brother. He had to stay awake, had to rally his strength to protect her, but oblivion beckoned, sucking him into the black beyond.

Chapter 13

Blood stained the rolled asphalt roofing of the building where Reagan had taken sentry. He spit again, trying to get his brother's blood out of his mouth. But he could still taste the metallic flavor of it.

And it sickened him, making his stomach roil.

He couldn't understand his cousins who'd gone rogue—who had enjoyed carnage. He shuddered in revulsion.

But he was more disgusted with himself than with what they'd done. How could he have attacked Warrick like that—in his weak spot—his wounded shoulder? Maybe he was the monster his brother thought he was.

But Warrick had been so enraged that he hadn't heard the sirens. It was bad enough that Kate had seen them in their changed form—but then she'd already seen Warrick like that once. She'd also seen that other member of the pack—the one who'd attacked her.

But whoever had been approaching her apartment with sirens wailing hadn't needed to see Reagan and Warrick in that form. Enough people were already in danger.

They didn't need to endanger anyone else.

And Warrick was so tough that Reagan hadn't realized that he had hurt him that badly. Even when they'd been kids and Warrick younger and smaller than Reagan, he'd been invincible. It hadn't mattered then that Reagan was older and bigger than him.

No, Reagan hadn't hurt him when they were kids. But he'd hurt him plenty as adults. He'd hurt him emotionally. And tonight he'd hurt him physically.

How badly?

Would Warrick be okay? Could he make it out of her apartment before the police arrived? Warrick wouldn't be able to forgive himself if more people were put at risk.

Warrick wouldn't forgive him, either. And he doubted that Sylvia would—after how the pack was treating her. Like a criminal...

And she'd done nothing wrong. No, she was paying for the mistakes that Reagan had made. Maybe he should have saved one of those silver bullets. Not for self-defense but for...

No, he had never been a coward. And he wouldn't be one now. He wouldn't give up. Not yet...

Not until he had absolutely no hope left.

Shivering with cold and fear in that strange, sterile room behind Club Underground, Kate stood over

Warrick. And just as he had at midnight, he began to change again right before her eyes. His fur receded to smooth skin over sleek muscle. His jaw turned back into human shape—square and hard and stubborn. Only his eyes remained the same—that eerie topaz as he stared up at her from the metal table on which he lay.

"What time is it?" she asked. She had dozed off sometime during the night but only after Ben had promised that he would be okay.

Of course he would be okay. He wasn't human. Or he hadn't been then. He was again now.

"Dawn," he replied despite having no window or watch to verify that the sun was rising. His watch had fallen off during his struggle with his brother; she remembered seeing it on her bedroom floor among the tatters of his and his brother's clothes.

"I always change back at dawn," he explained.

"And into a werewolf at midnight?"

He nodded and reached out. But his handsome face distorted as he flinched in pain. Blood oozed from beneath the bandage Ben had put on his rewounded shoulder. The doctor would probably need to change the bandage now that Warrick had changed. But Ben had gone home, leaving Kate to watch over his patient.

They were alone in that creepy room. Ben had assured her they would be safe there. Maybe safer there than anywhere else...

"Are you okay?" she asked. "Should I call Ben back?"

He shook his head. "I'm fine. What about you?" He eased up and reached out, trailing his fingers along her cheek. "Did he hurt you again?"

She shook her head, and his hand slipped away from her face. She released the shaky breath she hadn't known she'd been holding. At just that slight touch, her pulse quickened and her skin had heated with desire. She forced herself to focus on what he'd asked her and on what she'd learned. "Reagan claims he's not the one who hurt me last time."

"Then why was he at your apartment." Jealousy hardened those topaz eyes. "In your bedroom?"

Now that she was certain he was okay, her anger flashed back. "Don't act like a jealous fool again," she snapped at him. That was why she'd gotten angry with him earlier—when he'd been jealous of Dwight. And because he wouldn't confirm the suspicions she'd already had. "Your brother wasn't there to seduce me."

"Don't trust him," he warned her. "He's a master manipulator."

She had considered that, too—that he'd been manipulating her. But his actions had spoken even louder than his words.

Reagan had told her—by giving her the bullets— what Warrick had refused. But had Warrick changed his mind and decided to share his secrets with her?

"Why did you come back?" she asked. Had he been about to break the rules? For her?

"I caught his scent," he said. "I followed him back to your apartment." His voice grew nearly as gruff as his growl when he added again, "To your bedroom."

"So you didn't come back for *me*," she said, her heart hurting with rejection. Reagan hadn't hurt her, but Warrick had. "You came back for *him*."

"Kate…" He sat up fully, and the sheet Ben had put over him fell down—revealing his muscular chest and the rippling muscles of his abs. "I came back because I was scared he was with you—that he was going to hurt you."

"*He* didn't hurt me," she repeated.

He reached out and slid his fingertips across her cheek. "I'm sorry. I didn't mean to hurt you. That's why I wanted to stay away from you—to keep you safe. But I just can't—" his breath shuddered out, and desire lit up his topaz gaze as he continued "—keep away from you…"

His touch had her skin again tingling in reaction. All he had to do was touch her and her common sense fled, leaving her incapable of thought. Incapable of anything but feeling. And she wanted to feel him— to make sure he was once again the man she knew. The man she loved…

She slid her palms to his chest, careful of the bandage on his shoulder, and leaned into him. Her lips touched his softly. But then passion caught.

He tangled his fingers in her hair and clutched her mouth to his while he made love to it. Sliding lips across lips, tongue across tongue—their breathing mingled into one breath—their chests rising and falling in unison.

His hands were on her waist now, and he lifted her onto the table so that she straddled his lap. The sheet and her jeans were all that separated his erection from the part of her that ached for his possession.

Careful of her bandaged arms, she dropped the sweatshirt she'd unzipped back at her apartment. Then she pulled her tank top over her head, leaving her breasts bare to his gaze. And his mouth. He closed his lips around a nipple, tugging and nipping.

She nearly came—sensations rushing through her from her breasts to the very core of her and even lower so that her toes curled in her shoes. She kicked them off then unsnapped and pushed down her jeans. Leaning on him, she managed to wriggle out of the denim.

The room was cool, the air lifting goose bumps on her skin. But he covered her. With his hands, with his lips—caressing and kissing her until she was so hot perspiration beaded on her upper lip.

Tension built inside her, and she shifted her hips, thrusting against his erection. He shoved down the sheet so nothing separated skin from skin. Then he lifted her again—his lips closed over the tip of her breast as his shaft nudged between her legs.

She reached between them and guided him inside her. On top, she was the one in control of the depth. Sliding down, she took only the tip of him before rising up again.

He groaned and gently bit her breast.

She clutched his long hair in her fingers, pulling him closer. And she slid farther down, taking him deeper and then deeper still until he filled her. She rocked against him and whimpered at the sensations racing through her. So much pleasure and the promise of so much more.

He caught her hips, lifting her up again and driving her back down—helping her find the rhythm that would free them both from the madness gripping their bodies and their minds.

And their hearts. She was crazy to love a man like him—a man who wasn't only a man. But her heart was already his. And now so was her body. She gave it up to him, riding the waves of pleasure that shuddered through her.

He thrust deep and groaned as he filled her, his passion spilling inside her. She collapsed onto his slick chest and nearly rested her head on his shoulder before she remembered his injury.

And where they were.

"What did we just do?" she wondered, scrambling off him to grab up her clothes from the floor.

"I can't resist you," he said. "And I can't stay away from you—even when I know I should."

"Warrick…" She paused in dressing and met his hot gaze. How could she not love him?

"But it doesn't matter if I'm with you or not," he said. "You're still in danger."

"Yes," she agreed. "Both times I was attacked, I was alone."

"Then I shouldn't leave you alone again."

Shouldn't. But he would. They both knew it.

"We don't know that those attacks were related," she said. "Anyone could have hit me in the head with that flashlight. It could have even been Bernie the homeless man since it was before I found his body. Or it could have been some suspect I arrested during my years on the force."

"But the second attack was definitely—"

"I don't think it was Reagan," she interrupted, wishing she could end their grudge.

"If he didn't hurt you, what did my brother want?" he asked.

She reached into her jeans and held up one of the silver bullets she had pocketed. "To give me this. He loaded them into my gun."

He narrowed his eyes. "That's how you figured it out."

"That you're a werewolf. And so is whoever's after me." She nodded. "I already had my suspicions, though. That night I shot you in the alley…" Regret tugged at her. "If only you'd spoken to me then…"

He shook his head. "That would have scared you as much as seeing me for the first time had."

Her lips lifted into a grim smile. "You're probably right." In his changed form, he was intimidating enough—but if he'd spoken to her…

"And then you had the same wound where I'd shot you that night…"

Guilt and regret filled his eyes now. "I should have stayed away from you. I shouldn't have…"

She had no regrets over what they'd done—over making love with him. "I would have figured it out that night I was attacked outside my apartment," she said. "There was no way that was a dog or even a regular wolf. I knew for certain then that whoever attacked me was a werewolf."

"My brother is after you," he insisted.

"Why?" she asked. "He doesn't even know me. Why would he want to hurt me?"

"To hurt me," he said.

She couldn't argue that Reagan hadn't hurt him. He had tonight—with his teeth. And months ago when he'd killed their father. But why did she think there was even more bad blood between the brothers? Something that neither had admitted to her yet.

She skimmed her fingers lightly over his bandage. She had inflicted that initial wound; Reagan had only reopened it. "I'm sorry you got hurt again…"

"He gave you the bullets," Warrick said. "Why didn't you shoot him?"

She sighed. "I couldn't."

"Why not?"

She hadn't been certain who was who, but she wasn't about to admit that to Warrick—not with as much as he currently hated his brother. But she knew what she was about to tell him would probably upset him even more.

"I didn't shoot him because I believe him," she admitted.

"I told you I witnessed it—"

"He didn't deny what he'd done to your father," she said. "But he had a reason. And I really don't think he was the one who attacked me. I don't think he's the threat."

But there was someone else out there—someone far more dangerous than Reagan because they had no idea who he or she was.

That son of a bitch...

Reagan was doing it again, trying to woo away the woman Warrick loved. God, he loved Kate—with all his heart. What he'd felt for Sylvia paled into insignificance in light of his overwhelming feelings for Detective Kate Wever.

"Don't let him manipulate you," Warrick warned. "That's what he does. He's smart and charming. And a total sociopath."

"This isn't just about your father, is it?" she asked, her blue eyes narrowing with familiar suspicion.

"Kate..."

"I saw you change—both into a wolf and back into

a man. I know your biggest secret, so you might as well tell me the rest of them."

He sighed in resignation. He might as well. But telling her would lay him bare and vulnerable. So he couldn't do it naked. He found the clothes Ben had left out for him, jeans and a sweatshirt, and hurriedly dressed.

"You're stalling," she said. "Why? What else did your brother do?"

"He stole my fiancée," he replied.

She gasped in surprise. "You were engaged?"

"To a human girl," he shared. "I met her when I was traveling."

"You don't always stay in a pack?"

He shook his head. "Not always. We have lives. Careers." Especially when they weren't believed to be strong enough to lead the pack. Reagan was the one who had been groomed to take over for their father.

"What do you do?" she asked. "When you're not seeking justice?"

"I'm a security consultant," he replied. "I make sure nothing and no one can get into places like banks and museums. Sylvia was an art curator."

Concern flashed in her blue eyes, as if she was worried that Sylvia had passed. "Was?"

"She gave up her job to come home with me, to become part of the pack," he said.

"She must have really loved you—to give up so much," Kate said. There was something in her voice— something he couldn't figure out. It wasn't jealousy. Maybe awe? Surprise?

And he knew that she wouldn't willingly give up

her career or her friends. Which meant she would probably wind up giving her up her life.

Kate...

What was he going to do? How was he going to protect her?

"So what happened?" she asked.

"She met Reagan," he said, and all his bitterness rushed back. "And he turned on the charm. Then he turned her."

"Turned her?" Her brow furrowed. "Oh, into a..."

She couldn't even say it. How could she ever be one?

"Is that how he stole her away?" she asked.

He nodded. "A human is bound for life to whoever turns them into a werewolf. That is their mate."

"So Reagan is Sylvia's mate?"

He nodded again.

"Is she here in Zantrax, too?"

"No. After he killed my father, he left her with the pack and fled alone." Reagan had left her alone with people who didn't respect her trading in one brother for the other. And so had Warrick...

He hadn't realized then that she could be in danger, too. But Uncle wouldn't let anything happen to her whereas their father might have ordered it.

"Reagan told me that he killed your father to protect you," she said.

"He's a liar." His father hadn't always been pleased with the decisions Warrick had made, but he had never threatened his life.

"I believe him," she said.

And Warrick's blood ran cold. It was happening again. Reagan was already manipulating Kate, just as he had manipulated Sylvia. "Don't make the same mistake I did," he warned her. "Don't trust him."

"It's not a matter of trust," she said. "It's a matter of motive. Why would he kill your father?"

With a manipulator, it was always about power and control. "To take my father's place in the pack," he said. "To become the leader."

"Did he?" she asked.

Usually he was amused when Kate became Detective Wever, but tonight her questions annoyed him. Because she was using them to try to prove the innocence of his enemy. "Did he what?"

"Did he take over the pack?"

Warrick shook his head. "No, he's been on the run ever since he shot that silver bullet into our father's heart. He even left Sylvia."

"So he left behind the woman he took from you and the pack he'd wanted to control?" Kate summarized. "What, exactly, did he gain?"

Warrick had believed it was all about taking away everything from Warrick that mattered to him. But now Reagan had less than he had. He had lost everything that had mattered to him, too. "I don't know…"

"I think you need to find him," she said. "But not to kill him. You need to find him and let him talk. You need to figure this all out."

"It doesn't matter why he did what he did back home," Warrick said. And it really didn't matter to him anymore. Sylvia was no longer the woman he wanted as his mate. He wanted Kate. For life. "It just matters that you stay safe."

She lifted the silver bullet between her thumb and forefinger. "I have this. I'm in no danger anymore."

Armed as she was, she would be safe. Even if his brother had just laid an elaborate trap for him and Warrick never made it back to her. He kissed her goodbye and hoped it wasn't the last time.

Despite the fact that it completely creeped her out—even worse than Club Underground, Kate had remained behind in the clinic after Warrick had left through the secret passageway. Finally alone and fed up with secrets, she'd had a chance to thoroughly investigate the place.

"Why are you still here?" Ben asked as he opened the door between the club and the clinic.

Paige followed him inside. "Kate? What are you doing here yet? Are you all right?"

She shook her head. "No."

"Did your wounds get infected?" Ben asked, already reaching for his gloves.

But she shook her head again. "No. Physically I'm fine. Mentally I'm reeling."

"I understand," Paige said. "After what happened to you last night—what you saw…"

"I learned that werewolves are real," she said. "Not just some myth or a character in fiction. They really exist."

Ben and Paige exchanged a glance. "You really shouldn't be talking about this," Ben advised her, his deep voice lowering to a whisper as if he was worried that someone might overhear them.

She shook her head, needing to talk—needing to sort out everything she had seen. "At midnight I watched a man change from a man into a beast and then, at dawn, back into a man." Into the man that she loved. "I know for a fact that werewolves are real."

Hell, she had known even before she had watched Warrick and his brother change. That first night Warrick, as a beast, had found her in the alley she'd begun to suspect that he and the beast were the same. And then, when one of them had attacked her, she had known for certain.

"Kate, you need to forget about that. You need to pretend you never saw a werewolf," Ben said, his voice almost hypnotic in his intensity to brainwash her back into ignorance.

She'd been oblivious long enough. "No. I've seen too much. And it got me wondering what else is real…"

What little color Paige had in her pale skin fled, leaving her deathly white. "Kate…"

"What other myth is actually reality?" She held up the blood-saturated wooden stake she had found in the medical waste disposal bin. That explained all the blood from the other night, when Ben had treated the wounds on her arms. She'd seen the blood spattered across the walls and steel surfaces and had realized that Ben had treated someone with far more serious and potentially fatal injuries than hers.

"Kate, you want to put that back," Ben said, as if she held a bomb instead of a splintered piece of wood. "And you want to forget you ever saw it. Hell, you want to forget about this whole damn clinic."

"You would like that," she replied. "You'd like to keep all your damn secrets." She focused on the woman who had been her friend for so many years, but Paige's face blurred as tears filled Kate's eyes. "Even you…"

"These aren't secrets a human can learn and live," Paige said, tears glistening in her eyes, too.

Kate blinked furiously. She wouldn't cry. And she shrugged off her friend's concern. "Someone was already trying to kill me when I knew nothing at all."

"Even then, you were safer than you are now," Ben advised, his dark eyes as filled with worry as his wife's were. "There are rules…"

"I know all about rules," she said. "I took an oath to protect and serve all of Zantrax. But I never knew about all of Zantrax. I never knew that werewolves and vampires are real and not just figments of someone's imagination. Not just nightmares."

"Discovering what you've had," Ben said, "you're living a nightmare now—for however long you have left. No human is allowed to learn of the Secret Vampire Society and live."

Just when she had thought it couldn't get any worse. "I don't understand…"

Ben gestured to the bloody stake she hadn't realized she still held. "That's what happens when humans learn of the existence of vampires. They react out of fear, thinking all vampires are bloodthirsty killers, and they try to eradicate the entire society."

Her fingers trembled on the stake. "Someone was killed with this?"

"I saved him," he assured her. "But that's not always possible. So to protect the society, it must remain secret. Any time a human learns about it, they become a threat that must be eliminated."

"You both know about it," Kate said as another horrible realization dawned on her. "So that means…"

Paige nodded, and now her tears streamed down her face.

So they weren't her friends anymore, they were strangers. And according to Ben, perhaps her killers. She probably should have tightened her grasp on the stake but instead she dropped it.

She couldn't hurt them.

What about them? Could they hurt her? Would they—in order to uphold the rules of their secret society?

Chapter 14

A strong hand clutched Reagan's arm and spun him around on the barstool. He tensed, expecting another of his brother's blows. But instead of a fist, it was a hand that slapped his face. It was a strong slap—one that nearly knocked him off that stool—despite the petiteness of the blonde woman who delivered the slap.

He was certain she'd left her small handprint on his face—probably etched into his skin. "Excuse me?"

"There is no excuse for what you've done!" she yelled at him. "How dare you show your face in my club again!"

Her club? She was Paige Culver, the proprietress of the underground club and a vampire.

"He's not Warrick," the bartender told her.

"I know who he is," she said. "He's the other one—"

He lifted his hands in a gesture of peace. "I didn't attack her. That wasn't me."

Despite it being early and the club nearly deserted, the woman lowered her voice to a raspy whisper, and said, "You didn't have to attack her to kill her."

Alarm clutched his heart. He hadn't taken away another woman Warrick loved—had he? "What happened to her?"

"Nothing yet," she said. But she glanced nervously at the people gathered in the other part of the club. They weren't just people—at least, they weren't human. They were vampires. And they were out quite early. Of course they didn't have to worry about the sun shining into the underground club.

"What's going on?" he asked.

"The society called a special meeting—"

"I didn't tell her about the society," he said. "I wouldn't do that—"

She looked at him with such fury that he expected her to slap him again. "You did enough to put her in danger—grave danger."

"I was trying to protect her," he said. "That's why I gave her the silver bullets. She was already beginning to suspect what Warrick is and what attacked her."

Paige nodded. "But now that she knows werewolves are real, she figured out the rest…" She glanced again at the group. They were obviously waiting for her. Sebastian had already stepped from behind the bar to cross the club and join them. And Ben, the surgeon, emerged from the hall that led to his surgery room and joined the group, too.

"She knows about the society?"

Paige nodded, and now a tear spilled from one of her eyes. She wasn't just angry. She was scared. The female detective obviously meant a lot to her. "She figured it out when she brought Warrick here—after you injured him."

"Is he okay?" That was why he had risked another visit to the bar—to see how his brother was.

"He's a fool," she said. "He should have stayed away from her. If he'd cared about her at all, he would have."

Reagan shook his head. "It's because he cares about her so much that he couldn't stay away." He knew about that—about that bond that drew souls together. "They have a connection that can't be denied."

No matter who got hurt...

He'd had that connection with Sylvia. But after he'd killed his father and fled the pack, leaving his mate behind—he'd no doubt severed that connection.

Sylvia was lost to him.

Like Warrick had lost her. And now it sounded as if he was about to lose Kate, too. He could hear the raised voices coming from the meeting they'd started without Paige. If they were deciding Kate's fate, it didn't sound good.

The silver bullets wouldn't protect her from the Secret Vampire Society.

"Uncle, I'm sick of trying to track him down," Warrick said, barely resisting the urge to slam his fist into the wall of the vault as frustration gnawed at him. At least Sebastian and Ben and Paige had promised to keep an eye on Kate and keep his brother away from her.

But like her, they seemed to believe in Reagan's innocence, too. He had seen him kill their father; Reagan had even admitted it. No matter what the circumstances, he was a killer who Warrick suspected would kill again.

Not Kate...

"You're giving up?" Uncle Stefan asked, his gray eyes rounded with surprise. "I thought you were more your father's son than that."

"I'm not giving up."

"Good. I will help you find him—as I promised. I caught his scent last night," the old man said, grinning with pride. "I can catch it again."

Warrick shook his head. "No. I want you to do something else for me."

"Anything, my nephew," he generously offered. "What do you need?"

"I need you to bring Sylvia here," he said, "to Zantrax."

"If you want to see her, why not just return to the pack?" Uncle Stefan asked, his silver-haired head tilted as he waited for Warrick's answer.

Home wasn't that far from Zantrax. The small town of St. James was in Michigan, too, but in the farthest point north in the Upper Peninsula. He shook his head. "I can't leave."

"Because of him or her—this woman who is important to you?"

"Because of both of them," Warrick honestly replied. "I can't leave her alone in the same city where he is."

But if Reagan was truly a threat to Kate, why would he have given her the silver bullets?

Warrick didn't share that revelation with his uncle, though; the man was too much about honor. If he knew that Kate knew about the pack...

Hell, she would have to use that silver bullet on him.

"I thought you were over Sylvia," Uncle Stefan remarked with a sniff of disdain for the newest member of the pack, "after the way she betrayed you."

"I am over her," he insisted, not because of her betrayal but because he now knew what true love was. Because he felt it for Kate; it filled his heart so that it actually ached for her.

"So then you are just using Sylvia to lure him out?" His uncle's silver-haired head bobbed in approval. "That is how a leader thinks. Your father was wrong to groom Reagan to take over when you are the son who was meant to lead."

Warrick had once cared about things like that, cared about his father's respect and love. Now he cared only about Kate. And he would do anything to ensure her safety.

It wasn't as if he was putting Sylvia in danger, though. Reagan would never hurt her. While Warrick's love for the blonde beauty hadn't been deep or true, he now suspected that his brother's had been.

Maybe Reagan hadn't gone after her just to take her away from him. Maybe he'd done it because he hadn't been able to control his feelings for her, like Warrick hadn't been able to control himself around Kate.

He'd wanted to stay away from her for her protection. But that hadn't been possible—the attraction between them was more than compelling or irresistible, it was surreal, like kismet or destiny.

Nerves unsettled him, quickening his pulse and tightening the muscles in his stomach. Should he have trusted the vampires to keep her safe?

Or was she in more danger from them than from

Reagan? At least Reagan had given her the silver bullet to protect herself. Why had he done that?

He almost asked Uncle, but the older man was already heading for the door—almost as if he was eager to bring Sylvia to Zantrax.

And the muscles tightened more in his stomach. Had that been a mistake—bringing Sylvia here? It was his last resort, though. He had to end this war with Reagan for once and forever.

Light glinted off the metal. She'd polished it up, but had she sharpened it enough? She ran her fingertip over the makeshift blade, and a bead of blood oozed from the cut on her skin. Her handcrafted weapon was sharp—especially for having been fashioned from the metal edge she'd pulled off the shower door.

She would have broken glass and used that as a weapon, but she'd worried that she might have hurt herself with it, too. The metal strip was easier to wield.

But now the question was if she could actually wield it? Could she sink it into another person's flesh?

Her babies shifted within her swelling belly. For them—to protect them—she had to.

A lock clicked as a key turned and the chains rattled. A guard was coming. This was her chance. She had to escape. She moved quickly, stepping behind the door before it opened fully. She needed the element of surprise.

But when she jumped out, swinging her weapon, she was the one who was surprised.

Kate needed one of those damn wooden stakes now. Her silver bullets wouldn't protect her from the

Secret Vampire Society, and yet she sat among them, as she had unknowingly so many times before. Glancing around the bar, she took note of the drinks they lifted to their crimson lips. What she'd once thought were Bloody Marys, she realized now was probably just blood.

She shuddered and turned toward the bartender. "So you're one of them, too?"

A muscle twitching in his cheek, he nodded. "For a long time now."

"Why do I suspect we're not talking about just years or even decades?" She reached for the glass of whiskey he'd poured for her. But she only lifted the glass and studied the amber liquid; it reminded her too much of Warrick.

"Centuries," he whispered his reply as he glanced furtively around the club.

He was worried about the others overhearing her and realizing that she knew.

She lowered her voice but could not stop with the questions. She had learned the big secrets, but there was so much she still didn't know. "Then you're not really Paige's younger brother?"

He shook his head. "I'm actually her father."

"Is no one who I thought they were?" she wondered aloud, blinking against the sudden rush of tears. She couldn't fall apart now, not when she needed all her wits about her. "What about Lizzy? And Campbell?"

"They're human, like you," he said. "Actually they're better off than you are. They know nothing of the society." He breathed a sigh of relief. "And that is how it must remain. For their protection."

Because of the damn rules…

"And Renae?" she asked of the young trauma surgeon.

He rubbed at his chest, as if pressing his knuckles against a sudden pang. "She learned about it, but the society has made an exception for her—as they had Ben before he became one of us."

"She can help them…with her medical skills," Kate guessed.

He rubbed his chest again and nodded. "They would make an exception for you, too."

"But I can't help them with anything." She only answered to the laws she had sworn to uphold—not to laws that authorized murder in order to maintain secrets.

"That is not why they would make the exception," Sebastian replied.

She leaned across the bar, anxious for the answer. "Why would they?"

"You would no longer be a threat to the society—"

"I'm not a threat," she protested. Unless they broke the rules she had sworn to uphold: the law.

Sebastian shook his head. "They don't believe that."

She glanced nervously around. Was she in danger? Had she been a fool to even risk a visit to Club Underground? She would have reached for her weapon, but she knew it wouldn't be any more effective against the vampires than it had been against the werewolves.

Against Warrick…

A pang struck her heart, but it had already been aching—for him.

"What are they going to do?" she asked.

"We tried lying to them," Sebastian said.

And her heart swelled with love. No matter what he

and Paige and Ben were—they were still her friends. "Tried," she said. "It didn't work?"

He shook his head. "No, we bought you some time to make your decision. But it's only a matter of time…"

"A matter of time before what?" she asked.

He didn't answer her. But she knew. It was only a matter of time before they killed her.

"So what do I do?" she asked. Could he give her a stake like Reagan James had given her a silver bullet to protect herself?

"You would no longer be a threat to the society," he began again, "if you joined a pack…"

Her breath caught in her throat; she had to expel it to ask, "If I became a werewolf?"

"Their secret is as big as ours," he explained. "We respect each other's rules."

"So my choices are death or…" What kind of choice was becoming a werewolf? What would she gain from the transformation?

As if Sebastian had read her mind, he answered her unspoken question, "Love."

"Damn."

She loved Warrick James. But did he love her? Even after realizing she had learned the truth, he hadn't offered to turn her—as his brother had turned Sylvia.

Sylvia…

She was the woman Warrick had chosen as his mate, the one he'd intended to spend the rest of his life with. Was that why he hadn't offered to change Kate—because he didn't want her as a mate? She wasn't the woman he wanted to spend the rest of his life with…

* * *

A noise, something shifting in the darkness, had Warrick's every muscle tensing. Uncle would not have had time to get home and back with Sylvia already. So that left only Reagan...

"I'm surprised you have the guts to confront me here," Warrick remarked.

"I thought you would have figured out by now that I have guts," a female voice replied. "Sometimes more guts than brains."

"Kate?" Shock staggered him as she stepped into the faint glow of the lamp sitting atop an old desk. Then her beauty staggered him, her blue eyes sparkled in the light and her black hair gleamed. "How did you find me?"

"I am a detective," she said, as if she needed to remind him. "A damn good one."

"But..." It had taken all of his senses for him to track Reagan down to this place. If only he had been a little faster...

Then she smiled and admitted, "Sebastian told me where to find you."

"How the hell did he know?" Warrick wondered. He had always been so careful to make sure that he wasn't followed.

"I think he might be able to read minds." She sighed. "As if it wasn't strange enough that he's a vampire..."

"You know?"

"About the Secret Vampire Society?" She nodded. "After you left the clinic, I looked around and figured it out."

Once again he shouldn't have left her. Every time he did she put herself in danger. He wanted to wrap her up in his arms and never let her go—to keep her safe and just to keep her. Forever. But that wasn't possible anymore; it had never been. "But you can't know about them and live…"

"I know," she replied wearily. "Sebastian, Paige and Ben are trying to buy me some time while I decide what I want to do."

"You don't have a choice," he pointed out. "If you don't turn into one of them, they'll kill you."

"I don't have a choice?"

He wanted to offer her one. His heart ached with the overwhelming desire to ask her to become his mate. But he would be asking her to give up everything for a future he wasn't certain of.

Reagan had silver bullets. If it had been him instead of Kate stepping from the shadows, he could have shot Warrick—could have killed him just as he had their father.

How could Warrick ask her to become his mate when he might not be around?

He couldn't leave her as Reagan had left Sylvia alone with strangers. And because she had betrayed him, Sylvia was truly alone; the pack would not accept her.

They might not accept Kate, either, if they knew he had willingly given up his life to protect her. Kate would be safer in the Secret Vampire Society anyway; she already had friends in it.

And feeling as he did about her, her future and her safety mattered more to him than his own. He'd already put her in danger because he'd been too selfish to fight his attraction to her.

Now he had to do what was best for her.

"No, you don't have a choice," he forced himself to reply even though his heart constricted with each word. "I think you would be happiest as a vampire."

Her voice sounded odd—almost hollow—when she asked, "Really?"

"You'll be immortal," he reminded her. And knowing that would give him peace.

"Yeah," she said with another sigh, "and people would literally kill to live forever."

"They would," he agreed. And probably many of them had.

Was that any kind of family for Kate? Would she be safer in the pack? Being Kate, she would probably win them over—just as she had won him over.

She sucked in an audible breath. "I just wonder..."

"What?" he asked, barely resisting the urge to reach for her. He wanted—he needed—to touch her, to kiss her...

"Will I really be happy living forever...*alone*?"

"You'd have Paige and Ben and Sebastian."

She nodded. "Of course. By becoming a member of the society, I will never lose my friends. But there's more to life than friends. There's you..."

Did she want to become his mate? But she had no idea what the pack was really like, had no idea of the responsibilities he would have.

He shook his head. "I have nothing to offer you."

Her throat moved as she swallowed hard, and her eyes glistened, as if she was fighting back tears. His strong Kate? He had thought she needed no one. Could she need him as much as he needed her?

"I'm sorry…" If he only knew how everything would turn out…

If he only knew what kind of future he could give her, if he could give her one at all, then he would beg her to become his mate.

She shook her head. "No, it's okay. I get it. What's happened between us… It didn't mean anything to you."

"It didn't mean anything?" he repeated. "It meant…" Everything. But if he told her that, she might wait for him—and what if he didn't make it? Then the Secret Vampire Society's offer for her to become one of them might expire and they would kill her.

"Nothing," she finished for him when he didn't. She lifted a trembling hand to her face and pushed her hair off it. Then pride lifted her chin.

He fisted his hands to keep them from reaching for her, from dragging her into his arms and never letting her go. But he had to make her leave before his uncle came back with Sylvia.

Uncle Stefan couldn't discover that Kate had learned about the pack; he couldn't learn that she had silver bullets loaded in her gun. Or she wouldn't be in danger from just the secret society.

He choked down the emotion strangling him and told her, "There's no reason for you to stay, Kate."

She jerked her head in a sharp nod. "I appreciate your honesty. It's better to know the truth. Now I know what my options are." She turned and walked out with her head held high and her back rigidly straight.

She was proud. So proud that she would never give him another chance—should he survive a silver bullet. When she was gone, she was gone to him forever.

Chapter 15

She was gone. He didn't need to step inside the cabin to confirm it. He didn't *feel* her there anymore. And if he emerged from the shadows of the woods, he might be seen. It would all be over then. For him.

For Warrick.

For Sylvia.

It was probably already over for the human detective; the vampires would have already decided her fate.

Had someone decided Sylvia's? Or had she decided her own? His heart beat furiously, the blood pumped so fast and violently through his veins. He wanted to track her down—wanted to make sure she was safe.

But if she'd escaped the locked cabin—if she'd made it away from the pack, she would be safer on her own than she would have been with him.

She was gone. He hoped it was a good thing.

* * *

Kate couldn't stop shaking, and it had nothing to do with the cold night air. The sun had just disappeared with dusk. Shadows grew longer and darker. This area of the city had other buildings like the bank that were abandoned due to the economy. So there was no else walking the streets with Kate, or even driving along them.

Perhaps she should have driven, but she had needed the walk to build up her courage to talk to Warrick, to tell him that she loved him and wanted to spend her life with him.

She would have gladly given up immortality and her friends for love. *His* love.

But he hadn't offered it.

Thank God she hadn't actually professed her love. She would have felt even more the fool than she did now.

Making love with her had obviously meant nothing to him. She meant nothing to him. But then why had he always seemed so concerned about her safety? Why had he been so determined to protect her if he didn't care?

Did he think he was doing that now? Was he somehow protecting her by letting her go?

"Warrick," she whispered as hope lightened the heaviness of her heart. Maybe he did care about her. She stopped walking, wondering if she should turn back.

A sound of shoes scraping across cement caught her attention. She wasn't alone.

Had he changed his mind and come after her?

As hope filled her, she whirled around. But no one stepped from the shadows, and an eerie silence fell.

"Warrick?" she called out. "Is that you?" But she already knew it wasn't. He wouldn't try to scare her; he wasn't that cruel. But hadn't he just been cruel if he'd lied about his feelings for her?

Tears threatened again, but just as she had back at the vault, she blinked them away. She wasn't a weeper; she was a fighter. So when she turned back around and started walking, she listened carefully for the sound of someone following her.

And when she heard the telltale scrape of shoes on the sidewalk, she reached for her gun—the one Reagan had loaded with silver bullets—and spun around with her weapon drawn and ready to fire.

"That won't protect you from me," Dwight said.

"The gun or the silver bullets?" she wondered. Could it have been him that night? Could he be a member of Warrick's pack? They hadn't seemed to know each other, though. So he would have had to belong to some other pack.

He lifted a blond brow with surprise and a question.

She nodded. "I know everyone's secrets now." And back when they'd been married, she had known Dwight was keeping secrets from her. Secrets that would have devastated her as much as his sudden fits of violence.

He uttered a ragged sigh of resignation. "Then you need to know that if you want to stop me, it would take a wooden stake."

"So you are a member of the Secret Vampire Society."

"Yes."

Her head pounded with confusion. "But we had an outside—daytime wedding. You couldn't have always been…" One of the creatures of the underground.

How had she lived in Zantrax so long and not known about the creatures? Even Bernie—poor brutally murdered Bernie—had known.

And how in the hell had she been married to one and not known?

Her confusion turned to humiliation. She had always prided herself on being a good detective. But she'd failed to detect the biggest dangers in her city— in her life. Of course she hadn't realized that those dangers were real.

"I wasn't a vampire when we got married," Dwight said.

Her mind eased a little. At least she hadn't been a total fool.

He continued, "I got turned not long after we'd been married, though. It was during a late-night bust—something bit me."

"I remember your being hurt. You acted so strangely after that. Then you started—literally— pushing me away. And down on the ground. And into walls." He'd suddenly become so strong, too. Like Warrick. Superhumanly strong.

"I'm sorry, Kate. I never meant to hurt you, but I couldn't tell you," he explained. "Not without putting you in danger—the same danger that you're in right now."

She needed a wooden stake. But despite buying her time—to live—her friends hadn't offered her any protection against the society.

"I know about the rules," she said. And she, who

had always loved law and order, had begun to despise rules.

"You don't have much time," he told her. "If too many society members find out that you've learned the secret, you'll be killed."

"I know. I have a decision to make."

"What decision?" he asked. "You need to turn into a vampire. That's the only way you can save your life. You can have immortal life then."

She would rather have Warrick. If only she knew for certain why he had denied having feelings for her...

Because he really didn't or because he had too many?

"I need to think about that," she said, "before I rush into anything."

"Kate, it's simple," he said as if she was a dim-witted idiot. "Death or life."

"It's not that simple."

"Is this about that damn werewolf?" he asked, his eyes growing hard and hot with jealousy. "Is he trying to make you join his pack?"

She finally understood Warrick's impatience with all her questions. Perhaps detectives could be annoying. "That's not any of your business," she reminded him. "I'm not any of your business. So why were you following me?"

"Someone has to keep you safe, Kate. You're not thinking clearly," he said.

Actually, she was finally thinking clearly—because she knew her fears weren't just crazy notions. They were reality. The werewolves. The vampires.

It was all real.

There were no more secrets. She was finally and fully aware.

"I'm thinking quite clearly," she assured him.

"But you're not taking care of yourself," he said. Moving closer, he offered, "Let me take care of you."

Goose bumps lifted on her skin, and she shivered at his obsessive tone and the strange gleam in his eyes. "I can take care of myself. I've been doing it for years."

She'd even been doing it against them—werewolves and vampires—before she'd realized they existed.

"You can't protect yourself against the society, Kate. You need to join them. Now. Let me change you, Kate." He stepped closer, his arms reaching for her. "Let me be your husband again."

She flinched and stepped back, not wanting him touching her. She cringed with disgust. "No. We were over years ago—the first time you struck me."

"I had my reasons, Kate," he insisted. "I did it so that you would leave. Then I didn't have to worry about you finding out the secret."

"You could have told me that you were cheating." It wouldn't have been a lie since she'd suspected he had been seeing someone else—always at night. She'd probably been a vampire, too. "I would have left then without the bruises and the scars." Both physical and emotional.

His broad shoulders slumped slightly as if he actually had a conscience, as if he actually regretted how he'd treated her.

She doubted it—his sincerity ringing false to her. She doubted him.

"I'm sorry, Kate. Let me make it up to you. Let

me spend eternity making it up to you." He reached
for her again.

She shrank back. "I don't want to spend another
minute with you—much less eternity. Leave me
alone!" She definitely needed a wooden stake. But
would she be strong enough to bury it deep in his
chest—in his heart?

"I will never leave you, Kate. You just have to accept that you belong with me."

"No…" She shook her head. She belonged with another man—the man she actually loved. But he didn't
love her back.

What Dwight felt for her wasn't love, either, though.
It was obsession.

She shivered in the cold night air and tightened her
grasp on the gun. But even the silver bullets wouldn't
hurt him. She would just be wasting them if she fired
her weapon at him. She needed to run.

But then she remembered Bernie's warning about
the humans that weren't human that could fly. The
vampires. They were the ones capable of flying.

She couldn't outrun a man who could fly. But before she could even turn to run from him, he lunged at
her. "Once I've changed you," he said, "you'll realize
that we are meant to be together. Forever."

If only a silver bullet could have stopped him…

He had to find her; he had to beg her forgiveness.
His heart ached with the pain he had seen in her eyes,
which had filled with tears. It killed Warrick that he
had hurt her. Even if he didn't survive the next skirmish
with his brother, he had to tell her how he really felt.

She deserved to know that he loved her—though she would probably be too proud to accept his love now.

Or to offer him forgiveness.

Had he turned the wrong way out of the building? He'd gone toward Club Underground, believing she would head back there to be changed. And he didn't want her to change into a vampire thinking that it was her only option besides death.

He wanted to give her another option: love.

But she hadn't been at the club, so now he rushed into her apartment, through that damn bedroom window she always left open. "Kate!"

A shadow hovered near the bed. Unmoving. Stoic. She had to be so mad at him, or worse, so hurt that she wouldn't speak to him.

"Kate, I'm so sorry," he said, his heart wrenching over how he'd hurt her. And the words he'd denied her, the feelings that had overwhelmed him spilled out, and he shouted, "I love you! I love you!"

"I love you, too, brother dear," Reagan remarked as he stepped from the shadows.

"Son of a bitch!" He gasped for breath, shocked at his brother's sudden appearance.

"Yeah, we both are sons of a bitch," Reagan replied with a brief chuckle.

Their mother hadn't stayed with Father or his pack; she hadn't understood that whole mating for life promise she'd made. Kate would understand, though. But would she want to spend her life with him after he had acted like such an ass?

"I can't deal with you right now," Warrick said with a shake of his head. Why now? After days of looking for his brother, why had he showed up again when Warrick was worried only about Kate?

"You're looking for that female detective," Reagan surmised. "What have you done that you're so sorry about?"

Ignoring his brother's question, Warrick asked his own. "What the hell are you doing here? Are you looking for Kate, too?"

If Reagan had intended to hurt her, why had he given her silver bullets? Warrick had looked at them; they were real. She would be safe from his brother. From him…

It was the damn vampires she had to worry about—that Warrick had to worry about. Had they already changed her?

"No. I'm looking for you," Reagan replied. "I knew you'd come back to her."

If only Kate had known that…but she thought she didn't matter to him. He hated himself for letting her believe that.

"I—I can't do this now," Warrick said again. "I have to find Kate."

"I gave her the silver bullets," Reagan reminded him. "She'll be able to protect herself."

"Only from you. Why would you do that?" he asked. That question had been burning within him since Kate had revealed what Reagan had loaded into her gun. "Why would you give her silver bullets if you intend to hurt her?"

His brother shook his head and his voice was deep and full of sincerity when he vowed, "I would never hurt her. I can tell how much she means to you."

"And I figured that's *why* you wanted to hurt her," Warrick said. "Because it would hurt me."

Reagan sighed every bit as raggedly as Warrick had. "I never wanted to hurt *you*, either." His eyes darkened with regret and guilt and he shook his head. "I can't explain what happened with Sylvia…"

He didn't need to explain because Warrick understood now. If Reagan had met Kate first, Warrick would have tried to steal her away. As much as he had loved his brother, he wouldn't have been able to fight his feelings for that incredibly strong and sexy woman. Even as much as he loved Kate and wanted to protect her, he hadn't been able to deny his feelings for her. At least not for very long…

Just long enough that he might have lost her forever.

For eternity…

"I can only apologize," Reagan said with that sincerity that began to reach Warrick. It rang very true.

But he shook his head, refusing to accept. "I don't want your apologies."

"No, you want my life." Reagan's eyes gleamed in the darkness—with more regret but no fear.

"Your life for my honor," Warrick reminded him. "You know the rule." If he didn't kill Reagan, he wouldn't be able to rejoin the pack. A werewolf without honor wasn't allowed to live among the pack—or at all.

Reagan nodded. "I know the rule. That's why I killed Father."

"I don't understand." How had killing their father been about Reagan's honor? Then a horrible thought occurred to him. "Did he hurt Sylvia?"

"No." A muscle twitched along Reagan's tightly clenched jaw. "He was going to hurt you. He'd loaded his gun with the silver bullets to take your life."

Reagan had started saying something like this that horrible day that Warrick had found one of his idols standing over the dead body of the other. By that time, Reagan had already been a fallen idol, so Warrick had refused to listen to his explanation and had attacked him. But Reagan had gotten away from him and instead of staying to explain his actions to everyone, he had fled St. James.

"Why my life?" Warrick asked, needing the explanation now. He needed Kate, too, but Reagan had seen to her protection. And Sebastian, Paige and Ben had bought her time with the society.

Even if she'd decided to join the society, it probably wouldn't happen right away. So he could deal with his brother now; then he would know exactly what kind of future he could offer Kate when he found her.

"Father believed you had lost your honor when I took Sylvia," Reagan explained almost reluctantly. "So he was going to take your life."

Warrick understood now why Reagan hadn't been eager to explain his actions. Because his reasons hurt Warrick, too. If he was telling the truth...

The sick feeling in the pit of his stomach told Warrick that his brother was telling the truth. And maybe he'd always known it.

Maybe that was why he had never tried harder to kill Reagan—because he'd known that he hadn't deserved to die. According to the rules, Warrick was the one who should have been killed.

"Father believed I was weak," he said. Reagan had

always been the old man's favorite. "And he would not tolerate anyone weak in the pack. He was going to kill me?"

That muscle twitching in his cheek, Reagan grimly nodded.

Warrick dragged in a deep breath, bracing himself before he asked, "So you killed him to save me?"

Reagan nodded again.

Warrick wasn't entirely convinced. His brother and father had been so close. They'd gotten along so well. He couldn't believe it. He couldn't accept his brother's explanation.

"And you expect me to believe that you would kill a man you loved and idolized for *me*?" He snorted. "You almost had me. You're so good with the manipulations."

"He was my father," Reagan said. "But you're my *brother.*"

"A brother you had no problem betraying when you stole my fiancée," Warrick reminded him. "You killed Father because you wanted to lead the pack."

Reagan snorted now. "I'm not the one who's been manipulating every situation to his advantage."

"What are you talking about?" Warrick asked, taking offense at the implication. "Do you think any of this has been to my advantage?"

"While chasing me down, you met Kate," Reagan reminded him. "Wasn't that to your advantage?"

"Yes." Even if she never forgave him, he would never regret loving her. Now he finally understood what true love was. He'd been a fool before.

"But I'm not talking about you," Reagan said, interrupting Warrick's thoughts. "You're not a manipulator."

Warrick sighed.

There were things his brother did not know about him. Warrick had changed after everything that had happened between them.

"If you're not talking about me," he asked, "then who?"

"It's obvious," Reagan said. "Who's leading the pack? Who's got everything he always wanted but that Father always denied him?"

He sucked in a breath of shock and dread. "No."

"I suspect he even manipulated Father into deciding your fate," Reagan said with the wisdom of someone who had spent a long time alone, thinking about what had happened.

Warrick had been so busy falling for Kate that he'd been too distracted. Otherwise maybe he would have figured out what his brother had—because what Reagan was saying...

It all made horrifying sense.

"Father killed Uncle Stefan's sons because they were weak," Reagan said.

"They were killers," Warrick reminded him. "They went rogue and were attacking innocent humans. Father had to take care of them or risk the whole pack being hunted down and killed by humans. Uncle Stefan understood that."

"Understood, but did he forgive?" Reagan shook his head. "I don't think so. Then when..."

"You stole Sylvia?"

He nodded. "He jumped on it—called you weak. But Father would never admit something hadn't been his idea. He wouldn't back down once he'd made a decision. It was killing him, but he was determined to…"

"Kill me." His heart ached with a betrayal that was far greater than what he'd thought Reagan had done. "He was going to kill me."

"Uncle Stefan made certain I knew what Father was planning," Reagan said. "He was even there when I fought Father for the gun and got it away from him."

"He came and got me," Warrick remembered. "Said I had to stop you…" That was the reason that he had showed up when he had—why he'd seen what he had. "But I was too late…"

Reagan shook his head. "You were right on time for Uncle. He made certain you knew that I killed Father."

Warrick couldn't deny what he had witnessed himself. He wouldn't have been able to defend his brother—even if he hadn't already been angry with him over Sylvia.

"He orchestrated it all," Reagan said. "He's brilliant really—smarter even than Father."

"Smarter than I am," Warrick admitted. But not smarter than Reagan, who had figured it all out. If only Warrick had listened to him sooner…

"Damn!" Regret knotted his guts. "I sent him back home to get Sylvia."

Reagan cursed. "I thought she got away from them—"

"You've been back to St. James?"

His brother nodded.

Just as Warrick hadn't been able to stay away from Kate, Reagan hadn't been able to stay away from Sylvia.

"But I didn't see her," Reagan said. "She'd been

locked up in the cabin…until the last time I went back." His breath caught. "I thought she got away…"

He'd hoped she had—Warrick heard it in his brother's voice. But he shook his head. "He went to get her a while ago."

"Why would you send Uncle to bring her here?" Reagan asked. "Did you intend to use her to lure me out?"

"That's what Uncle thinks. Maybe that's even what I convinced myself," Warrick said with a heavy sigh of regret. "But I needed to talk to Sylvia."

"Then you should have gone home yourself!"

"I didn't want to leave Kate."

"That's right," Reagan said. "You have Kate. So what do you want with your ex-fiancée?"

"With your mate," Warrick reminded his brother of the woman he'd stolen and then abandoned. "I wanted to ask her if she loved you."

Reagan tensed, that muscle twitching in his cheek again. "Why?"

"Because then I could accept what happened between you two. If she loved you and you loved her." He studied his brother's tense face and body. "And you do. Then I could forgive you." And he wanted to forgive him. He wanted to forgive them both. Now he understood that love wasn't something that could be denied and that it was far more important than honor. It was more important than anything.

"I was a selfish fool to act on my feelings for her," Reagan said, his voice heavy with regret and guilt.

"You would have been a bigger fool to not act on those feelings." Like Warrick was for letting Kate leave thinking that he didn't care about her—that he didn't love her with his entire being.

"So Uncle thinks he is bringing Sylvia here to use her as bait to lure me out?" Reagan shook his head. "I don't think he'd waste his time with me."

"What do you mean?"

"I'm not the threat to his role as leader." Reagan pointed a finger at him. "You are."

Warrick shook his head now. "No. But even if he thought that, why not just kill me?"

"He can't just kill you in case the pack starts to figure out his real motive," Reagan explained. "He's trying to manipulate us into killing each other. Then he's rid himself of the only threats to his leadership."

"But we haven't killed each other." Because Warrick really hadn't been able to bring himself to end his brother's life. That was why he'd never carried that gun on him. "So won't he get sick of waiting and pull the trigger himself?" It had already been months since their father's death.

"He'll try one more time," Reagan surmised. "He'll put us in a volatile situation—make you think that someone you love is in danger from me again."

"So Sylvia will be safe," Warrick assured his brother. "He knows that I don't care about her...if he thinks that I was willing to use her as bait for you."

Reagan shook his head "No. He's not going after Sylvia. He'll go after whoever matters most to you."

Fear clutched his heart. "Kate."

She—a mere human—wasn't strong enough to fight him off. And the gun wouldn't stop him. But she tried anyways, kicking and punching and trying to wriggle free of his grasp. His grip was painful, so tight that it threatened to snap her bones.

"Don't," she said. "I don't want this. I don't want you."

"But I want you!"

And their brief marriage had been all about what he'd wanted and nothing about her needs. No wonder he couldn't respect that she didn't want or need him.

She needed Warrick. But he didn't care enough to rush to her rescue this time.

"Help!" she screamed. Maybe someone else— Sebastian or Paige or Ben—would rush to her aid.

The street remained deserted. And Dwight lowered his head, his fangs glittering in the faint light of the streetlamp. Hunger filled his gaze—hunger and obsession. But then his eyes widened in surprise, and he jerked back.

Kate slipped from his grasp. Off balance she stumbled and fell onto the sidewalk, cement scraping her hands and knees.

Dwight cried out—as she had in fear. She jerked her gaze up, to where he fought with another man. The other man was older, his hair silvery. But he was not weak. His fist knocked the younger man back against the building.

Before Dwight could regain his breath, the older man launched himself at him. And this time he didn't swing just his fist but the wooden stake he grasped. The sharp point sank deep into Dwight's chest, impaling his heart. Blood gurgled from the vampire's mouth and pumped from the open wound in his chest. He slipped down the wall and dropped into the pool forming of his own blood.

"Thank you," she said, nearly sobbing in her relief. "Thank you so much. You saved my life."

The man didn't turn to her, though. Instead he groaned and lowered his head.

"Are you hurt?" she asked. After surging to her feet, she stepped toward her rescuer. "Did he hurt you?"

The silvery hair spread down the man's neck and then his back. His shirt split as his muscles expanded and contorted, changing shape as he changed form. He turned to her finally, his pale eyes gleaming in the face of a beast.

Warrick did not look like this when he changed. Nor had Reagan. They were fearsome just because of their size and strength. But this man was terrifying. His pale eyes didn't just gleam with murderous intent. They gleamed with madness.

He hadn't killed Dwight in order to save her life.

He'd killed the vampire so that he could kill her himself. She reached for her gun, but his claws closed around her wrist. Before she was able to draw her weapon, he would cut off her hand. So she pulled it away from her holster and lifted her palms up.

"What do you want with me?" she asked.

"I don't want you," he replied. "I want Warrick. Dead. And you're going to help me kill him."

Chapter 16

The sweet, metallic scent of blood hung thickly in the air, filling Warrick's nostrils. Voices raised in anger and fear created a low rumble that Warrick could feel like a vibration that rattled his nerves and his senses. Oh, God, he was too late. His heart lurched, beating painfully hard in his chest.

Not Kate…

Not his beautiful, vital Kate…

He dropped to all fours, using all his legs to close the distance between him and Kate. Was she already dead? He pushed through the crowd gathered on the sidewalk not far from the deserted bank. How had he missed her when he'd left?

Because he'd thought she had headed to the club when she had turned instead for home. But she had never made it there. Would she ever make it home again? Not to her messy apartment but to his arms?

The scent of blood was overpowering—it rose from the pool of it congealing on the sidewalk. It spattered the wall of the building behind the pool, running in rivulets down the bricks. So much blood…

No, she was never coming home again.

He didn't want to look. Didn't want to see her like this. But he owed it to her to face what he had caused—what danger he had brought to her that had ultimately ended her life. Before he could shove through the crowd, someone stepped in front of him and blocked his way.

"Did you do this?" Sebastian asked. He suspected the bartender was not the only vampire gathered around; that they all were. That was why he hadn't hidden himself from them. He doubted there were any humans among them that would see him in werewolf form. But then, he cared about nothing other than Kate.

"I would never hurt her." But he had. He'd hurt her badly. And she had died with that pain being the last thing he'd given her…when it should have been his love.

"It's not Kate," Sebastian said.

Relief shuddered through him that she was alive. But then who was dead? He shoved through the last few people gathered around and stared down at the vampire lying on the sidewalk. A stake embedded deep in his chest. "It's Kate's ex—the detective."

"You were seen fighting with him," Sebastian said, speaking for the crowd who'd turned to him now.

"I didn't do this," he vowed. Even though he hadn't liked the man, he hadn't wanted him dead. Just a little roughed up—like Dwight had roughed up Kate.

"That'll be up to a secret society council to de-cide now," Sebastian said. Werewolves and vampires could coexist peacefully until one committed a crime against the other; then the injured society or pack had the right to enforce their justice on the vampire or wolf responsible.

Beneath the blood, he picked up another scent. Two scents actually: one Kate's sweet, innocent one and the other dark and musky.

"I don't have time for that." He needed to follow the scent before it faded. But these vampires were strong; he couldn't fight them all off to escape.

"You don't have a choice."

Just as Kate didn't have a choice now. Death had been decided for her.

"I have an alibi."

"It's not Kate," Sebastian said. "You thought she was lying here dead."

Warrick shook his head. "It's my brother. I was with Reagan."

"He'll have to testify—"

"A trial or council won't be necessary. I know who the killer is," Warrick said.

Sebastian's blue eyes narrowed. "It can't be your brother—if he's your alibi."

"It's not my brother. He's not the one who's caused all the trouble in Zantrax and back home." And if only he would have buried his stung pride and talked to Reagan, he would have figured it out long ago.

"Then who? Give us a name," Sebastian demanded.

"I'll give you his body," Warrick promised. "If you'll let me leave, I'll take care of him." That was the man that he should have spent these past few months trying to stop—not his brother. He hoped that it wasn't already too late. Uncle had taken Kate.

But thanks to Reagan, Kate had the silver bullets. "Warrick—"

He snapped. "Kate's in danger. The man who did this…" He gestured at the mutilated body. "…he has Kate."

If he hadn't already killed her…

The rope cut into Kate's skin, but she ignored the burning pain in her wrists and her bandaged forearms and strained against the bindings. Her ankles were also bound—together—and to a reinforced bar on the wall. Despite having claws instead of hands, he had tied her tightly, so tightly that she had not been able to escape them even though she'd had all night.

He had left her alone.

He'd left her gun, too, on a table close to her. Its nearness taunted her—had her fighting even harder to free herself. He must not have known she had silver bullets, or she doubted he would have left her weapon in the same room with her. Not that she could reach it…

And what the hell kind of room was this? It reminded her of the bank vault with no windows and soundproofed walls. The only exit was one steel door, as reinforced as the ones in the underground clinic. So even if she had managed to free herself from the ropes, she wouldn't have been able to escape the room.

Or her captor. The door rattled as the locks—there were several—were unlocked. Finally the door opened and the man stepped inside. He was a man again—

all trace of the wolf-beast gone but for the madness in his pale gray eyes.

"Good to see you're still here," he said with a maniacal laugh. "I brought someone you need to meet."

He stepped back into the hall outside the room and moments later a young woman stumbled through the door. Platinum-blond hair tangled around her delicately featured face, which was pale with fear. Her hands were bound, too, but with a heavy-link chain, not ropes.

The chain dangled in front of her swollen stomach. She was pregnant. But the man did not care, as he shoved the woman again, so that she fell to her knees next to Kate.

"Are you okay?" Kate asked her, her heart filling with concern for the woman's condition and her fear. "Did he hurt you?"

The woman shook her head, as if afraid to even speak.

"Kate, meet Sylvia. Sylvia, Kate," the man performed the introductions with great irony.

A pang of jealousy struck her heart. This young beauty was Sylvia—no wonder Warrick was unable to forgive his brother for stealing her away. The woman stared at Kate with curiosity, no doubt wanting to know who Kate was to whom. But Kate needed to satisfy her own curiosity first.

"Who are you?" Kate asked the man.

He pressed a hand to his chest. "Have I been remiss? I thought you already knew who I am. Didn't my nephew tell you all about the leader of his pack?"

Kate shook her head. "Warrick told me nothing about the pack."

"But you know about us," the man said. "And humans aren't allowed to learn about us and live."

"I only know about the pack because you attacked me," she pointed out. "It was you that night outside my apartment building."

He chuckled. "I would have finished you off then but I figured you might come in handy to get my nephew to do what I need him to do. It was better to just hurt you a little—just enough to infuriate him."

"You want him to kill Reagan," the young woman finally spoke, her voice raspy with anger and fear, "so you have no threat to your leadership."

"There is no threat to my leadership," the old man insisted.

Sylvia's full lips curved into a mocking smile. "No? Then why are you so determined to pit your nephews against each other?"

"I didn't do that," the man said. "You did."

Sylvia flinched, and regret darkened her silvery green eyes.

"You never told me your name," Kate said, wanting to draw the madman's attention away from the pregnant woman. She did not know how much more stress Sylvia would be able to handle in her condition. Her friend Paige had once lost a baby under a lot less duress.

"I am Stefan James," the old man said with great pride. "The leader of the St. James Pack."

"Shouldn't you be with them?" she asked. "How can you lead your pack if you're here?"

"My pack understands that I need to be here," he insisted, "that I need to make certain there is justice for my brother's murder."

"A murder you orchestrated," Sylvia said, "just like you're trying to orchestrate Reagan's and Warrick's murders."

Panic clutched Kate's heart. "You want Warrick dead, too?"

Sylvia nodded. "Like Reagan, Warrick is a threat to his leadership."

"Warrick is a threat to no one. He has done nothing to restore his honor, nothing to avenge his father's death." Stefan snorted his disgust. "The only thing he has done in Zantrax is get involved with this *human*."

It was apparent that he had no respect for human life—for humans.

He had only one use for her.

"So you're going to use me," Kate said, "to get Warrick to do what you want. But why bring Sylvia here?"

"I brought her because I'm not sure Warrick is certain which of you he really wants," Stefan James replied. "The beautiful human or the young woman he'd chosen as his mate only to have his brother steal her away before he could claim her as his."

After their last meeting, Kate believed Sylvia was the woman Warrick wanted. That he had never stopped wanting the blonde. Kate had only been a temporary substitute.

"He didn't love me," Sylvia whispered, as if she'd noticed Kate's pain and wanted to comfort her.

"Shh," Kate shushed her. If Stefan thought Sylvia could no longer be of use, he might get rid of her now. There was no way he would let her go back to the pack, not with what she'd learned.

The young woman nodded and rubbed her hands

over her swollen belly. She wasn't worried about her own safety but that of her unborn baby.

Kate had to make certain she protected them both. For Warrick. He would never forgive himself if something happened to them.

"Now I need to get this show on the road," Stefan said, reaching in his pocket for a cell phone. "It's dragged on long enough." But before he could dial a number, the phone rang. He glanced at the screen and grinned. "Well, well..."

"Who is it?" Kate asked. "Warrick?" Had he figured out that he'd trusted the wrong man?

He picked up Kate's gun and trained it on her. "If either of you makes a sound, I will kill the human."

He could have killed Sylvia, too, with the bullets in that gun. But he must not have known what Reagan had loaded into her weapon.

"Hello, nephew," Stefan greeted his caller. "How nice of you to finally get in touch with me."

Reagan. It had to be him because from what he'd already shared, he had recently been in contact with Warrick—when he'd asked the man to bring him Sylvia.

"I don't know if I can meet you now," Stefan replied. "I'm a little busy with something—kind of all tied up."

A deep voice rumbled from the phone, but the words were unintelligible to Kate.

"Do not leave the city yet," Stefan snapped. "I will come see you."

Sylvia leaned in front of Kate and began to scream, "He'll kill—"

But Kate, despite her bound wrists, clasped her palm over the younger woman's mouth, silencing her.

Stefan dropped the gun back onto the table and his phone back into his pocket. "Don't worry," he told Kate. "I will not kill you over her outburst. He had already hung up."

He leaned down and connected the end of Sylvia's chain to that bar on the wall, tethering her like an animal. Like Kate. He shook his head at his niece-in-law. "With your disregard for human life, you would have made a good member of the pack. Too bad that I will have to kill you, too."

He straightened up and sighed. "But that will have to wait...until I get back from killing Reagan since Warrick has been too weak to do it." Whistling in anticipation he opened the door then locked it behind himself, locking the two women in alone together.

"I wouldn't have let him shoot you," Sylvia said. "I was going to take the bullet. It wouldn't kill me."

"Those bullets would," Kate said. "Reagan put silver ones in there for me."

"Reagan?" she asked, her breath catching. "You've met Reagan?"

"I don't know that we were ever officially introduced, but yes, I've met your...mate." Was he also the father of her child or had Warrick fathered her baby before Reagan had stolen her away?

The thought—that Sylvia's baby could belong to the man Kate loved—had her feeling empty and achy inside. She wasn't even sure she would be able to give Warrick a child—if he wanted one. But then he didn't even want her...

"His uncle is going to kill him," Sylvia said, tears

glistening in her eyes. "Stefan has another gun all loaded with silver bullets. Reagan and Warrick trust and respect that man. They don't see how evil he is."

"He's crazy," Kate agreed. "We need to work together to get free. We'll need to have that gun when he comes back." It was the only way they could stop him from killing them and Warrick. If they couldn't get to the weapon in time, they would be joining Reagan in death.

"He's not coming here to talk to you. He's coming here to kill you," Warrick warned his brother.

Reagan shrugged off his concern. "He'll come alone then. And it'll give you time to track Kate and save her."

"I don't think she's alone."

Reagan's breath audibly caught. "You caught her scent, too?"

"He's brought Sylvia to Zantrax." Just as Warrick had asked. He shook his head in self-disgust for having been stupid enough to trust the man.

"Yes."

"Are you putting your life at risk for her or me?" Warrick wondered.

"For everyone I love." Reagan's throat moved as he swallowed hard, as if struggling with emotion. His brother definitely loved the woman he had claimed as his mate. But when he'd chosen to protect Warrick from their father, he had been forced to leave her.

Warrick truly let go of the last of his resentment and bitterness. His brother had not chosen to betray him; he'd just chosen love.

Like Warrick wished he'd done with Kate.

Crossing the bank vault, Warrick hugged the man on whom he'd once vowed such bitter vengeance. He hoped like hell it would not be the last time he would see his brother. But their uncle was too powerful to vanquish without a bitter fight. And there were always casualties in a bloody battle.

As the door closed behind his brother, Reagan breathed a deep sigh. At least Warrick had forgiven him. What about Sylvia? Would she ever forgive him for what he'd done to her life—for how he'd messed up everything?

She was alive. For now…

He could feel her close. He could feel her fear, too.

Hopefully Warrick could track down the women in time to protect them. Because Reagan didn't have any silver bullets. He had given them all to Kate.

So he would only be able to stall Uncle Stefan. He wouldn't be able to stop him. And he wasn't even sure how long he would be able to stall him—because Uncle would be prepared. He would have silver bullets with him.

The door rattled and Reagan tensed. Warrick hadn't been gone long, but he was too focused on finding the women to have come back for any reason. No, it was Uncle. Along with the older wolf's scent, Reagan picked up his aura—of evil.

He'd arrived quickly. So the women were close. Warrick would find them. He would protect them. Reagan trusted his brother to do that. And he would take care of Sylvia, too.

Regret filled Reagan that he would never see his

mate again. He would never again be able to kiss and touch the woman he loved.

"I'm sorry," he murmured. She was close. But not close enough to hear him.

Could she feel him—like he could feel her? Did she feel his love?

"I'm sorry," he murmured again. Sorry that he'd claimed her when he wasn't able to keep the promises he'd made her. That he would protect her. That he would take care of her.

The only promise he could keep was that he would love her forever. The door rattled again before opening. This was it. The end...

Chapter 17

Tears stung Sylvia's eyes, blinding her. He was going to die. She knew it—that Reagan had offered up his life for his brother's. For hers…

He was using himself as bait now to lure his uncle away from her and the human. But even though the woman was human, she was strong—far stronger than Sylvia. There were no tears in her eyes as she leaned close.

"Come on," Kate urged her. "We need to fight."

It was too late for Reagan—too late for her to save the man she loved. "He's going to die…"

Kate shook her head. "We don't know that," she said. "But we do know that Stefan could come back anytime. We have to get loose. You have to get me loose."

The human wanted her help?

"You can do this," Kate urged her. "You're stronger than me."

A sad chuckle slipped through Sylvia's lips. "You don't know me at all."

"You're stronger than me," Kate repeated. "I'm human. You're not."

"I'm not strong enough." Physically or emotionally. Sylvia held up her wrists. "I can't break the chain."

"You don't have to get loose," Kate said. "You just have to get me loose."

What did it matter if Reagan was already dead?

But then her babies moved, kicking and punching. They were fighters. She couldn't give up. She had to get them a chance. She blinked back her tears and focused.

Even in her human form, Sylvia's teeth were sharp. Painfully sharp where she'd nipped Kate's flesh. Blood from the torn skin of her wrists saturated the bindings that Sylvia worked free with her mouth. Finally the last fiber of rope snapped and Kate managed to break free of the bindings.

But the rope around her ankles held, tethering her yet to the wall where Sylvia was bound. She reached for the rope and tried to work the knot loose with fingers that were numb from being circulation deprived.

"You can take a minute," Sylvia said as she leaned against the wall gasping for breath. "Let the feeling return to your fingers."

Kate shook her head, the knot of nerves in her stomach as tight as the knot of the rope. "I don't trust him. He's playing games with us."

One of those games was not allowing much air into the underground room. That was probably why Sylvia struggled so hard to breathe, not from her exertion, but from lack of oxygen. They had to get free soon, or they wouldn't have the chance.

Sylvia nodded and began to help. "He's been playing games with the whole pack. He has them all turned against Reagan and Warrick."

"And you?" Kate asked, wondering how the woman had survived, especially given her delicate condition.

Sylvia nodded.

Kate's respect for the young woman grew, especially when she made short work of the rope around her ankles. "Now we have to free you," she said. She had to get the pregnant woman and unborn child out of the stifling room.

Sylvia shook her head. "The chain is too heavy. We can't break or cut it. You need to get out of here and bring back help."

Warrick. He would help—if his uncle didn't get to him first with those damn silver bullets. But then Kate remembered the door. "There's no getting all those locks picked, not from the inside," she admitted. "But I wouldn't leave you anyway. All I need is the gun."

The door rattled. It couldn't have been Stefan back already. Without the silver bullets he'd given her, Reagan wouldn't have been able to stop the man for long. But maybe he'd given her just enough time…

"Warrick?" she called out.

"The room is soundproof," Sylvia reminded her. "And mostly unventilated. I don't think Warrick could have found us."

And if he hadn't that left only them to take care of themselves. As the door swung open, Kate jumped to her feet and reached for the gun. But her legs, numb from being tied so long, folded beneath her. She fell into the table, knocking it over and falling on top of the splintering wood. The gun slid across the floor toward Stefan James.

He sneered at their efforts to escape him. "I've never known two bitches to work together before." Their captor left the door open behind him, allowing a blast of air into the room, but his body blocked their escape. He chuckled. "But you are no more a match for me than my foolish nephews."

"Why are you back already?" Sylvia asked. "Was Reagan that close?"

The question she really wanted to ask, the one filling her green eyes with fear, was if her mate lived. Kate wanted to know, as well.

"Reagan was trying to trick me," Stefan said with a slight smile of respect. "The boy was always more like me than his father—not that his father would have ever admitted it."

"Warrick's smart, too," Kate defended the man she loved. "I'm sure he's figured out that you're the one he really needs to bring to justice. Not his brother."

"They're probably working together," Sylvia added with a chuckle. "Doing the exact opposite of what you wanted."

"Your plan is falling apart," Kate said, trying to edge closer to where the gun lay on the floor. The splintered boards cracked beneath her, digging into her hip and thigh.

"You think I would fall for such a ploy?" Stefan asked with outraged pride.

Kate stilled, daring not even to breathe. He had figured out she was trying to reach the gun. But he made no move for it, as if unconcerned that the weapon was so close to her.

"Even working together, those two would not be able to outsmart me," he arrogantly claimed. "They are not about to lure me away from the two of you."

"What is your plan?" Sylvia asked. "How are you using the two of us for bait?"

"Even in his human form, Warrick is an incredible tracker," he admitted. "Once he turns…" He glanced at his watch and continued, "…in just a few minutes, he will follow your scents here."

"But the ventilation system is mostly shut down," Sylvia remarked, still breathing heavily from her efforts to free Kate. "How will he smell us?"

The blast of air from the hall wasn't enough to make up for the lack of oxygen in the room. Kate's head grew lighter. Or maybe that was just exhaustion coming over her; instead of sleeping she had spent most of the previous night and day trying to escape the ropes Sylvia had made short work of.

"Once I turn, I will begin to spill your blood," Stefan matter-of-factly informed them.

Kate glanced at Sylvia, whose eyes had widened with the same fear that gripped her—nearly paralyzing her. She forced herself to move, just inching closer to that gun. But she was also inching closer to the madman who spoke calmly of killing her.

"Blood is the strongest scent to track," Stefan said. "He will find you easily when you're dead."

"What are you going to do when he gets here?" Kate asked. She waited for him to reach for her gun.

But instead he patted his jacket. "I am armed. With the very gun that killed the father, I will kill the sons.

My brother thought his boys were so clever, so far superior to my sons."

"You have sons of your own?" Kate asked, trying to keep him talking. Trying to keep him from killing…

"I *had* sons of my own," he replied. "Until my brother deemed them unfit for the pack and ordered their deaths."

Kate gasped over the actions of Warrick's father. No wonder he had never spoken of him with much love—just respect and fear.

"They were murderers," Sylvia explained. "They killed innocent humans."

Stefan snorted. "There are no such things as innocent humans."

"Kate is innocent," Sylvia insisted. "She has nothing to do with the pack. You should let her go."

"She knows about the pack," Stefan said. "You are new to it, but you are aware of the laws of it. Once she learned of our existence, we can't let her live."

Was that why he had attacked her earlier—to give himself an excuse to kill her? The man was that manipulative and that evil. And if they weren't able to distract him long enough for Kate to grab her gun, they wouldn't be able to stop him from killing them all.

Warrick fisted his hands at his sides and held his breath, so that he would not give away his presence too soon. His uncle didn't know him at all. Warrick didn't need blood spilled to track someone's scent—at least not Kate's. He had picked up their trail from where Uncle Stefan had killed her ex, and he'd followed it back to the abandoned building near the bank. This one had once been a restaurant, the room in which Stefan held the women captive a cooler. At least the refrigeration unit had been shut down, so Kate wasn't freezing.

Warrick had found the building but not the room—until Uncle Stefan had come back. Too soon. He hadn't fallen for the trap Reagan had tried setting for him. The man was really very clever.

And too dangerous for Warrick to make any sudden moves without thinking them out first. But then Uncle Stefan stepped closer to Kate and farther inside the room. Before the old man could swing the door shut behind himself, Warrick jumped from the shadows of the hall and burst into the room with them. "Let her go!"

Stefan's pale eyes widened in surprise. He had underestimated Warrick.

But Warrick had underestimated him, too. He had never realized how clever—and complicit—the old man really was. Warrick had loved him—even more than he'd loved his own father, who he had never been able to please. While his father had denied him affection or respect, Uncle Stefan had always seemed to care about him. He had always taken an interest in him…but his only interest had been in planning Warrick's destruction.

"Here you are, my boy, just in time for the party." Madness hardened the old man's gaze and he grabbed for Kate's hair, yanking her to her feet.

Warrick swung his fist and connected with Uncle Stefan's jaw. The contours of it were already beginning to change, as were Warrick's, the bones stretching and reshaping as hair spread over his skin. The old man stumbled back—over the broken table on which Kate had been lying. When he fell, she twisted free of his grasp.

"Get out of here!" he yelled at her. Nothing stood between her and freedom now.

But she shook her head.

"Sylvia, get her out of here!" Warrick ordered. Sylvia was beginning to turn, too. And the links of the chains that held her to the wall snapped as her muscles grew.

"I'm not leaving you!" Kate said.

"Good, then you'll die together." Uncle Stefan pulled a weapon from his shirt just as the material split and fell from his hairy torso. But before he could tighten his claws around the gun, Warrick knocked it from his grip. It flew across the room toward Kate.

"Grab it!" Warrick yelled at her.

But she already held a gun. Had she kept the bullets in it that Reagan had given her? Had Reagan given her real silver bullets? Warrick had thought so when he'd inspected him.

But he had spent so long distrusting his brother that he couldn't entirely shake off his suspicion of the other man's motives. And why would he have armed Kate when she might have used one of those silver bullets on him?

While Warrick was worrying about Kate, his uncle rallied his strength and attacked. He launched himself at Warrick, who fell to the ground. His uncle clawed at his throat, digging through the hair to the flesh.

Sylvia screamed as Warrick's blood began to flow. "Shoot him!" she yelled at Kate.

Kate tightened her grasp on her gun and lifted the barrel. This time she would shoot the right man. Actually the right beast.

Both men had turned into werewolves, and they looked so much alike with their black-and-silver hair and enormous, muscular bodies. And they kept rolling across the floor, tearing at each other.

If only she could see their eyes…

Then she would know.

Sylvia gasped as blood spurted across the walls from fresh wounds. "You have to shoot," she said, breathing hard with fear and lack of oxygen.

She had changed, too. Her coat was golden, her eyes that brilliant green. She studied the fighting wolves and shook her head. "But if you shoot Warrick instead…"

Then he would be gone to Kate—to both of them—forever. And she would be left alone in a small room with werewolves whose law was to kill any human who learned of their existence. She only had so many silver bullets; she had to make each one count.

So she steadied her hand, directed the barrel and fired. Once, twice, three times…

Sylvia screamed again before uttering Kate's greatest fear aloud, "You shot the wrong one!"

Chapter 18

"I can't believe he's dead," Kate murmured, still trembling in the aftermath of all that had happened that night.

Paige wrapped her arm around Kate's shoulders and offered a comforting squeeze. "He's gone. He can't terrorize you anymore."

"Which man are you talking about?" Kate asked. "Warrick's uncle or my ex?"

Paige smiled slightly. "Both."

Kate sighed and leaned back in the booth in Club Underground. Daylight now, the bar was closed. She and Paige were the only two people—or whatever—in the place. "Yes, they're gone." Despite Sylvia's fear, Kate hadn't shot the wrong wolf. All her silver bullets had gone into the uncle—not the nephew.

"What about Warrick?" Paige asked, glancing toward the hall that led to that strange back room of the club. To their secret clinic. "After Ben patched him up from the injuries his uncle had inflicted with his teeth, he took off. Do you think he left Zantrax?"

"I don't think he's gone yet," she replied. If he was, he hadn't said goodbye. But then, if she truly meant nothing to him, why would he have bothered? "He will need to return to his pack soon."

"Part of his pack is in Zantrax, isn't it?"

Kate shrugged. "Sylvia is still here." Ben had checked her out, too, making certain that she and her baby—babies, actually—had survived the ordeal. "I don't know about Reagan."

"So if Reagan is gone, why is Sylvia still here?" Paige asked.

"Maybe she realized that she picked the wrong brother." That Warrick was the better man.

"You have your own choice to make," Paige said. "You've been given a reprieve."

"Because you, Ben and Sebastian pleaded my case," she surmised.

Paige nodded. "Time's up, Kate. You have to decide or we won't be able to protect you anymore."

"So I guess I'm not done being terrorized," she said with a weary sigh.

"Is it wrong that I'm glad you found out?" her friend asked, her blue eyes clouded with guilt. "It was horrible keeping such a secret from you. And it was horrible to think that one day, when you began to notice that we weren't aging, that we would have to leave."

Kate's breath caught. "I hadn't thought about that—that I won't be able to stay here, to stay friends with Lizzy and Campbell."

"We have some time. Maybe years even."

She chuckled. "We can claim that Ben hooked us all up with plastic surgeons."

Paige smiled, her face beaming with relief. "So you've decided? You're going to join the secret society?"

"It's that or death, right?"

"I thought you had another choice," Paige said. "The pack…"

Kate shook her head. "That's not a choice for me." Warrick had made that absolutely clear to her.

"But you love him," Paige said, squeezing Kate's shoulders again. "I know you do."

"I love him, but I'm not the right woman for him." He had already chosen his mate. Reagan may have stolen her away, but the young woman was too smart to not have come to her senses by now.

And if Reagan was already gone, as Kate suspected, then Sylvia would need help raising the babies she carried. "So if the society will have me…"

"I'm sorry," Sylvia said, her voice cracking with regret and sincerity.

"Why?" Warrick asked, turning back to her. He'd been packing the few belongings he'd brought to Zantrax back into a duffel bag. He had no reason to stay in the vault any longer. There was someplace he needed to be more.

Sylvia stood nervously on the other side of the vault, as if she was afraid that he was still as angry as he'd once been, and those old brass bars might protect her from him. "Because I hurt you."

"You hurt my pride more than my heart," he admitted. "That's why I acted like such a jealous fool." He had accused her and his brother of being selfish and unfeeling. But they had actually felt too much—for each other—to deny their love.

"You realize that you never really loved me?" she asked.

He didn't want to hurt her but he nodded in reply. "I'm sorry…"

"No, that's great," she said with a breath of relief. "You realize you never loved me because now you know what true love is."

Sylvia had always been a romantic, more a dreamer than the practical, no-nonsense woman for whom he had really fallen. "And why did I realize what true love is?" he asked her—even though he knew the answer.

"Because you love Kate," she replied, her smile fading as she added, "the way that I love your brother."

"Reagan's a fool," Warrick said. "I can't believe he took off without even seeing you."

Sylvia's eyes widened with pain. "He knew I was here?"

Warrick nodded. "But I don't think he knows about…" He gestured toward her swollen belly.

She slid her palms over it, already stroking the babies she carried. "He had left before I even found out for certain that I was pregnant," she said, her eyes brimming with tears. "And I haven't heard from him…"

"He feels such guilt over breaking us up," Warrick said. He'd seen the misery in his brother's eyes. "And over everything else that happened."

"So instead of dealing with it, with me, he's going to just keep running?" she asked. "Uncle Stefan is dead now. There's no reason he can't come back to the pack unless you still want justice for your father's death…"

Warrick shook his head. "Kate killing Uncle Stefan is all the justice I need." She'd hurt the man who had hurt her, who had hurt them all. "Reagan can come home and resume his rightful place as leader of the pack."

"But he doesn't want it," she said. "He's giving it to you to make up for how he feels he wronged you."

Warrick pushed a hand through his hair. "I'll talk to him. I'll explain that the only one he's wronging now is you by staying away when you need him."

"You don't have time to track him down now," Sylvia said. "You need to go back to St. James and lead the pack. After everything they've been through, they need a strong leader. You can be that strong leader, Warrick."

He shook his head. "My father didn't think so."

"Your father was an egotistical ass," Sylvia replied, coming out from behind the bars to offer him her support. "He had no idea who you are. But Reagan always believed you would prove to be a better leader than him. You can do this."

Warrick reached out and caught her delicate hand in his. "Don't worry about you and the babies. I will take care of you."

"What about Kate?"

"What about Kate?" he asked, his heart pounding faster at just the sound of her name.

"She's the woman you love."

With all his heart. But after she'd shot his uncle, she had never looked at Warrick again—as if she couldn't bear to face him after his rejection. He'd wanted to explain and apologize, wanted to give her the words she deserved. But could he give her what else she deserved?

If leading the pack made him as busy as his father had been, he would have no time for Kate. And then she might grow as bored as his mother had and just leave...

His mother leaving had nearly destroyed ten-year-old Warrick. All the tears he'd shed were why his father had thought him so weak. Kate leaving him, after becoming his mate in every way, would kill thirty-year-old Warrick.

"If I am to lead the pack, I cannot shirk my responsibilities," he said. It wasn't as if Kate would even give him another chance. She probably hated him for all the trouble he'd caused her.

Sylvia's silvery green eyes filled with sadness as she studied him. "You would choose responsibility over love?"

He straightened his shoulders. "I will do what I have to do."

She shook her head as if disappointed in him. At least the romantic in her had to have been. "Then you are the one who is meant to lead the pack."

"I intend to take the responsibility very seriously. I will take responsibility for you and your babies, too."

"As part of your duties as leader?" she asked, again with disappointment. "Because I don't want to be just another one of your responsibilities."

"No, as their uncle and your friend."

She blinked as tears filled her eyes now. "I don't deserve your friendship. But I hope we can be friends."

He nodded. His anger and disappointment—even

his infatuation with her—was completely gone. "Of course we can."

"Then as your friend…" she drew in a deep breath, and continued, "I'm telling you that you're making a big mistake. You love Kate, and she loves you so much. I didn't know which wolf you were. I couldn't tell you apart, but Kate just knew. She loves you that much that she instinctively recognizes you no matter what form you've taken."

"I don't deserve her love," Warrick said.

"You love her the same way she loves you," Sylvia said. "I see it in your eyes. I saw it when you looked at her, when you thought your uncle was going to hurt her—it nearly tore you apart."

He gasped as the remembered pain and fear rushed over him. If his uncle had carried through on his threat to spill her blood…

Kate, as a human yet, would have died quickly and painfully—because of him.

"That's the kind of love that defies all boundaries— between human and werewolf—detective and leader." She smiled. "It's the kind of love that lasts forever. It's rare and wonderful and…" Her smile faded as she said, "…sometimes miserable but always special. It's the once in a lifetime, mate-for-life kind of love."

The kind of love she must have thought she would have with Reagan until everything had gone so wrong.

"You can't walk away from that," she urged him. Not like his brother had.

Warrick couldn't—not even for the role of leader of the pack that he'd always coveted. He couldn't leave Kate.

But Sylvia could leave him.

She hugged him first, kissed his cheek and then walked away—passing another man who'd slipped into the bank unnoticed.

After she'd passed him, Sebastian turned to Warrick and asked, "So you've chosen her over Kate?"

Was the vampire freaking invisible as well as occasionally telepathic? Warrick hadn't detected his scent or his presence. Neither had Sylvia as she'd walked right past him.

"What?" There was no choice.

"That's what Kate thinks," Sebastian said. "It's why she asked me to turn her."

"You're turning her into a member of the Secret Vampire Society?"

"And not a moment too soon," Sebastian replied. "If I don't do it right away, she'll be killed. Other members of the society are upset that she's lived this long after discovering the secret."

Once again Warrick had failed her. He had left her alone and in danger. He had waited too long to make her his mate. She had made her decision, and as stubborn as Kate was, he didn't know if he would be able to talk her out of it—if she would talk to him at all.

"Where do you think you're going?" a deep voice asked.

Stunned, Sylvia stopped on the sidewalk outside the bank building. Her voice soft, she admitted, "I don't know…"

And she had no idea.

"You could go back to the pack," he suggested.

She shook her head. "They wouldn't welcome me."

"Warrick offered you..." his voice cracked with emotion, "...his protection."

"You heard that?" He had been that close to listen to their conversation and she hadn't felt him? But then she'd been convinced that he was gone. "You're still here?" She winced as she heard how ridiculous her question was. Of course he was still in Zantrax.

He was talking to her. Or was she only imagining his voice in her head?

She drew in a breath and turned toward him. He was leaning against the brick wall of the old bank building—his face in the shadows. But then he stepped forward and she noticed the bruises and scrapes.

And gasped. "Are you all right?"

He shrugged off her concern and instead reached out, his hands settling on her swollen belly. "Are you?" he asked.

"Yes." She nodded. But he wasn't really concerned about her; he was concerned about their babies. He hadn't even looked at her, his gaze instead on her stomach. She couldn't *not* look at his face. Even battered, he was so handsome. "What happened to you?" she asked. "Uncle Stefan said he didn't fall for your trap—that he didn't see you."

"He didn't," he said.

"Did Warrick do this to you?" She'd thought that the brothers had made up and had been working together. And these bruises looked fresh.

"No," he said. "He finally let me explain what happened—why I did what I did."

She nodded. "That's good. But that doesn't explain..." She lifted her hand to his face, and as her palm slid across his cheek, she shivered in reaction.

It was still there—even all these months later—that undeniable attraction. She glanced up and found his gaze on her face now.

And the look in his eyes had her shivering again.

"It's cold," he said. "Let's go someplace where you'll be warm."

His arms. That was the only place she wanted to be, and she would be more than warm in his embrace. But so much had happened...

"You still didn't say what happened to your face," she murmured.

He grimaced. "Damn Secret Vampire Society..."

"They did this?"

He nodded. "I thought it was Uncle Stefan coming, but it was them—dragging me off to some inquisition."

"Inquisition? About what?"

"They questioned me about a murder," he said. "Uncle Stefan had killed one of them."

She gasped. "Yes, Kate told me about that—that she'd thought Uncle Stefan was saving her. But he was the greater danger."

Reagan shuddered now. "I'm not so sure about that," he said. "They're pretty dangerous."

And he had faced them alone. But he had survived.

He moved his hands from her belly now to her arms. "I should get you out of here," he said.

She shook her head. "I have no place to go."

"Warrick offered you his protection," he repeated. "But you turned him down?"

"I am not Warrick's responsibility," she said.

"You're mine," he said.

She shook her head again. "No."

"Sylvia…"

"I am responsible for myself," she said. "For the decisions I've made." For falling for the man she had—even after she'd promised herself to his brother.

He glanced back down—at her belly. "You and those babies are my responsibility," he repeated.

She didn't want to be his responsibility. She wanted to be the woman he loved. "I'll be fine alone," she assured him. "I was fine the past few months."

She'd been miserable and scared. But she was not about to admit that to him. His guilt was already apparent—it bowed his broad shoulders. Or maybe that was the damage the vampires had done to him.

"I can go back to my old life," she said. "I can go back to my old job." She had worked days at the museum, so she had no reason to be out between midnight and daybreak.

"No," he said, and his eyes had an eerie glow to them. "You can't."

She sighed. "Is there some other rule I don't know about?"

"There are a lot of them," he pointed out. "That's why you can't raise these babies on your own."

"Reagan—"

He lifted his hand and pressed a finger across her lips. She shivered again at that brief, sensual contact. "You're cold. Let's go someplace warm."

She shook her head.

"Warrick gave me a chance to explain my actions," he said. "Will you?"

She understood his actions. It was his heart she didn't know anymore. Did he love her? Or did he see her and their unborn children as just a responsibility?

Part of her was afraid to learn the truth. But the night before and the bravery of Detective Kate Wever had taught her to face her fears and fight for what she wanted.

"So you will do this?" Kate asked, her pulse pounding hard and fast with nerves and revulsion. "You'll turn me into one of…you?"

Sebastian nodded. "But only if you're sure this is what you want."

What she wanted was Warrick. But he hadn't come for her. He had probably already returned to lead his pack with the woman he'd really wanted. Sylvia.

"Because once you've turned, there is no going back to the life you used to know," Sebastian warned her. "You have to be certain."

"I am certain," she said, but she stepped away from where he stood in front of her couch. "I'm certain that this is the wrong choice."

"She has *no* choice," a female voice murmured as a woman stepped from the shadows of Kate's bedroom and joined them in the living room.

Was there a damn beacon in her bedroom window that guided every damn creature in Zantrax inside? As a detective, she really should have had better security. But an alarm system wouldn't have kept out any of the creatures of the underground.

"If she refuses to turn," the woman continued, "the human will have to die."

"Ingrid…" Sebastian greeted the raven-haired woman with a coldness Kate would have never guessed he possessed—especially with women. "You don't need to be here."

"I need to make sure this is done," she insisted. "That the threat she poses to the society is finally neutralized. She has dragged this out long enough. Too long."

As if he knew arguing with the woman was futile, Sebastian turned back to Kate and whispered, "You have to let me turn you now."

Kate shook her head. "I've changed my mind. I don't want this…"

Not this life. Not these people. Sure, some of them were her friends. But not one of them was Warrick.

"If you don't choose immortality, then you choose death," Ingrid said, stepping even closer. "Now."

Sebastian moved forward to shield Kate from the female vampire, but other men came from the shadows of her bedroom and caught his shoulders, holding him back. He was strong—superhumanly strong, but he couldn't break free of their grasp. They were as strong as he was.

And so was the woman who started toward Kate.

A gun with a silver bullet would not save her now. She had no protection from her fate. She had chosen Warrick over the society, but instead she would wind up dead.

Chapter 19

"What is this place?" Sylvia asked as he led her inside the building in which he had taken refuge after Warrick had discovered the bank vault.

"An old museum," he said. And staying inside it had made him feel closer to her. "This was where the paintings and books had been kept, so it's temperature controlled." And the walls were thick enough that Warrick hadn't been able to track him.

"What's all this?" she asked as she gestured at the candles he'd lit and the food and flowers he'd set out.

"Hope," he replied.

She turned toward him, her green eyes intent on his face. "Hope?"

"That you would give me a chance to explain," he said. "And to apologize..."

"I understand," she told him. "I know why you had to kill your father—to protect Warrick."

She was more understanding than he was of himself. "I should have protected you, too."

She shook her head. "There was no time. And I was never a threat to Uncle Stefan," she said. "It was you and Warrick who were in danger." She lifted her hand to his face. "Those vampires really hurt you."

"I'm fine," he said. "Or I will be…"

Concern stole color from her already pale skin. "You're in pain?"

He nodded and admitted, "I hurt."

"Where?"

He moved her hand from his face to his chest, to his heart. "Here. I ache…for you…"

Her eyes darkened as her pupils dilated. "Reagan…"

"You have every reason to doubt my feelings," he said, "with the way I left."

"I understand why you left," she said. "I just don't know why you've brought me here."

"To explain…"

"Or to assume your responsibilities?" she asked. She pulled her hand from his chest to place it on her belly. "Is this about them?"

His heart thudded hard and he expelled a shaky breath. "I didn't know…"

"I should have told you," she said. "But I wasn't absolutely certain and there was already so much tension between you and Warrick and your father…"

Then it had all blown up and Reagan had killed. "And then, after I did what I did, you probably didn't want me for your mate anymore—let alone a father to your children." He couldn't blame her for not trusting him, for fearing his violence. "I understand…"

She pressed her fingers across his mouth now, her skin so silky and warm. "I couldn't have a better father for these babies," she said. "I know you'll do whatever necessary to protect them—just like you protected Warrick."

"And failed you."

She shook her head. "I'm fine, or I will be if you answer my question honestly…"

He touched his swollen face. "I'm not sure I can handle another inquisition."

"I'm not going to hurt you," she said.

"You're the only one who really can…" Because if she rejected him, he wasn't sure how he would survive—if she went back to her old life and excluded him. "What's your question?"

"All this…" She gestured at the candles and flowers and food. "Is it for them…" She touched her belly again. "Or me?"

He settled his hand beside hers and a tiny foot kicked his palm. He gasped in shock—the shock he'd felt when he'd overheard his brother's conversation with her. "When I set all this up, I didn't even know about them. I didn't know until I overheard you and Warrick talking about the babies."

Her face flushed. "I'm sorry…"

"I left you," he reminded her. "You had no way of telling me."

She shook her head. "You heard me telling Warrick that he'll make a better leader."

"He will," Reagan readily agreed.

"But you're the one your father was grooming to take over the pack."

He flinched. "And that's why Warrick will be the better leader. He'll be his own man. I was my father's."

Her lips curved into a smile. "No. You're your own man."

"I'd rather be yours," he said. "If you'll have me…"

Tears shimmered in her beautiful green eyes as she stared up at him.

And his heart broke. He hated to see her cry. He touched her cheek. "It's okay if you don't feel the same way anymore…" He wouldn't force her to honor the rule of mating for life. Those had been his father's rules. Hopefully Warrick would make his own.

"I don't," she admitted.

And his heart shattered.

"I love you more."

He grabbed her then—gently pulling her burgeoning body into his arms. "I love you, Sylvia. I love you so much. I will never leave you again."

He lowered his mouth to hers, kissing her with all the love and passion burning in his heart and soul for her. But when he tasted her tears, he pulled back. "Are you really okay?"

She nodded. "I'm happy for us, so happy…"

"But?"

"I want that happiness for Warrick."

Guilt tugged at him. "Me, too. I hope he took your advice," he said. "I hope he went to Kate."

But they both knew how stubborn Warrick could be. Had he waited too long? Had he already lost her to the Secret Vampire Society?

Just as the grandfather clock chimed for the twelfth time, Warrick snarled and growled as he stepped from the shadows of Kate's bedroom into the faint light of the small, crowded living room. "Get away from her!"

"This doesn't concern you," Ingrid said. "Go back to your pack. Get the hell out of Zantrax. You and your brother brought enough trouble to our city. If not for you, the human would never have discovered our secret. Perhaps you need to die with her."

"I would have learned about the society even if Warrick had never come to Zantrax," Kate defended him.

He did not deserve her loyalty—not after leaving her alone and in danger. Not after waiting so long to claim her as his mate. "Kate is no threat to the society. She's known your secret for days and has revealed it to no one."

"We cannot let her live," Ingrid insisted. "You know the rule."

"I know an exception to that rule."

The woman's face distorted to an ugly mask of bitterness. "She would not let Sebastian turn her into a member of the society."

"Let *me* change her," Warrick urged.

"Into one of your pack?"

"Into my *mate*."

Kate turned toward him, her blue eyes wide and unreadable. Did she want him?

He couldn't blame her if she didn't—not after the fool he had acted. He'd thought he'd been protecting her, but he had really only been protecting himself. Afraid that some day she would leave him, he hadn't dared to give her the chance. So he had left her first... when she'd needed him most.

"She refused Sebastian," Ingrid said, as if no woman

had ever refused the vampire bartender before. "What makes you think she will accept your option?"

"Because she loves me." Or at least he hoped like hell she did.

Her face flushed, her cheeks growing pink.

"Then she should have chosen you already," Ingrid said. "She waited too long."

"No, I was the one who waited too long to claim her as mine." And he'd risked her life. And his own. Because he could not live without Kate.

"It doesn't matter who waited," the woman replied, shaking her head with disgust in both of them. "You both need to die."

Kate gasped. She couldn't lose Warrick now, after he had finally chosen her as his mate. But there were too many of the vampires. No matter how hard they fought together, she and Warrick could not win this battle.

Her true hero, in his wolf form, leaped toward the woman. He had a wooden stake clasped tight in his claws. "I'll take you out," he warned Ingrid. "You're the one whose immortality will end tonight."

"But you will die, too," the dark-haired woman warned him. "The society has only been able to co-exist with packs because we've stayed out of each other's way and honored each other's rules. Killing me will end that peaceful coexistence."

"And killing me won't?" Warrick asked. "You'd be killing the leader of the St. James Pack. The rest of my pack will be duty bound to come after the society."

The woman sucked in a breath, as if only now re-alizing the implication of killing Warrick James. No trace of fear or intimidation was apparent in her imperious tone when she said, "You will be spared if you leave now. We will just kill the human."

Warrick shook his head. "You won't be able to hurt Kate with this stake buried in your heart."

The woman's throat moved as she swallowed hard, fear filling her dark eyes as she realized how serious the werewolf was. "The rest of the society will kill you," she warned him. "And the human."

Sebastian shook his head. "I won't kill him. He's given her another choice, one the society will accept."

"But will she?" Ingrid asked.

Warrick turned to her, his topaz gaze intense and questioning. He had claimed that she loved him, but from the way he looked at her, he wasn't certain of her feelings. But she hadn't actually told him what she'd felt for him. He hadn't given her the chance, and then after she'd shot his uncle, she hadn't wanted to burden him with another responsibility when he already had so many others. The pack, Sylvia and her unborn babies...

"Will you?" he asked. "Will you become my mate for life, Kate?"

She feared he was only offering her that option over death—that he was just trying to protect her as he had been since she'd first been attacked in the alley. But if she refused him now, in front of all these members of the Secret Vampire Society, she would be putting them both in mortal danger. So, even though she wasn't certain of his motives, she accepted his proposal. "I will."

"See," Sebastian said as he tugged free of the men holding him. "There is no need for any violence."

Ingrid nodded. "All right."

Warrick dropped down and stepped back from her. But he still clasped the stake tightly, ready to strike if Ingrid changed her mind.

"As long as she's turned from a human into something else," the vampiress said, "we will let her live."

"I will turn her as soon as you all leave," Warrick promised.

The woman stared at him, as if unwilling to leave— as if determined to witness the transformation.

"I will not share such an intimate moment," Warrick said. "A moment that is just for me and the woman who has agreed to be my mate. You need to leave."

Finally the dark-haired woman nodded. Then she gestured at her men and headed toward the door of Kate's apartment with them falling into line behind her. The vampiress stopped at the door and stared over her shoulder at them. "But she must be turned tonight."

"She will check tomorrow to make sure Kate's been turned," Sebastian warned them before following the other members of his society out.

"Are you sure you want to do this?" Warrick asked her once the door had closed behind all the vampires.

Had he changed his mind?

"Because changing you into a werewolf will be quite violent," he continued. "I have to bite you."

"I'm fine with however much it will hurt," Kate assured him.

"You've been through so much pain already though," he said, his voice gruff with regret.

It couldn't hurt any more than the thought of losing him forever had hurt her. "I need to know why we're doing this, though," she said.

"You heard them. It's this or death," he reminded her.

She shook her head. "There was another option. I could have become one of them."

"But you didn't. Why not?" he asked. "Your friends are part of the Secret Vampire Society. I would have thought you'd choose them."

She sucked in a breath and braced herself for the admission she needed to make. "I didn't want to become one of them and risk never seeing you again, never being able to be with you again. I chose you."

His pupils dilated, nearly swallowing the topaz. "Kate…"

"But I didn't think you would choose me," she said, her voice catching with all the fears and doubts that had been pummeling her.

"Kate…" He stepped closer, still on all fours even though dawn was beginning to break, light streaking through her blinds. "There was no choice."

"Over Sylvia," she continued as if he hadn't spoken. "She's the love of your life, the woman you were willing to kill over losing."

"I was a fool," he said. "I had no idea what love was until I met you."

Hope swelled her heart. "What are you saying? You really want me as your mate?"

"Did you think I was just offering in front of the vampires but that I wasn't really going to change you?"

"I thought you were just offering to change me in order to protect me," Kate admitted. "You're always trying to protect me."

"That was why I didn't ask you sooner," he said. "I wanted to so badly, especially that day you found me in the vault in the old bank. But I had no idea what the future held for me—or if I even had a future. I didn't want you to wind up like Sylvia—alone even in the pack—with no mate."

"So Reagan is gone?"

He nodded.

"And you didn't offer to take Sylvia back?" She had been so certain that he would—if his brother didn't come forward to support his mate.

"I offered her and their babies support and protection," he said. "And friendship. That's all I feel for her."

"Now," she said, letting the jealousy bubble up. She had been married before, but she had never cared enough about anyone to want to kill over them...until she had fallen for Warrick.

He shook his head. "You're the woman I love. The only woman I have ever really loved."

"I was married before," she reminded him. "But I never loved Dwight—not like I love you. I love you so much that I really can't let you do this."

"What?"

"Maybe you can choose me over Sylvia," she said, "but you can't choose me over your pack."

"I don't have to choose one or the other."

"They won't accept me as your mate." She was certain. He was young and virile and needed to have sons to carry on the pack like he and his brother would carry on for his father. "I'm older than you are. You'd be better off with someone young like Sylvia. I may not be able to give you children." Not after the beatings she'd taken from Dwight.

"I don't care about anyone or anything but you," he said, as he began to turn back from a beast into a man. Into the man she loved—all powerful muscles under naked skin. Thick hair dusted some of the muscles, of his chest and lower. And that dark beard clung to his jaw as it shifted from canine back to man. "I don't need to be a leader or even a member of the pack. I just need to be with you, to be your mate for the rest of our lives."

"Then turn me." And as she told him, she began to undress—pulling off her sweater and pushing down her jeans along with her panties. A quick snap of the clasp of her bra and she stood before him entirely naked. Vulnerable like she had not been vulnerable in years. Because she loved him like she had never loved anyone else. Because she needed him like she had never needed anyone else.

"It's not going to be pretty like the bite on the neck Sebastian was going to give you," he warned.

She shuddered in revulsion. "Sucking my blood would not have been pretty."

"Biting you hard enough to brand you will not be pretty, either." He lifted her in his arms and carried her into the bedroom.

"I don't care," she said, sliding down his body—naked skin over naked skin and hair that tickled and scratched. "I just want to be with you. In every way. Forever."

"You really chose me over your friends, over the life you've known," he murmured, as if stunned that she would. "Over immortality?"

"I really had no choice to make. Love was the only choice I could have made," she said. "I *love* you."

"You won't change your mind?" he asked, worry

evident in his voice and in the depths of his eerie topaz eyes. "You won't regret turning for me?"

"My only regret is that I didn't meet you sooner, so that we would have more time to spend together."

"Wolves don't live for eternity like vampires," Warrick said. "But we can live a long time, much longer than humans. It can be a *very* long time. My mother had decided she didn't want to spend the rest of her life with my father."

"Your father sounds like he wasn't an easy man to love, though."

"No, he wasn't," Warrick admitted. "But she didn't leave just him. She left me and Reagan, too."

Tears stung her eyes as she imagined the pain he must have felt over his mother's abandonment. And she understood him so much better than she already had. "I will *never* leave you. I will *never* stop loving you. Please turn me now, so that we can be together in every way."

"I wish this wouldn't hurt you."

"Make it hurt good," she teased him, rubbing her naked body against his.

He groaned and pulled her tight against him, muscles rippling in his arms and chest. "You feel so good—so perfect—in my arms."

"Because we're meant for each other," she mused in wonderment. It didn't matter that he was younger and not even human. He was her perfect mate.

He lowered his head and pressed his mouth to hers. She parted her lips and slipped her tongue out, teasing him with the tip, running it over his lips and then into his mouth. He nipped at it before tangling his tongue with hers.

His hands moved over her body, skimming down her back to her hips—then lower. He cupped her buttocks and lifted her, his fingers splaying between her legs. He teased the core of her.

She arched and whimpered and wrapped her legs tightly around his lean waist. He lowered his head to her breasts, teasing a nipple with his tongue as he slid his fingers deep inside her.

"Warrick…" She sighed his name with pleasure.

He chuckled deep in his throat as he continued to tease her—with his lips and his fingers. Pressure built inside her, winding tight as her body begged for release. She shifted against him, trying to lower herself onto his straining shaft. But he held her up so that only the tip of him rubbed against her, against the most sensitive part of her.

It wasn't enough. But then it was too much. And she came, screaming his name now. His body shaking with the need for his own release, he carried her the few short feet to the bed and dropped her onto it. He followed her down and kissed her lips, then her shoulder.

"Are you going to do it now?" she asked.

"Not yet."

She reached between them, stroking her fingers over his chest then trailing them down his stomach to his shaft. Before she could close her hand around him, he pulled back. Then he turned her over, so that she lay on her stomach. He kissed his way down her spine.

She shivered at the sensation of his lips skimming over her skin. Maybe he would do it now. But he slid his palm between her and the sheets and lifted her slightly, until she knelt on the mattress. She leaned some weight on her arms, on all fours like he had been as the wolf.

And he joined them, sliding deep inside her. Pleasure spread through her, so that her breasts tingled and warmth and wetness pooled around his shaft. He withdrew and then thrust deep. His hands moved from her hips to her breasts, cupping the weight of them in his hands as he continued to pump in and out of her.

Panting for breath, he warned her, "I'm going to do it now."

"Do it," she urged him, her pulse pounding with excitement. As he continued to thrust deep and then even deeper, he lowered his head to her shoulder.

She braced herself. He didn't just nip her skin. His teeth sank deep into the flesh. She tensed at the pain tearing through her. But he kept making love with her, his body pumping into hers—his hands cupping her breasts, his thumbs stroking back and forth across her sensitive nipples. And the pain turned to intense, mind-blowing pleasure as she came, pouring over him. She arched into him and screamed his name.

He clutched her close and gave a guttural cry as he joined her in ecstasy, his desire spilling inside her—filling her with warmth and love. He leaned over her shoulder and kissed her lips gently. "I'm sorry I had to hurt you."

"It's done?" she asked, having already forgotten the pain for the pleasure.

"You're my mate now."

"And you're mine," she said possessively.

He grinned. "I've been yours since you shot me in that alley. It's just official now."

She'd had the big wedding with Dwight and family and friends. This private ceremony meant much more. It—and Warrick—meant everything to her.

Epilogue

She was a magnificent beast. All lean muscles and velvety raven hair with those pale blue eyes that could cut through a man, straight to his heart. When he saw her like this, like him, Warrick loved her even more. And he wouldn't have believed that was possible.

"Now you can call me your bitch, huh?" Kate teased.

"I wouldn't dare," he said. "You've already shot me a few times."

"But never with a silver bullet."

"You didn't doubt yourself that day," he said, still in awe of how calmly she'd pulled that trigger. "You had no doubt which wolf I was."

"I would know you anywhere."

Sylvia hadn't. His brother had done him another favor when he'd stolen away the blonde beauty. She hadn't been the woman for Warrick; Kate Wever was the only woman for him.

His mate.

Everyone was with whom and where they belonged. He smiled as he watched Sylvia and Reagan head toward their cabin, their bodies rubbing against each other. He couldn't believe he had once been so selfish as to resent their love.

But now that he had found love—real love—of his own, he understood. They hadn't been able to help how they felt about each other—just as he hadn't been able to help falling in love with Kate.

"Sylvia will be having those babies any day now," Kate murmured with concern. For him she had left her friends behind in Zantrax, but she and Sylvia had forged a close bond—maybe in that restaurant freezer when they'd all fought Uncle Stefan.

Or maybe when they'd all returned to St. James together. The four of them—she and Sylvia and he and Reagan—had presented a united front. There was no *one* leader among them; the four of them led as a team. And because of that united front, the pack had accepted and respected them all.

Kate should have had no doubts that she was the right mate for him. Hell, she was so beloved within the pack that she could have probably become the sole leader herself. But she had suggested instead that they become a team. Reagan had been harder to convince. He hadn't thought the pack would ever accept him after what he'd done. But they had understood and appreciated that he had acted in the best interest of not just Warrick but all of them.

And Warrick didn't have to worry about being too busy to give Kate the attention she deserved because she was always at his side, sharing her intelligence and strength with him.

And her love.

He followed her into their own cabin that she and Sylvia had decorated together. With its wood and brightly patterned curtains and linens, it was warm and beautiful and so big that it was never as cluttered as her apartment had been.

The last of six chimes rang out from her grandfather clock. It had the place of honor against the arched wall that led up to the high, beamed ceiling. He appreciated their home and the life they'd built together.

He appreciated, too, that she stood before him now in all her glory—all naked skin and seductive beauty. He couldn't wait to get her to their bed in the loft, so he swept her up in his arms and carried her up the stairs.

She clung to him, rubbing against him—all naked skin sliding over naked skin. He laid her on their bed and followed her down, covering her body with his.

"And I know that you are my heart, wife," he told her as he kissed her cheek and then her lips. "Not just the love of my life but my life itself."

"As you are mine," she said, her fingers sliding along his jaw.

Their hands moved greedily over each other, stroking flesh. And his mouth moved over hers before moving lower to her breasts and then the very core of her. When she was wet and ready, he slid inside her—thrusting deep—thrusting home. Her muscles clutched around him, holding him inside her—where he belonged.

They were meant to be mates—fitting each other

perfectly. She arched up, meeting his thrusts, and her body clenched him even more tightly as she came. His control snapped and he filled her with his passion. With a growl of satisfaction, he rolled onto his back and held her closely against his chest.

She uttered a contented sigh and murmured, "We will have to make sure to always make time for each other."

"We always do," he reminded her, her comments puzzling him.

"But the pack will be getting bigger."

He nodded in understanding. "I know Sylvia's babies will be coming soon." He and Reagan had already called Ben. The special surgeon and his wife would be coming up soon for a visit and a house call.

Kate hadn't had to leave her friends completely behind; they came up to visit often and he and Kate returned to Zantrax often, too. She had even gone recently by herself. It might have concerned him—if he'd been his old insecure, jealous self. But her love had given him a security and confidence he'd never known. He knew that she wouldn't leave him like his mother had left his father. He knew that she truly loved him.

Kate moved his hand from her side over the faint swell of her belly. "Our babies aren't due for a while yet," she said. "But they will be adding to the pack, too."

Love and happiness swelled within him, filling the heart that had been full of rage and bitterness until he met Kate. "You are expecting our babies?"

"Ben thinks at least two," she said, which explained that recent solo visit home to Zantrax to visit her friends. She had wanted to confirm her condition before sharing her news with him.

She hadn't even been gone the entire day, but he had missed her. He couldn't imagine his life without her in it and knew that he would never have to. She'd already given him so much. And now she was giving him more.

Babies. They were going to have children of their own; they were adding to the pack. Just when he thought he couldn't be happier…

She made him happier.

"You are…" His voice cracked with the emotions overwhelming him. "You are…*everything* to me."

Tears glistened in her eyes along with the love that brimmed in them. "And you have given me everything I've ever wanted. Love. Babies. A purpose and a future I had never realized were possible."

She hadn't known all the secrets then—about the pack or the Secret Vampire Society. She hadn't believed that the impossible was possible.

And even though Warrick had known all the secrets, he hadn't known her. He hadn't known *love*.

"Together—everything's possible," he said. "*Everything…*"

* * * * *

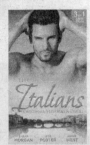

MILLS & BOON®

The Rising Stars Collection!

1 BOOK FREE!

This fabulous four-book collection features 3-in-1 stories from some of our talented writers who are the stars of the future! Feel the temperature rise this summer with our ultra-sexy and powerful heroes. Don't miss this great offer—buy the collection today to get one book free!

**Order yours at
www.millsandboon.co.uk/risingstars**

MILLS & BOON®
n o c t u r n e™

AN EXHILARATING UNDERWORLD OF DARK DESIRES

A sneak peek at next month's titles...

In stores from 20th November 2015:

- **Wild Wolf Claiming** – Rhyannon Byrd
- **Otherworld Protector** – Jane Godman

Available at WHSmith, Tesco, Asda, Eason, Amazon and Apple

Just can't wait?
Buy our books online a month before they hit the shops!
visit www.millsandboon.co.uk

These books are also available in eBook format!